"Do you still dream, Rose?"

"Dreams are for children, Mr. Castle."

"Jade," he said harshly. "Don't you think you could call me Jade?"

The light was on his face, and in the indigo depths of his eyes Rose saw anger, frustration, and something else she didn't dare put a name to. Fighting for calm, she said, "It hardly seems appropriate. You're my employer."

"A technicality. And some of the people I hire, depending on what we've shared, call me Jade. I'd like you to be one of them."

"And just what have we shared, Mr. Castle? As I recall, you *took* something from me, and without asking."

His laugh was sardonic. "What did I take from you? You mean the kiss? I rather thought I was giving you something—something you accepted readily."

Dear Reader,

When two people fall in love, the world is suddenly new and exciting, and it's that same excitement we bring to you in Silhouette Intimate Moments. These are stories with scope, with grandeur. These characters lead the lives we all dream of, and everything they do reflects the wonder of being in love.

Longer and more sensuous than most romances, Silhouette Intimate Moments novels take you away from everyday life and let you share the magic of love. Adventure, glamour, drama, even suspense— these are the passwords that let you into a world where love has a power beyond the ordinary, where the best authors in the field today create stories of love and commitment that will stay with you always.

In coming months look for novels by your favorite authors: Maura Seger, Parris Afton Bonds, Elizabeth Lowell and Erin St. Claire, to name just a few. And whenever you buy books, look for all the Silhouette Intimate Moments, love stories *for* today's women *by* today's women.

Leslie J. Wainger
Senior Editor
Silhouette Books

IMRL-7/85

Kathleen Creighton
Double Dealings

Silhouette Intimate Moments
Published by Silhouette Books New York
America's Publisher of Contemporary Romance

SILHOUETTE BOOKS
300 East 42nd St., New York, N.Y. 10017

ISBN: 0-373-07157-4

First Silhouette Books printing September 1986

America's Publisher of Contemporary Romance

Printed in the U.S.A.

Books by Kathleen Creighton

Silhouette Intimate Moments

Demon Lover #84
Double Dealings #157

KATHLEEN CREIGHTON

has roots deep in California's rural Kern River Valley. Into this setting came a young Hungarian refugee with a dream in his heart and, against all odds, their marriage has survived twenty-three years and produced four children. Writing is, along with her family, her great joy.

Chapter 1

Hello, Jordan Rose, this is Titan."

A voice on the telephone. A whisper from out of the past. It ricocheted off her eardrums, generating an adrenaline surge that left her with tingling nerves and an accelerated heartbeat, like a sprinter at the starting blocks.

There was a muted sound of amusement. "Earth to Jordan Rose...come in please. Do you read me?"

"Yes, I'm here." She was gratified to hear that her voice sounded calm and, except for that long pause, unperturbed. She glanced over at the young man who was patiently perspiring under the lights. He was watching her closely, but with no more than the usual half arrogant, half wary appraisal of a male adolescent scoping an attractive female. She hadn't betrayed herself. It was unexpectedly gratifying to discover that her protective reflexes were still sharp.

"How nice of you to call," she said pleasantly into the telephone. "It's been a long time."

"Yes," the voice whispered in her ear. "Too long." There was an expectant pause; Rose, recognizing the tactic, waited it out. Finally, almost reluctantly, "Sorry, Rose. This isn't a social call."

"I never thought it was." She watched the young man shift uncomfortably and insert a finger between his collar and his neck. He gave her a look of resentment. She smiled reassuringly and turned her back to him.

"I'm very busy," she said quietly, her voice cold. "And I can't think of anything the Bureau could have to say to me that I care to hear." Damn the Bureau anyway. Just when she'd begun to forget.

"Forget the Bureau, then—*I* need you." Simple, short and arrogant. Typically Titan. *Damn Titan.*

"Tough." Emotion crept into her voice, and she choked it off. "I don't work for the Bureau anymore. Or you."

"I know that." There was a long pause, and what might have been a sigh. "You must know I wouldn't have turned to you except as a last resort. I need a favor, Rose." Was there actually entreaty in that quiet voice? How untypical of Titan.

After a long pause of her own she murmured, "I'm sorry."

"I really do need you, Rose."

The voice was as pervasive as a virus. She shook herself, took a deep breath and said flatly, "Then I guess you're in big trouble."

"Come now, Rose. This isn't like you. I don't blame you for quitting after Beirut, but it's been two years. Aren't you the least bit . . . curious?"

She hesitated, staring down at the white-knuckled hand gripping the edge of the counter. "Absolutely not," she lied, smiling in spite of herself. The smile was a mistake. It leaked into her voice, and the answering chuckle was complacent. Oh, how well he knew her. And, she thought with a familiar chill, I don't know him at all.... Which was strange, considering he had been, at one time, the most important man in her life, the single controlling factor. And she didn't even know what he looked like, how old he was, whether, in another part of his life, he had a wife, a family, a dog, a mortgage.

"At least come talk to us." The voice was cajoling now. "Remember your pattern codes?"

"No."

"Liar. I'll make it easy for you...."

Her mind recorded the meeting sequence out of deeply ingrained habit, working against her will and better judgment. She hung up slowly and turned back to where the young man sat slumped and surly before the camera.

She thought, I don't work for the Bureau anymore. I don't have to go.

But, that whisper taunted her, aren't you the least bit curious?

"Sorry for the interruption." She turned a dazzling smile on her unhappy subject and ducked her head to squint through the viewfinder. "Are you sure you wouldn't rather wait for that hair to grow out? These are your senior pictures, you know. They're going to haunt you for a long time."

The boy grinned, touching the side of his head where the hair was artistically shaved in one-inch diagonal stripes. He muttered, "Naw, get it over with."

Rose St. James sighed and reached for the remote shutter release. "All right, then. Let's try shooting you from the other side. A little more to the left, please. Sit up straight . . . chin down a bit . . ."

And all the while in her head a whispering voice was repeating, like a prayer of supplication, *Rose . . . I need you.*

"Will she come?" The younger man, whose name was Michaels, sounded dubious.

The one who had identified himself as Titan sat regarding the phone, lost in private thoughts. After a moment he turned abruptly to gaze out the window. He shrugged. "Who knows? Two years is a long time."

"Long enough to forget?"

The man called Titan grimaced. "Forget? No . . . but to forgive—maybe."

"I wasn't thinking about Beirut. I mean the Bureau. Things like loyalty . . . training . . ."

"Loyalty . . . training. You never worked with her, did you?" Titan said, keeping his gaze on the smoggy skyline of Los Angeles. He was silent for a long time, and when he spoke again his voice held a husky burr of regret. "What she had went beyond training. She had . . . instincts. You don't measure what she had with statistics and test scores." He shook his head, and swore briefly and mildly. "Lord, how I hated to lose her."

"I've heard she was good."

Titan snorted. "She was the best. Resourceful, inventive, unflappable—a consummate actress." His voice was flat and remote, and his eyes had focused on something only he could see. "She could play Madonna or Medusa, virgin or vamp. And then, five minutes later, you could pass her in the street and, if she wanted it that way, you'd never even recognize her. She has the most flawlessly symmetrical features you've ever seen—though none of them are individually remarkable. You'd think she'd be unforgettable with a face like that, and she can be. Oh yes, she can be...when she wants to. I don't know what it is about her. She has thick, shiny...beautiful hair. But when she doesn't want you to notice it, you don't. If you had to describe it, I guess about all you could say is, it's brown. Same goes for her body. Nothing remarkable, nothing spectacular. About all you can say is, she's average height and weight. But believe me..." He caught himself and laughed softly, ironically. "Never mind. Suffice it to say that there was a time when every male agent in the department would have given a lot for first-hand data."

Michaels smiled. "Including you, by the sound of it."

Titan's face closed. "An impossibility, under the circumstances," he said distantly. "At any rate, she was a strange woman in some ways. Very private, very self-contained. The only person I ever saw come close to opening her up was Thad Moses, and after he was killed in the Beirut fiasco..."

"What makes you think she'll come out of retirement to help you now?"

An odd smile hovered over Titan's mouth and then disappeared, leaving his face almost bleak. "Old habits are hard to kick, Michaels. Maybe you're too young to know that. Yet." He checked his watch and picked up a file from his desk. "It's time you were leaving. This is the file." He smiled again, grimly. "Everything the Bureau has on Castle Industries, including the most up-to-date dossier on the maverick and mysterious Jade Castle. If Rose keeps the rendezvous, give it all to her. And don't forget to give her the call-code sequence."

"Are you sure you want to do this?" Michaels asked, staring down at the file.

"I'm sure."

"You seem pretty certain she'll come."

"We'll soon find out, won't we?" the man called Titan said.

Rose stood motionless, watching the limousine move toward her. It was gray, like the fog, and almost as silent, so that its appearance seemed more like a materialization, a ghostly visitation born of an overwrought imagination.

The car rolled to a stop beside her, its powerful engine purring faultlessly in the damp chill of the early August morning. A typical California coastal summer morning, Rose thought with a shiver, tolerable only when you considered that the sun was going to shine warmly enough in January to make up for it.

And a typical time for a meeting with Titan. He had always preferred the inconvenient and lonely hours. The fog was a nice touch—added a bit of melodrama. A pity I'm not in costume, Rose thought with a tight little smile. A trench coat, of course, and a fedora with the brim tilted down...

But a trench coat would have been noticed on a Venice street in August, fog or no, and that had never been Rose's style. A glance into the car's dark-tinted windows reflected back a face that was moderately flushed and framed by a white sweatband and straggling wisps of dark hair that had managed to escape a haphazard ponytail. She was wearing plain gray sweats and well-worn running shoes. Just one more jogger, out for an early run on the boardwalk. She was satisfied no one would give her a second glance.

Her hand was steady on the cold chrome of the door handle. Her movements as she pulled it open and slipped

into the plush, insulated interior were graceful and economical; no one could have guessed at the sudden accel-
eration in her heartbeat, the surge of heat and blood and
adrenaline that rolled through her body in a single wave
and then receded, leaving her fingers and feet tingling,
and all her senses in overdrive. For a moment she sat still
on the soft leather seat, assessing her reactions like a sci-
entist monitoring the effects of a powerful drug. Incredible, she thought; after all this time it's still there...the
thrill, the exhilaration.... And then, unbidden and in
mild surprise, I've missed it.

The car pulled away from the curb so smoothly that its
movement was barely perceptible. Rose was alone in the
passenger compartment; the shade across the driver's
window was firmly shut. A cut crystal goblet of orange
juice and crushed ice stood in the bar, shedding conden-
sation droplets onto the polished surface. Next to it, in a
crystal bud vase, a single rose shivered slightly with the
car's vibrations. A half-opened bud, almost, but not
quite white...touched with pink just where the petals
curled. Rose stared at the exquisite blossom for a long
moment before sitting back and picking up the manila
folder on the seat beside her. She smiled at herself and
shook her head. She had been foolish to hope, even for
a moment, that this time Titan would come in person.

"Good morning, Jordan Rose," the intercom said.
Not Titan's resonant burr, but a pleasant, featureless
tenor.

"You're new," Rose observed without looking up.
"What do I call you?"

"Uh...my name is Michaels."

"Good morning, Michaels," Rose said pleasantly, and
then very casually, still glancing through the files, "Is
Titan with you?"

"No...sorry." The voice held a trace of embarrassment. "Titan felt...he seemed to think it best to give you a chance to weigh the...um...data without undue...pressure."

Rose snorted softly and frowned at the dossier in her hands. The snort was one of surprise at her own acute sense of disappointment. The frown was to cover it. "Jade Castle...odd name. I once knew someone named Jade."

"Oh really?"

"Yeah." Rose gave a dismissive sniff and grinned wickedly. "She was a belly dancer—a featured attraction at Mama Califa's in Cairo. They said she could take a dollar bill from a man without using her hands."

There was a brief silence. When he spoke again Michaels sounded amused and more assured than he had seemed before. "I...um...think I can safely guarantee that this is not the same Jade. One of the few things that is known for certain about Mr. Castle is that he is now and has always been completely masculine."

Rose glanced up, alert to the unusual timbre of laughter coming through the intercom. Interesting, she thought, and went back to her reading.

"Interesting," she said aloud sometime later. "Sketchy, though. So toxic chemicals bearing the Castle Industries label have been turning up in Costa Brava, where they're being made into chem-warfare weapons and used against the rebellious populace. Dirty, but hardly criminal, by the world's standards."

"Not just any toxic chemicals—experimental and highly classified materials manufactured under top secret contract solely for the U.S. government. Shipments destined for the Pentagon have been diverted to Costa Brava. Not all of them, you understand, but enough."

"What makes you think it's an inside job, rather than a deliberate anti-U.S. smear? Seems to me somebody could get a lot of mileage out of the negative P.R. You know, U.S. aid to Costa Brava killing innocent civilians...."

"No," Michaels said flatly. "In the first place, there's been no attempt to capitalize on this by the other side. We can only assume that's because they don't know about it—yet. But it's only a matter of time before they do find out, and then our position in the Western Hemisphere is going to be in big trouble. And second, the shipments are being diverted by computer."

"Hacker?"

"Probably. But he'd still have to have certain information available only to someone in tight with the highest levels of Castle management. Those shipments are very highly classified. That's why—"

"Why Jade Castle himself becomes the number one candidate. Tell me something. If so little is known about this man, how did his company acquire such classified government contracts?"

"That's classified," Michaels said austerely. Rose snorted, and then hearing something in the silence, laughed out loud. The answer from the intercom was a low chuckle.

I like you, Michaels, Rose thought. You have a sense of humor, at least. "Is this all the data the Bureau's vast resources have been able to dig up on the elusive Mr. Castle, or is Titan holding out on me?"

"I assure you, you have everything the Bureau has," Michaels said. Rose, keyed to every nuance in his voice, detected the hint of evasion and was puzzled. What could Titan be hiding? Was this a tactic, designed to intrigue her into joining the Bureau again? Titan's "pressures," she knew only too well, could be very subtle.

She made a disgusted sound and placed the file back on the soft gray leather beside her. It was insane for her to be here in the first place. She shouldn't have come. Glancing out the windows and discovering familiar streetscapes, she snapped, "Let me out here. I'll jog home. It's been nice talking to you, Michaels."

The car pulled obligingly to a stop at the curb, but the doors remained locked.

"Aren't you even going to listen to Titan's proposition?" Michaels's voice sounded almost hurt.

Rose laughed without humor and settled back against the cushions. "Do I have a choice?" She reached for the glass of orange juice and let her eyes roam around the car's interior as she sipped. Her glance fell on the rose. Very slowly she reached out and touched a finger to the cream and velvet petals, then picked up the vase and brought the flower close enough to sniff its delicate, spicy fragrance. Michaels's idea, she wondered...or Titan's? She rather thought it would be Michaels's.

"All right," she said with a sigh of capitulation. "I'll listen. I guess I owe him that much. What's the proposition?"

"Meet him," Michaels said. "Just...meet him. That's all."

Rose's heart gave one lurch before she realized that Michaels meant the target, not Titan. She frowned. "Meet Castle? That's it?"

"That's it. Meet him, get a good look at him, give your instincts a go, and then decide. Yes or no."

"No pressure? No persuasion or coercion? Not even a little friendly blackmail for old-times' sake?"

Michaels's chuckle was sympathetic. "Nothing. Titan's word."

Rose's snort was wary. "He must be even more arrogant than I remember." And more devious. He had something up his sleeve. "Tell me, Michaels. If Jade Castle is so elusive and mysterious, how am I supposed to meet him? Any ideas, or am I supposed to come up with something?"

"I have no doubt that you could," Michaels said placidly, "but, as it happens, circumstances are on our side. Ever hear of Tessa Freedom?"

Rose frowned and leaned forward to set the rose and its vase back in the bar. "The rock singer? Sure."

"Then you probably know about that big rock concert at the Coliseum Saturday—the charity benefit." Rose acknowledged that with a murmur, her curiosity piqued in spite of her better judgment. "On Friday..." Michaels paused for dramatic effect. "Tessa Freedom is hosting a big party at Castle's estate in Bel-Air. Kind of a kickoff for the concert. All the beautiful people will be there, at a thousand dollars a ticket, I'm told. They expect to raise an additional million or so, and of course the pledges of the rich and famous then become inspiration for—"

"Why Tessa Freedom?" Rose interrupted. "What's the connection with Jade Castle?"

Michaels's shrug was almost audible. "They've been friends for a long time. A lot more, if the pop press is to be believed. The tabloids are always full of romantic rumors, but as far as we know that's all they are—rumors. At any rate, that's immaterial. The point is, Tessa's little bash is to be well covered by the press—including photographers."

"Ah," Rose said. "I see."

"I thought you would. Your press pass and necessary corroborating identification are in the folder."

Rose fingered the laminated ID card and engraved press invitation. "These will get me onto Castle's estate. I presume the place will be crawling with celebrities, which means security people by the jillions. And if Castle's as private as the thinness of this file would seem to indicate, he's going to have some security of his own."

"That's right," Michaels said softly. "But from what I've heard, that should pose no problem at all for the Jordan Rose...."

Rose St. James, of St. James Photography Studios, stood in a copse of white birch and juniper in a quiet corner of the Castle estate, surveying what appeared to be a gypsy encampment. The laminated tag clipped to the front of her dress declared her to be an employee of the West Valley Daily News. No one had questioned it.

She was wearing what she thought of as her working clothes: simple knit dress of gray and white and low-heeled shoes, with her hair held securely in place with combs and rubber bands. Like any good photographer, she hoped to blend into the scenery, so that her prospective subjects would forget she was there. But she'd miscalculated. It had become obvious to her very soon after being admitted to the Castle estate that for once Titan's research had been inadequate. In order to blend with this scene what she really needed were gold bangles and scarlet ribbons.

The grounds of the Castle estate had been transformed into a gypsy camp, flawlessly conceived and crafted, like an enormous movie set. Rose had seen enough of Eastern Europe firsthand to know that this bore little resemblance to the real thing, which was more apt to be dirty and squalid than colorful and romantic. But she had to admit that, as a party theme, it was wonderfully photogenic, had energy and originality, and provided endless opportunities for show-biz excess.

As she squinted through her camera lens she was smiling a thin, chilly smile. If so inclined, she could probably turn some of her best candid shots into a small fortune, either through sale to the tabloids or out-and-out blackmail. But she would gladly trade them all, every last frame, for one meager portfolio of the man just coming into focus in her telephoto lens.

Oddly enough, even though he was the reason she was there, she hadn't really been deliberately stalking him. From her place in the shadows she'd been surprised to see him approach, quietly and unobtrusively, like a wary and reclusive jungle animal. She thought it strange that, in the midst of his own party, on his own estate, he should elude his own protectors and seek out solitude. Strange . . . and intriguing.

She lowered the camera for a moment, the better to study the man as he leaned casually against the trunk of a tree. Of all the people in costume she'd seen today, this man in a stark white shirt and black pants, without so much as a gold earring for adornment, most looked as if he belonged in the exotic setting. One thing was certain: the Bureau's surveillance photos hadn't come close to capturing him. Maybe no one could; it might be a challenge to try.

So this was the target, her quarry. As Rose brought the rugged face into stark close-up in her viewfinder she felt a little shiver of excitement. The thrill of the hunt. She'd almost forgotten what it was like.

He was a dark man, broad-shouldered, but hard and lean. He had blue eyes, so the dossier said; now they seemed dark, deep set and brooding. An intelligent face; an arresting face. A face without softness... He wasn't handsome—not in the Hollywood sense—but even here, in this elaborate playpen full of the famous and beautiful, he stood out. Around him everything faded into silence and insignificance, the way a hush falls in the forest when the tiger walks. He exuded power and grace, and a subtle aura of mystery.

As she looked at Jade Castle in the twilight, Rose felt her body quicken with awareness, and a certain yearning.

Well, well, she said to herself, smiling a little inner smile of surprise and chagrin. For these, too, were sensations she'd almost forgotten....

Interesting, she thought wryly. But most unprofessional. And dangerous. This could be a very wicked man. He could be responsible for the ugly deaths of innocent people. He could be a traitor, a worse sin in some people's eyes.

The dossier had been stamped EYES ONLY—MEMORIZE AND DESTROY. It hadn't taken her long to commit it to memory; it contained tantalizingly little. Jade Castle, naturalized citizen, birthplace NDA—No Data Available. Emigrated from Australia in 1975. Currently head of Castle Industries, chemical manufacturing conglomerate; personal and company logo: black rook (chesspiece); networth (estimated)—somewhere in nine figures. Activities prior to 1975 NDA. Rumored to have been in Southeast Asia. Next of kin NDA. Birthdate NDA. Approximate age: 35-40.

And that was all—nothing but rumors and unknowns. And the ever-popular NDA. Bureau euphemism for I don't know, something no self-respecting computer would ever admit.

Who are you, Jade Castle? she wondered. A man with no past...a man without softness...a man with secrets... Where did you come from? Were you ever a boy, a baby? Somewhere a woman must have held you and rocked you and touched you with gentle hands. What happened to forge you into cold steel?

Rose tightened her own jaw and pressed the shutter release. As small as the sound was, it was enough to alert her subject. He grew taut, like a bow string, and turned his head unerringly toward the source of the disturbance.

"Ah," he said. "The press." His voice was dry and carried traces of Australia.

Rose stepped out of her shadowed retreat, lifting the camera with a rueful shrug. "I'm very sorry. I was trying to be unobtrusive. Rose St. James—with the West Valley Daily News."

"Unobtrusive? A member of the press?" His voice sounded amused rather than sarcastic. "That makes you unique, Rose St. James." He watched her approach with a dark appraisal that made her both uneasy and strangely exhilarated. Suddenly he held out his hand. "Nice to meet you. I'm Jade Castle."

Both the gesture and the ingenuous introduction were so unexpected that they were disarming. Rose found herself smiling as she placed her hand in his. "Yes, I know," she murmured. "Something to do with Castle Industries, aren't you?"

He threw back his head and laughed, not loudly, but with real appreciation. "You are unique for a member of the press, aren't you?" He was regarding her with an odd intensity, rather like someone sizing up an opponent in a contest. Rose felt a thrill of warning go shivering down her spine. This man would be a dangerous adversary.

"Well, I'm not really a member of the press. I'm a photographer, not a reporter." He hadn't released her hand. His was large, warm and dry. Hers felt... vulnerable. She disengaged it and filled it instead with the comfortable bulk of her camera. "I'm not even a photojournalist, actually. I'm a studio photographer." Experience had taught her that it was better to volunteer too little information than too much. People tended to fill in blanks with their own assumptions, which satisfied them better than anything she might come up with. Jade Castle was no exception. He merely inclined his head slightly and said, "Ah, of course—I'm sure you must be finding this a gold mine. And I won't ask you how you came by your press pass, if you promise to stay as... unobtrusive as you have been so far."

Rose took a deep breath and exhaled. "Thank you, Mr. Castle. I really—"

He took her arm suddenly and waved his hand in the direction of the lights and music. His fingers, though not holding her tightly, felt like steel bands. "Tell me, Rose St. James, what do you think of all this?"

"What do I think?" He had caught her off guard. She was finding that she had to concentrate very hard in order to stay in character. Oh yes, she thought, a very formidable adversary.

He was walking her slowly back toward the semicircle of painted wagons at the party's center. The scene was illuminated by torches and kerosene lanterns; it reminded Rose vaguely of Disneyland. All the sinister introspection and undercurrents of danger began to seem a bit silly. Rose cleared her throat and said cautiously, "Well, I'm very impressed."

Castle's chuckle was dry. "Rose St. James," he said, "I have a feeling very little impresses you."

The hairs on the back of her neck rose in the same reflex that lifts the hackles of a wolf. She glanced at the
lean form moving easily at her side and found him
watching her. The look in his eyes was one she'd seen in
men's eyes before, but it had never affected her like this.
She felt confused. Threatened, vulnerable and...yes,
frightened. But excited, too, and full of a kind of vitality
she hadn't known in a very long time. All her senses were
humming at a pitch that seemed almost supernatural. She
was keyed to this man in ways she couldn't remember
ever having been to any man before, and on several different levels. She'd already acknowledged the physical
attraction, and there was no doubt that it was electric.
But the presentiment of danger was just as vibrant, and
it kept her instincts for self-preservation humming full
volume every second she was with him. And yet there was
a kind of instant camaraderie between them, as if they
had known each other for a long time.

All of which told her one thing: Jade Castle, guilty or
not, could be a danger to her, and the greatest challenge
of her life. And as much as she wanted to pick up the
verbal gauntlet he'd tossed at her feet, she knew it was
vital that she stay in character. Rose St. James, studio
photographer, simply would not engage in a verbal sparring match with the lord of the manor!

And so she tilted her head and widened her eyes and
said guilelessly, "Well, maybe 'impressed' isn't the right
word. But I can see that you've gone to a lot of trouble
and expense. It all seems very authentic."

"It isn't, and you know it." He looked down at her
with hooded eyes that seemed to see right through her
pose of vacuous innocence. He sounded almost disappointed. Rose mentally kicked herself for having vio-

lated the undercover operative's cardinal rule: never lie
unnecessarily. Use the truth whenever you can—it gives
your cover story that unmistakable aura of sincerity.

She laughed ruefully. "You aren't going to let me get
away with it, are you, Mr. Castle? You absolutely must
have the truth."

"I insist on it. Always." His voice was low and even;
she wished she could see his eyes.

"Oh dear," she said fearfully. "All right, here goes.
Are you going to have me thrown out if I tell you what I
really think?"

He looked startled. "Is it that bad? Good heavens no.
Guaranteed. Take your best shot."

"Well..." She tilted her head and met his challenging
gaze. "As a party theme it has originality and a certain
flair. The food looks fantastic, the music is...different,
and the bonfire is a nice touch." She smiled and lifted her
camera. "It does photograph beautifully."

"But?"

"But..." Rose took a deep breath and faced him. "It
just seems..."

"Is *ostentatious* the word you're looking for?"

"Considering its purpose is to raise money to feed
people who don't have enough to eat, yes. I keep thinking of all the food you could buy for what it's costing you
to throw this party."

"Ah, but by investing the money in this party I can
increase it a hundredfold. Doesn't that make better
sense?"

It was Rose's turn to be startled. He didn't sound like
a man who was so callous that he would knowingly con-
tribute to the deaths of innocents. When he took her arm
again she was acutely sensitive to the strength in his fingers where they curved around her elbow, the vibrance of

his controlled energy as he moved her effortlessly through the crowd. She looked up at him, confused. He smiled down at her almost ruefully, as if he knew what she was thinking.

"As a matter of fact, this is all Tessa's doing," he said with a note of fond indulgence, raising his voice above the level of revelry. "Have you met her yet, by the way?"

"No," Rose shouted. "I've seen her on TV. I liked her. She had red, white and blue hair."

The man beside her laughed out loud. "Ah yes. Her concert tresses," he drawled. He smiled down at her, a flash of white teeth in a dusky face. "You might have trouble recognizing her tonight. I think she's wearing her own."

Rose watched the torchlight chase shadows across the rough-hewn planes of his jaw and her mouth went dry. She thought, Rose, you sure can pick 'em. The first man to make your heart go pitty-pat in ages, and not only is he prime candidate for villain of the year, but he's the consort of a famous rock star! Without a trace of levity, she added, Get a grip on it, Rose....

They had to side step adroitly around a waiter in gypsy regalia bearing a tray of wineglasses. Her escort not only emerged from the close encounter unscathed, but with a glass filled with amber liquid in his hand. He presented it to Rose with the air of a magician producing a coin from his sleeve. She smiled her appreciation and murmured, "Neatly done."

"Go on, take it. I only had time to snag one."

Rose hesitated. She was thirsty. She hadn't stopped to eat or drink anything since arriving late in the afternoon. But she had no idea how wine might affect her on an empty stomach, and she needed a clear head. In fact, she always made it her policy not to drink anything alcoholic while she was working with her cameras, though in times past there had been occasions when the Jordan Rose had found a limited consumption of alcoholic beverages to be of...strategic value. Especially when her quarry's consumption was unlimited...

"Come on," Castle said, misreading her reluctance. "You've been working hard."

His voice was low, husky. She could barely hear him at all in the cacophony of music and laughter all around her; surely she'd imagined the seductive quality in his voice. But though her mind told her so, her body wouldn't believe it. His words touched her like caressing fingers, roughening her skin with gooseflesh.

She was losing touch with reality, that's what she was doing! This man was a suspect! Acting a part was one thing, but feelings were something else.

"Or, if you'd rather not drink alone, we can always share it," he murmured, laughter in his eyes and in his voice. Without taking his eyes from hers, he lifted the glass to his lips, sipped the golden liquid, and then held it to hers.

She raised her hand to steady the glass, but instead of cool, moist crystal her fingertips touched the warmth of a masculine hand. Reflexively, she drank.

The wine was unexpectedly sweet. Rose looked at him questioningly, and across the rim of the glass Jade Castle's deep-set eyes crinkled at her in reply. "It's Tokay. Very Hungarian, I believe. If you'd prefer something drier..."

"No," Rose said, claiming the glass and turning abruptly, the only way she could think of to break that disturbing eye contact. "This is fine. Thank you." She was disgusted with herself, and more than a little worried. She had been away from the life too long; she had lost her ability to keep herself inviolate and detached. And she was dreadfully out of practice, slipping badly. She'd gone to a great deal of effort to look like a lamp-post. She shouldn't have attracted *anyone's* notice, let alone the focused attentions of a man as attractive and exciting as Jade Castle.

Chapter 2

She was slipping away from him; Jade could feel it, just as he'd felt her awareness of him as a tangible thing, a current of energy as real and vital as his own forces. His need to hold on to her became a compulsion so acute it was almost painful. But she was quicksilver... sea foam and moonbeams. And he was afraid that if he tried to grasp her, he would find his hands empty and his heart aching with a taunting sense of loss.

It was that mythical quality about her that had struck him first when he'd seen her there in the twilight shadows of the birch grove. She was all grays and browns, with soft slender lines and the gift of stillness. She called to mind words like wood nymph and sprite. He felt that if he closed his eyes for only a moment she would disappear into thin air.

And then she had moved and spoken, and he had seen the clean pure lines of her face, the unconscious grace of her body, and had been surprised at how young she looked. How young and, incredibly, considering who she was, untouched . . .

"Penny for your thoughts," he murmured, stopping and compelling her, with a light touch on the elbow, to do the same. They were standing beside a small yellow tent decorated with cryptic signs and symbols. "Care to have your fortune told?" When she hesitated he taunted her gently, "On me. I dare you."

Rose gave him a faint smile and shook her head. "Oh, no, thank you. I don't think so. I really don't believe in destiny, and consequently not in fortune-tellers. How can anyone possibly see what will happen if there's no destiny?"

"Oh, come now," Jade said, teasing. "Do you mean to tell me you don't believe in fate? In kismet?"

"No," Rose said, lifting her chin and looking him squarely in the eye. "Things happen either by random chance or human design." She lowered her eyes and added in a curiously flat voice, "Or human error . . ."

Jade shrugged. "Not all gypsies tell fortunes. Some claim to read minds. Do you believe in ESP?"

She frowned. "ESP?"

"Yeah, communication on a nonverbal, intangible level." Let her try to deny the existence of it—he knew she'd felt it too. "Some call it psychic energy. Mental transmissions that can be picked up by particularly receptive people."

"I know what ESP is. I'm just not sure I believe in that, either."

Very softly Jade persisted, "Haven't you ever felt or known something on a level more primitive than thought? A sense of danger . . . ?"

"Yes." She had become very still. "I guess I have."

"Don't you think a sense of danger could be the result of intercepting currents given off by strong, even deadly, emotions?"

She smiled. "It's an interesting theory, at least."

"And how," Jade said without returning her smile, "do you explain chemistry?"

"Chemistry?" She was watching him across the rim of the wineglass; the smoky golden light of the torches gave her brown eyes an amber fire.

"Yes. Instant electricity between two people who are destined—excuse me—*going to* become lovers..."

Without taking her eyes from his, she sipped the sweet heavy wine. "Or enemies," she said softly. "Sometimes it's hard to tell the difference at first."

Silence crackled in the air around them like static electricity. And then Jade laughed and took the glass from her hand. "That's true," he said easily, lifting the glass to her in a self-mocking toast before he drained it. "I can see I'm not going to convert you from skeptic to believer, but come see my gypsy anyway. Some people went to a great deal of trouble to find an authentic one for this occasion. She's supposed to be the very best. Aren't you the least bit curious?"

His grin was disarming, his hand on her elbow no more than friendly. For he had reminded himself that the way to capture a moonbeam is to open your hand and let it lie cool and shimmering upon your skin.

Aren't you the least bit curious?

Jade Castle's gentle challenge struck Rose like a bucketful of cold water between the shoulder blades. A chance remark or a fortuitous phrase, it was a timely reminder of who she was and why she was here rubbing elbows with the glittering elite of show business and Los Angeles society. At least she knew now why Titan had wanted her to meet Jade Castle. Titan's pressures could be very subtle indeed. But how did Titan know her so well?

She turned to the man beside her, lowering her eyes and smiling her capitulation. "Well . . . all right, for curiosity's sake." It was odd the way he'd changed all of a sudden. The power and charisma were still there, but the aura of mystery was gone, as if he'd turned on a light switch, dispelling shadows. For the first time she noticed that his face was asymmetrical; it gave his grin a lopsided, wry quality that could, under different circumstances, be very touching.

Even his chuckle seemed reassuring. It brushed her cheek like a caress as he stooped with her to go through the low opening to the gypsy's tent.

The fortune-teller was a surprise. Rose had expected a dark, exotic beauty with flashing eyes and a thick fake accent, straight from Central Casting. Instead the woman was big bosomed and blowsy. She greeted them with a cheery, "Hi dears, come right on in!" and her accent was pure New York. She had frizzy gray hair and a gold tooth, and wore rings on every finger. She didn't, Rose noted with uneasy amusement, even have a crystal ball. Or tarot cards or tea leaves, or . . .

"Sit down, dears," the gypsy commanded briskly, gesturing toward the chair that faced her across a small round table. The table was covered with yellow cloth, not terribly clean and, except for the gypsy's plump hands, bare. "And give me your hands."

Aha, a palm reader, Rose thought, beginning to be intrigued in spite of herself. She glanced at Jade. He nodded at her, indicating that she should take the chair, and then withdrew into the shadows. She couldn't see his face, but felt his presence as if he were touching her.

The gypsy didn't even glance at the hand Rose reluctantly surrendered, enfolding it instead in both of hers and closing her eyes. Rose had expected the gypsy's hands to be unpleasantly soft and moist, but they were surprisingly cool and quite dry. Rose felt inexplicably uneasy, sitting there with her hand in the grasp of a stranger, and had to control an impulse to look to Jade Castle for reassurance.

Just as Rose was beginning to feel acutely uncomfortable, the gypsy stirred and a small frown appeared between her eyes. After a moment she turned Rose's hand palm up on the tabletop and placed her own upon it, palm to palm. "Come, dear," she said peremptorily to Rose. "Put your other hand on the table." And then, with an intensity that was oddly contagious, "Quickly, quickly... before I lose the thread!"

To her surprise Rose discovered that her heart was beating hard against her ribs as she placed her hand palm up on the tablecloth like a small, helpless sacrificial animal. The gypsy covered it with her own, palm to palm. Her eyes closed and her frown deepened. Seconds became minutes; noises beyond the tent's walls receded. And still the fortune-teller sat silent and motionless. Rose felt a curious tingling sensation in her scalp, and a prickling awareness along all her nerves. She slowly turned her head to look at Jade Castle. Without surprise she found that he was watching her with an intent blue gaze so deep and brooding it seemed almost black. She swallowed and shifted her own gaze reluctantly back to the gypsy, but she could still feel the awareness of his eyes on her skin.

At last, when Rose had begun to wonder if her rusty self-discipline were going to be able to stand the strain a minute longer, the fortune-teller released her hands and straightened, expelling her breath in a long, slow exhalation. She opened her eyes and sat regarding Rose accusingly, like a mother confronting a child over an empty cookie jar.

"Your future is very difficult to see," she said severely, as if Rose were a personal affront. "Very difficult ..."

Oh yeah, sure, Rose thought, and lifted her eyes to give Jade an amused "I-knew-it" glance.

"Your threads are a tangled web of deception." The gypsy clasped her hands at her bosom and inhaled deeply through her nose. "I see doubt and uncertainty. Trouble ... danger."

The words were melodramatic; in a stagey Hungarian accent they might even have seemed amusing, part of the setting, part of the atmosphere. Rose wanted to laugh them off as pure nonsense, coincidence, stock phrases for theatrical effect. But somehow, delivered in the flat, nasal tones of a Bronx housewife, the words were incredibly affecting. In spite of all her self-discipline, Rose felt a cold trickle of fear.

Did she only imagine a certain stillness in the man beside her? Or were her own heightened senses bringing him into sharper than normal focus? Psychic energy, he'd called it. Intangible, nonverbal communication. *Or chemistry* ... Quite suddenly she didn't trust herself to look at him.

"Don't worry, dear," the gypsy said suddenly, beaming and waggling her fingers dismissively. "You'll come through it. I see happiness for you. Love ... a long life."

Rose laughed, an involuntary release of built-up tensions, then stifled the sound and threw a warning look at the man standing in the shadows. He met her gaze with a shrug and a wry grin, but turned away before she could evaluate the look in his eyes. She was dismayed by her own feeling of relief at the gypsy's lapse into the trite, cliched phrases. How could she have allowed herself to be sucked into the atmosphere like that, even for a moment? The woman was an actress, even if she didn't look the part. A brilliant showman, too, but no more psychic than Rose was.

Jade thanked the gypsy, tipped her handsomely and guided Rose through the tent flap with a casual hand at the small of her back. To Rose, the hand felt like the point of a knife.

Outside the air was moist and balmy and smelled of wood smoke. The breeze from off the Pacific would bring fog soon, but now its touch was just cool enough to clear her head of the last remnants of the gypsy's spell. It found a few loose wisps of hair on her forehead and played with them, tickling her. She raised her hand to brush them back just as Jade, for what reason she couldn't imagine, reached up to do the same. Their hands touched, and when she lowered hers, she was shocked to feel it tremble.

Oh God, I've lost it, she thought in panic. Two years were too long; her instincts were dead, her reflexes shot, her emotions out of control. Or in control. Something. She thought, I can't take this assignment. I'll blow it. I'll get myself killed. I'll just have to tell Titan I can't.

Jade laughed softly. "Well, that was quite a performance. What do you think of my fortune-teller now?"

Rose laughed, too, deliberately avoiding his gaze. "She was very good, I'll have to admit. Very convincing, for a moment or two. Believe me, I'll never try to crash a celebrity party on a borrowed press pass again. I've learned my lesson! And you were good, too. I never saw your signals."

"I don't suppose you'd believe me if I told you I had absolutely nothing to do with that?"

Rose shook her emphatically. "Not in a million years." She began to fuss nervously with her camera. "Uh, look, Mr. Castle, you've been very nice about this, and don't think I don't appreciate it. But I really think it's about time I left. I'm not a press photographer. I just wanted a chance—I mean, it's a photographer's dream, you must know that. Some of the most beautiful people in the world are here."

Jade's soft laughter interrupted her performance. She looked up at him, and in spite of her resolve not to let him affect her that way again, she felt her throat lock and her stomach tighten. And she thought, the one I'd most like to photograph, Jade Castle, is you.

She could shoot him a hundred different ways, but beginning with this—with firelight glinting in his deep-set eyes and casting mysterious shadows across his face. With his head thrown back and the lines of his neck and throat and the open front of his shirt a single tapering column—a slash of dark against pristine white. With shoulders straight and hands lightly resting at his waist, a portrait of unconscious arrogance, of power held in check.

For the first time she noticed that he wore a chain around his neck. Not the cliched gold circlet made to rest at the base of a masculine throat just where it could be glimpsed in the V of an open-necked shirt, but a longer chain of a dull silvery metal, with a small black pendant that nestled all but invisibly in the hair-crested hollow between his pectorals. It was a personal thing, not meant for display; with his shirt properly buttoned it wouldn't show at all.

"But you can't leave yet," he murmured suddenly. "You haven't met Tessa."

Rose jerked her eyes from the center of his chest back up to his face and saw that his eyes were focused over and beyond her head. His smile was indulgent. She remembered belatedly what the tabloids had said about Jade Castle and Tessa Freedom. God, *there* were a couple of names! But then, this was Hollywood, where nothing was ever quite what it seemed.

She turned to follow his gaze, but it was several seconds before she was able to identify the famous rock singer. A bonfire had been lit in a huge fire pit near a pool the size of a small lake. In the firelight's erratic illumination gypsy musicians were playing something wild and wanton. A small group of professional dancers had abandoned the spotlight to a crowd of enthusiastic and uninhibited beginners. And nowhere in the world, Rose thought, could there be anyone more enthusiastic or less inhibited than Tessa Freedom. She had obviously chosen her name to match her personal credo.

Castle was right. She was hard to recognize without the wildly frizzed and tinted hair and oddball clothes that were her performance trademarks. Her own hair was black and straight and shiny as a raven's wing, and she blended with the noisy revelers as if born to wear gypsy skirts and peasant blouses.

Her partner in the dance was a beautiful young man with a red sash around his narrow hips and the twitchy self-awareness of a male model or aspiring actor. They were doing an impromptu variation of a courtship dance that, when performed by the folk-dance troupe, had probably been innocently playful and flirtatious. With Tessa adding elements of flamenco and modern jazz, it was torridly erotic. Seduction set to music.

The crowd parted to watch, and to stamp and clap, adding a primitive beat to the soaring violins. Faster and faster, rising like a whirlwind, the music spread wildfire through the senses. Heartbeats quickened, lips parted, eyes took on a hungry light, and way down deep inside, elemental passions stirred.

Rose shifted restlessly and glanced at the man beside her, embarrassed in vague and inexplicable ways. But Jade seemed almost amused. His eyes held genuine admiration and nothing more, and his smile was only slightly awry.

A little surprised, Rose cleared her throat and said cautiously, "She's very good. I had no idea she could dance."

Jade laughed and murmured cryptically, "There's not much Tessa can't do." The music ended with a shout and a round of appreciative applause. He looked down at Rose and jerked his head toward the dancers. "Let's go break this up before we get raided. It's time you met the one responsible for all this.... Hello, love, having fun?" Jade deepened his Australian accent and casually placed his hand on the nape of Tessa's neck.

Laughing and disheveled and still out of breath, the rock singer turned into the curve of his arm and stood on tiptoe to plant a noisily affectionate kiss on his mouth. "Yes, love, loads. Lovely party. Did you catch my act?" Her speaking voice was a rather childish croak; when she performed, it was reduced to emotional essence, evocative of lost dreams and tormenting passions.

Castle squeezed her shoulder and laughed softly. "Sure did. Who's your friend?"

"Oh! This is, um, Raoul Somebody. Isn't he great? Come here, Raoul, I want you to meet Jade. This is his house." She hooked an arm around the elbow of the beautiful young man and drew him forward into their intimate circle. "Raoul, this is Jade, and this is . . . ?"

"Rose St. James," Jade supplied

"I'm a photographer," Rose explained when Tessa looked momentarily puzzled, holding out her free hand. Tessa took it and gave it a quick, firm shake.

"Oh! Lovely. Raoul, Rose. Rose, Raoul."

Rose exchanged a handshake and "Pleased to meet yous" with Raoul.

"Raoul is going to be in my next video, aren't you love?" Tessa winked at Rose and patted the dancer's glistening chest as she adroitly turned him back toward the party. "Go have some goulash, darling. I'll join you in a bit in the casino, okay? Bye bye." She turned back into Jade's arms with a husky laugh and a low growl. "He is *such* an animal!"

"Control yourself, Tess," Jade said dryly, and with an odd note of warning added, "Ms. St. James would like to take your picture. Best foot forward, love; this is the press."

"Oh, lovely," Tessa rasped cheerfully. "Where would you like us?" She snuggled closer to Jade, mugging outrageously.

Rose laughed, liking the rock star in spite of herself. She glanced around. "Right here is fine if you really don't mind. That fire makes interesting lighting, and there's the pool, too." The huge free-form pool was landscaped to give it the look of a natural pond. It hadn't been illuminated for the party, and its dark surface reflected the bonfire and torchlight in constantly shifting patterns.

Jade chuckled and moved away from Tessa. "Not 'us,' love. You're the one the public pays to look at."

Rose fiddled with her camera, rapidly changing lenses and meter settings. "Now then," she said, taking a deep breath and carefully glancing behind her to gauge the remaining distance to the edge of the pool. "If you'll just stand right there and turn just a bit—I want the firelight on your face. That's right . . . wonderful."

She never saw it coming. She was preoccupied, and it happened too quickly. And besides, they say you never hear the one with your name on it.

Something struck her hard and with purpose on her blind side, knocking her backward, completely off balance. She dimly heard a distant shout and a cry that might have been her own. Her body braced for painful impact, but instead, in surrealistic slow motion, she felt herself falling and falling . . . and then the stinging shock of cold water. . .and a whooshing, crackling sound in her ears. And then suffocating liquid blackness closed over her head.

She didn't panic; she was too well trained. And it wasn't the first time she'd unexpectedly found herself in life-threatening circumstances. She went into the water back first, which might have kept it from rushing into her open mouth. But the impact also drove the air from her lungs, robbing her of buoyancy as well as an oxygen reserve. Weighted down as she was with clothing and heavy cameras, she sank like a stone.

Consumed by her desperate need for air, needing all her concentration to fight the overwhelming compulsion to inhale, Rose forgot the equipment that was dragging her down like so many anchors. She was rapidly losing reason and consciousness. Even when she felt hard hands grasp her and begin to tug at the straps that crisscrossed her body, she didn't understand. She fought mindlessly against her rescuer's efforts to save her life. Her head was bursting, her body one awful silent scream. She shook her head and lashed out, kicking and struggling against the darkness and the unseen shackles that were keeping her from the light.

And then suddenly she was free. Her body was doing appalling things in its effort to expel water and drag in air, and what light there was was far too much. There were hands on her waist, lifting her, and hands on her arms, pulling her. She felt surrounded by concerned faces and worried voices, when all she wanted was a private place to escape to. Her dress was sodden and plastered to her body, and as she was hauled from the water the skirt clung to her hips in folds, leaving her covered only by sheer panty hose and skimpy underwear. Her hair was loose and streaming over her face like seaweed. She was coughing and retching, breathing in racking sobs and trying not to cry out loud like a frightened child. Rose had never considered herself to be particularly vain, but now that her escape from near-drowning seemed assured, she was discovering that in times of catastrophy no one spares much consideration for personal dignity. She wondered if it were possible to die of mortification.

Titan, she thought as great racking coughs tore at her body, I'm going to kill you for this. If it's the last thing I ever do, I'm going to find out who you are, and then I'm going to kill you!

That Titan's machinations were behind this she had no doubt whatsoever. The inebriated reveler who had knocked her into the pool had mysteriously vanished into the crowd.

"Are you all right now?" Jade Castle's voice was harsh and guttural in her ear. For the first time Rose realized that he was as wet as she was, and that it was his hands that had found her and lifted her from the water, his hands that had held her while she coughed and fought for breath.

Almost reflexively she turned toward him, hiding herself in the shelter of his body. She nodded, tried to speak and couldn't. His arm tightened around her. At last she managed to whisper, "Please, just let me get out of here...."

In one swift motion he had scooped her up and was carrying her through the crowd. She was too exhausted, too drained to protest, even if she'd wanted to. And she didn't want to. It was incredibly wonderful to be there, cradled in those strong arms, with his heartbeat thumping steadily against her breast. In all her life she'd never felt so comforted and secure. An unfamiliar weakness washed over her, prickling and tingling through her nose and behind her eyelids, and settling in an aching lump in her throat. She drew an uneven breath and shut her eyes as tightly as she could, but tears squeezed through anyway. She turned her face helplessly into Jade's shoulder and pressed against his chest with a clenched fist.

Jade lowered his head to bring his lips close to her ear and murmured soothing, comforting phrases as he carried her, the way one would reassure a frightened child. It wasn't until later that it occurred to Rose that, from the moment he'd lifted her from the water, his Australian accent had miraculously disappeared.

Jade's house had once belonged to a silent-movie star. It was a sprawling but graceful Tudor, built of stone and wood in the days when skilled labor and natural materials were plentiful and cheap. The great Bel Air fire hadn't touched it, so its trees were big and old and, along with a massive brick and wrought-iron wall, effectively shielded the house from tour buses and casual passersby. The approach from the street was a sweeping drive paved with stone and wide enough to easily accommodate limousines. In back of the house the grounds sloped downhill over several acres toward a view of the Los Angeles basin and the Pacific Ocean beyond.

At the moment the house was a hive of strangers, command central for an army of caterers, all of whom were too busy to spare Jade more than a curious glance. Nevertheless, conscious of his own appearance and the sensibilities of the woman in his arms, he avoided the main part of the house and passed instead through a side door that led to a private courtyard.

It was quieter there and smelled of honeysuckle. His footsteps rang on flagstone as he bypassed the small pool and grottolike Jacuzzi, and pressed a button half-hidden in the wall beside a heavy wooden door. There was an electronic beep, and a panel slid back to reveal what looked like a push-button telephone panel. Jade shifted his burden, quickly tapped out an access code and waited impatiently while the panel made busy computer noises. Damn thing. Air-tight security had been a way of life for him for more years than he cared to count, but he'd never quite come around to feeling comfortable with computers.

Rose seemed very still in his arms; he wondered whether she was asleep or just listening. The hand on his chest, he noticed, had curled around his pendant and was clutching it like a talisman. The feel of her skin on his was unexpectedly disturbing.

The panel stopped playing electronic music, and the door gave a soft click. Jade kicked it open and entered his bedroom. He almost put her down on his bed, but then, thinking of moonbeams and sea foam, he carried her into his study instead and placed her carefully on a big, comfortable leather couch.

When he tried to straighten he discovered that her hand was still clutching his pendant.

She released it hurriedly when she felt the tug, and murmured, "Sorry." Her eyes followed it as he tucked it back inside his shirt. "It's very nice . . . your pendant." She had to stop to cough. "I've never seen one like it."

"I'm not surprised." The pendant was still warm from her hand; he felt it against his skin as if she were still touching him. "I've had it a long time."

"It's a rook, isn't it? A castle."

"Yes," Jade said distantly. He walked to his desk, pressed an intercom button and waited.

"What's it made of? Some kind of stone?"

Jade smiled sardonically. "Jade, of course. Black jade." He straightened as his housekeeper's voice came from the intercom.

"Yes, Mr. Castle?"

"Kim, we'll be having a houseguest. See to a room for her, will you?"

"Yes, Mr. Castle. South guest room is all right?"

"No." He hesitated, glancing again at the small figure on the couch. She was sitting up very straight, watching him with grave and measuring eyes. She reminded him of a wet kitten, a pitiful sight, but with plenty of fight still in her. Without taking his eyes off her, he said into the intercom, "I want her here—in the cottage. It's quieter. She can have the upstairs room."

There was only a moment's hesitation, and then his housekeeper said imperturbably, "Yes, Mr. Castle. I take care of it right away."

"Thanks, Kim." With his fingers still resting lightly on the lifeless intercom, Jade frowned and said bluntly to

Rose, "I'm sorry about this. More sorry than you can possibly imagine."

She lifted her shoulders in a shrug; he saw her try unsuccessfully to repress a shudder. The gray dress was still plastered to her, delineating her breasts like a carving in pewter. "It wasn't your fault," she said in a low voice. "I was careless and clumsy."

Jade swore briefly under his breath. "You were knocked into that pool, and you know it." He stopped and then added harshly, "Believe me, when I get my hands on the idiot who did it—"

"Please don't," Rose said quietly. "I'm sure it wasn't done with malice. It was just somebody who'd had too much wine." She was beginning to shiver, despite all her efforts to control it.

He straightened and said brusquely, "Look, the least you can do is accept my abject apologies. And my hospitality. I can't let you go like this—soaking wet. And you probably should see a doctor."

She smiled faintly and murmured, "You're as wet as I am. I'm fine, Mr. Castle. Really."

She wasn't; he knew that. The incident had shaken her more than she would ever admit. She'd lost some very expensive equipment, and she was cold and wet and looked terrible. And yet she still had the quality he'd noticed before, that quiet, unassailable dignity.

"Come on," he said abruptly, taking her by the elbows and raising her to her feet. He had to fight himself to keep from pulling her right into his arms. "You're freezing. There's still the possibility of pneumonia, you know. You may have water in your lungs. At the very least you've got to get out of those wet clothes—"

"And into a dry martini?" she finished whimsically, through chattering teeth.

He laughed. "Who said that, anyway? W.C. Fields?"

"I don't know. It sounds like something he'd say. But I don't like martinis. I'd settle for some more of that Hungarian wine, though."

"You got it. But first..." He steered her to his bedroom doorway and pointed. "Bathroom's over there. The tub's a whirlpool bath, good for soaking the chill out of you. Take as long as you like. There are clean towels in the cupboard. I'll have my housekeeper bring you something to put on while your clothes are being restored. You can stay here tonight, and tomorrow morning I'll have someone bring up your cameras. I'm afraid we'd never be able to find them in the dark, that pool's not equipped with underwater lighting."

He saw her swallow convulsively as she nodded, and knew that the loss of her equipment had hit her harder than her own physical trauma. Cold anger settled into his bones. As soon as she had disappeared into the bathroom and closed the door after her, he drew the study doors shut and listened until he heard the sound of running water. Then he went back to his desk and pushed another button on the intercom.

"Michaels," he said in a voice that would etch glass, "you have a hell of a lot of explaining to do."

Chapter 3

A long time ago, when she had still believed in dreams and fairy tales, a little girl named Rose had looked out her window and dreamed that she was a beautiful fairy princess, locked in an enchanted tower. Mrs. Pomphrey was the dragon who guarded the tower, and the ivy that grew thick on the dormitory walls was a veil of thorns. In those days she'd never doubted that someday a brave knight would come to rescue her.

Rose remembered that little girl as she stood there in bare feet and Jade Castle's pajamas, looking out at the morning. Perhaps it was the window. It was a big, beautiful arched window with divided panes, nothing at all like the orphanage windows. In her memory, at least, they had been small and dingy. But it was surrounded by ivy, a few untrimmed tendrils of which hung down into view. And the view, itself, made her feel as if she were in the clouds. It looked out over the sweeping lawns and gardens of the estate, past the rooftops of Bel Air and the hazy skyline of Los Angeles all the way to the Pacific Ocean. Out there the sky was still lavender and smoke, as night and the morning fog slowly retreated. Out there somewhere it was night still... in Tahiti and China and Timbuktu.

That little girl named Rose had dreamed of those places, too, and of traveling to wonderful, magical lands of sunshine and flowers. But now... Well, that dream, at least, had come true; she'd traveled to those places and others even more exotic. But now she knew that there was no magic, and that in real life the princess was probably better off fighting her own battles. And that more often than not, it was the dragon who won.

Dragon or knight? Which of those, she wondered, was Jade Castle? Just now he was asleep downstairs, like a dragon guarding his tower, but there was no doubt that last night he'd come to her rescue in the very best knightly tradition. The wry smile faded slowly from her lips as she remembered the darkness and the cold, the awful pressure and the pain. Whatever else the man might be, it was entirely possible that he'd saved her life.

Who are you, Jade Castle? she wondered again. Suddenly it was as if she could hear Titan's dry voice saying, "Aren't you the least bit curious?" Oh God, yes, she was curious about the man who headed Castle Industries. More curious than ever, after meeting him. The more she learned about him, the more questions she had, and the more she wanted answers. And Titan, of course, had known exactly what would happen. Just meet him, he'd challenged her. And then decide. He'd known that her curiosity would decide for her.

Titan knew her too well...

Jade Castle. Was that even his real name? Was the pendant the symbol of his name... or the source of it?

How she would love to get a good look at it, in the light. Last night she'd held it in her hand, and it had felt warm from the heat of his body. It had felt almost like a living thing, or a living part of him. Odd, how secure it had made her feel just to hold it, and to be held.

There was a knock at the door, jarring her, scattering those unwanted thoughts like dry leaves. He was a suspect, not a man. She was the hunter and he the quarry. It was entirely possible that to further her investigation she might have to contrive to get close to him. Very close. But her emotions must remain uninvolved at all costs, and even to *think* of feeling safe with him was not only absurd, it was downright dangerous.

She took a deep breath and turned from the window, tugging at the pajamas as she called, "Come in." The pajamas were scarlet silk and appeared not to have been worn. A gift from a female friend, perhaps? One without much knowledge of or regard for her lover's personal tastes.

As the door swung slowly inward Rose was surprised and dismayed to find that her heart was beating faster. But it was only Kim, the Asian housekeeper, with a heavy breakfast tray.

"Good morning, Miss St. James," the housekeeper said with a surprised smile. "You are already up. I bring you some breakfast. Your clothes be ready soon. I bring them for you, okay? Mr. Castle say if you like to walk in gardens—"

"My cameras," Rose interrupted, putting a hand on the housekeeper's arm. "Do you know if anyone's found my cameras yet?"

Kim raised her slender shoulders and smiled sympathetically. "I don't know, Miss. My son Tran looking for them right now. Mr. Castle let you know, all right?" She set the tray on the bed and turned to go. At the door she stopped. "Mr. Castle say to tell you if you like to go for walk, see him first."

"Oh?" Rose asked casually. "Why?" Was there something on Mr. Castle's estate that he would rather she didn't see?

"He take you to meet dogs; then it be all right. Then you go wherever you like. Enjoy your breakfast, Miss St. James. I go get your clothes now."

Dogs, Rose thought as she sat down on the bed and picked up a piece of buttered toast. Electronic security systems. A wealthy man with a lot to protect? Or a guilty man with something to hide?

Whoever he was, he intruded on her thoughts while she ate breakfast.

Before she had finished her coffee, Kim arrived with her clothes, which had been cleaned and pressed. Even her sandals were dry and supple.

Jade Castle continued to intrude on her thoughts while she dressed.

She was supposed to be thinking about him, of course, but she found that she wasn't able to *think* at all. Rather, she seemed to be receiving a jumbled montage of sensual impressions that interfered with her mental processes. Give your instincts a go, Titan had told her. But her instincts were being short-circuited by other things. Things like the sound of his voice, a low resonant burr with traces of Australia that came and went. The sweet taste of wine on her lips, and the sheen of wine on his mouth. The unexpectedness of his hand beneath her fingertips, and the hot-poker shock of it on her back. A piece of black jade that absorbed his body heat until it felt more like a part of him than cold, lifeless stone.

That pendant intrigued her. It was no secret that a black rook was the logo for Castle Industries. It wouldn't be unusual for a man to have such an ornament made and to carry it with him as a symbol of his identity and power. But there was the coincidence of his name. Jade Castle. A man with no past. A man with a made-up name. A man who wore the symbol of that name like a talisman, next to his skin.

He was waiting for her downstairs, in the room he'd brought her to last night. It was a private study, a room that should have betrayed something of the private man. But although it was warm and masculine, done in soft leathers and polished woods and the rich glowing jewel tones of Oriental rugs, it was oddly characterless. There were no photographs, no diplomas or certificates on the walls, nothing that suggested hobbies and interests. Rose couldn't stop to look, of course, but she would have been willing to bet that the books on the shelves had been chosen by decorators for their visual impact and nothing more. The room gave away no more of the man than the bedroom she had passed through so briefly last night, or the bathroom where she had soaked away the chill of shock in a sumptuous tiled tub.

Rose felt a little jolt of surprise when she saw him standing in front of the window, at a slight angle to the light, so that shadows accentuated the asymmetry of his face. It wasn't anything about *him*. In fact, he looked almost exactly as he had the night before. She had thought the white silk shirt and dark slacks must be a concession to the party's gypsy theme, but now she realized that his only concession had been to unbutton a few extra buttons on his shirt. And she thought that even those had been at the insistence of the uninhibited Tessa. No, the surprise was at herself, for her reaction to him.

He'd called it chemistry. She'd felt it yesterday when she'd seen him for the very first time—that funny little contraction deep inside, right under her heart. This morning the sensation was more marked, a little like having the room drop out from under her.

His eyes swept over her with that familiar look of appraisal and challenge. She found herself wishing... dangerous things. Wishing she were wearing something other than the plain gray working costume of Rose St. James, photographer. Something soft and clinging that would swirl around her knees as she descended the stairs. Something jade green and low cut. Or better still, something sporty and elegant, camel suede riding clothes, with an ivory silk blouse and a jade green cravat.

"Good morning," Jade said coolly. "I trust you slept well?"

Rose advanced, bringing her hands together at her waist in a deliberately nervous, self-conscious manner. "Yes, Mr. Castle. I did. Thank you very much. And please, thank whoever did such a lovely job cleaning and pressing my clothes. It wasn't necessary, really. You needn't have gone to so much trouble. I'm sure I'd have been fine with a few moments' rest."

"You were in shock," Jade said abruptly. "And in no shape to go anywhere." His voice and expression made it very clear that, as far as he was concerned, the subject was closed.

Rose cleared her throat. It wasn't difficult to act nervous and ill at ease. Jade's manner was so austere and distant, almost grim. It was almost as if he were angry about something, though she sensed that if he was angry it was not with her. Schooling her mind to function with precision and clarity, she carefully filed that impression away. Later, at a safe distance from disturbing chemistries and psychic energies, she would be able to clear her mind of all the emotional and sensual clutter and assess that tiny piece of information along with all the others. And when she had enough pieces, she would solve the puzzle of Jade Castle.

"Well," she said now, carefully injecting the right proportions of polite withdrawal and sincere gratitude into her voice and manner, "I do appreciate all you've done. Do you know if…have my cameras been found?"

His expression softened slightly. "We'll go find out, if you like. In fact, I was waiting for you before going down to the pool myself."

"Kim said you wanted me to meet your dogs. Does that mean what I think it does?" She shivered. "Do you have…guard dogs? Are they dangerous?"

Jade's grin was without humor. "Only to those who represent a danger to me. Once you've been properly introduced they'll count you among their bosom buddies. Ready to go?"

"I guess so," Rose said doubtfully. "Are you sure…?"

"Absolutely." His mouth twisted. "You don't imagine I'd put your safety at risk on my property twice in less than twenty-four hours, do you? Take my arm if it will make you feel better." He looked down at her as she tucked her hand gingerly into the crook of his elbow, and she saw a sardonic glint in his deepset eyes as he drawled, "Trust me, sweetheart."

Trust me. Rose was smiling with the irony of that as Jade escorted her through the private courtyard to the door in the massive rock wall.

"Where are the dogs now?" Rose asked as they waited for the computerized lock to run through its program. "Where were they last night during the party?"

"Last night they were shut up. As for where they are right now, I couldn't say, but I rather imagine they'll find us. Let's see, shall we?"

The lock beeped and opened, and Jade patted her hand reassuringly and led her through the door. Almost immediately two enormous—and wet—Dobermans came bounding around a corner of the house. "What did I tell you?" Castle said, raising his eyebrows at Rose.

The dogs, hell-bent on launching themselves into Jade's arms, instead skittered to a stop at the unexpected presence of a stranger. They sat back on their haunches, ducking their heads suspiciously.

"Come on, Duchess . . . Clyde. Someone here I'd like you to meet." The dogs stood simultaneously and trotted obediently over to push their pointed muzzles into Jade's hand.

Rose, who had dealt efficiently with more than one unfriendly canine in her days with the Bureau, clutched Jade's arm and murmured nervously, "What do I do?"

"What you do for any polite introduction—hold out your hand and say, 'How do you do?'"

Acknowledging the note of laughter with a glance, Rose held out her hand, palm up, for the dogs to sniff, and said cautiously, "Hello, Duchess. And, uh, hello to you, too, Clyde." In a stage whisper she asked, "How am I doing?"

"Just fine. Now pet them. Okay, kids, this is Rose, she's a friend of mine. Give her a big kiss and then beat it."

Both dogs dutifully nuzzled her hand, licked it thoroughly and went bounding off. Rose drew in a breath and released it in a relieved laugh. "That wasn't so bad."

"They're pussycats," Jade grunted in his dry way. "A couple of frauds, actually."

"Yeah, I'll bet," Rose responded just as dryly.

Jade chuckled. "Come on, we'll have to take a roundabout way to the pool." He brushed gingerly at his muddied slacks. "I think the sprinklers must be on."

The grounds of the estate were serene and quiet; it was hard to believe that last night had ever happened. The gypsy camp had vanished. Where it had been the trampled grass was already perking up under the sprinklers' diamond spray.

"Incredible," Rose breathed as she stopped to look over the scene. "It's all gone. How did they clean it up so quickly?"

"Actually, I believe the cleanup crew pulled out about an hour before sunrise," Jade said. "The gardeners have been at it ever since."

It must take a small army of gardeners to keep the place looking like this, Rose thought, impressed almost against her will. In daylight it was incredibly beautiful. Their circuitous route took them through a good part of it, past the birch grove where she had first met her prospective quarry, and then down a slope landscaped with rocks and junipers and into an informal rose garden.

Here Rose slowed her steps, then halted. Her hand slipped from Jade's arm as she turned slowly, looking and looking.

Jade stood watching her patiently, without speaking. After a moment Rose murmured, "I've always been partial to roses."

"Ah yes," Jade said softly. "Your namesake flower. He went on watching her, and there was an odd stillness about him.

Rose reached out to touch the crimson velvet petals of a Mr. Lincoln, and then glanced up at Jade. "May I?"

"By all means."

For a few moments Rose walked in the sun-drenched garden, touching a petal here, sniffing a blossom there, allowing herself to forget for those few moments, at least, all she knew of ugliness and shadows. And as always she thought that there couldn't be so very much wrong with a world that had roses in it.

"No," Jade said, his voice a husky burr from very close behind her. "There isn't."

She hadn't thought she'd spoken aloud. But she must have—he couldn't possibly have read her thoughts. And yet the communion between them was so strong that she almost felt as though he might have. Once again he was standing just behind her, not touching her, yet she could feel him there as vividly as if his fingers were caressing her skin. She wondered what would happen if she turned. Would his arms come around her? And would she go into them, drawn to the warmth of his body like a moth to a killing flame? Would she lift her face for his kiss? What would it be like, to kiss such a man, a man of so many mysteries, a man without softness?

Her body shivered with a chill of excitement that was almost fear. To cover it, she reached out to touch a blossom on the bush closest to her. And then, as her vision cleared and focused on the flower, she slowly drew her hand back. Her fingers had suddenly grown cold.

It was a large bush, heavy and thick with thorns. Its blooms were exquisite—almost, but not quite white, touched with pink just where the petals curled. Rose had

seen one exactly like these before. Very recently, in fact—
in a cut-crystal bud vase, in the back of a gray limousine...

"Do you like that one?" Jade's voice entered her rec-
ollection without disturbing it, like thistle-down settling
on the surface of a pond. "It's one of my favorites."

"It's lovely," Rose said reflectively. "Do you know
what it's called?"

"Pristine, I believe." Jade lifted his arm almost casually, and a young Asian appeared, dressed in blue jeans
and tennis shoes and nothing else. He was very thin, but
muscular and wiry. Jade spoke to him in a low voice, in
a language Rose couldn't identify; she mentally ticked off
the dossier item that had mentioned Southeast Asia.

The boy grinned and, producing a pair of short-
handled clippers from a hip pocket, lopped off one perfect half-opened bloom. Before handing it over to Jade
he meticulously clipped all the vicious thorns from its
stem.

Watching him, Rose murmured, "Pristine...such a
delicate name. And so many thorns."

"Yes," Jade said. "It has more than any other bush in
the garden, I think. But..." He took the flower from the
boy and touched it briefly and unexpectedly to his lips
before handing it to Rose, "the flowers are more than
worth the effort it takes to get past them, don't you
agree?"

The communion between them was such that Rose
knew instantly he wasn't really talking about flowers. But
why, she thought as she murmured her thanks, should he
think I have thorns if he'd never heard of me before last
night?

They strolled on, Rose with her face lowered to sniff
the fragrance of the blossom, hiding the questions in her

eyes, and Jade with a casual hand at her elbow. Except that, for Rose, no touch of his hands would ever be casual. His hands, his voice, his eyes, just his *nearness* electrified her. She'd never felt so alive, nor so cognizant of danger. She would have to tell Titan that she couldn't possibly accept this assignment.

"Ah," Jade said in his unobtrusive way, "Tran has found your cameras."

As they approached the huge pool another Asian boy, every bit as thin as the gardener, hoisted himself out of the water, holding the strap of her camera case in his teeth. He added the streaming case to the small pile of equipment already on the grass, and stood looking down at it while he wiped water from his face.

"Is that all of it?" Jade's grim question was directed at Rose. When she nodded dumbly he murmured his thanks to Tran, who grinned shyly, picked up a towel and went jogging off toward the house. After a moment's silence Jade asked roughly, "Is everything ruined?"

Rose picked up her camera, hefted it and nodded. "I suppose so. I would imagine..." She stopped, swallowed and shrugged.

"I do know roughly what a nice Hasselblad costs," Jade said quietly. "I'm sorry. I'll replace it, of course."

Rose glanced at him, then quickly looked away. "It was insured," she said woodenly. "It's the film. I hate to lose the film I'd already shot. It was irreplaceable."

"I imagine it was."

"All those candid shots of celebrities letting their hair down. They'd have been worth a lot if they turned out as well as I think—oh well."

He was frowning at her, his hands deep in his pockets. "If it's only the money—"

Her bark of laughter cut him off. "*Only* the money? Spoken like a man who's never had to worry about having plenty of it!"

Jade's eyes were shadows; his voice had gone curiously flat. "I only meant that my intention to cover your damages extends to a fair estimate of the market value of your lost photographs, Miss St. James."

It seemed for a moment as if he would say more. Rose waited, watching him intently, and then shook her head. "That's very kind of you. But they really are—were— irreplaceable. If you knew anything at all about photographers, you'd understand. Even if I never tried to sell a single one of those pictures, I'd still feel a . . . a terrible sense of loss."

There was another silence, and then Jade seemed to relax. He touched her cheek with the backs of his fingers and said softly, "Believe it or not, I do understand. And I'd like to try to make it up to you. How's your schedule for the next few weeks?"

It was Rose's turn to frown. "I'm not sure. Some high school seniors to finish up, a wedding next Saturday—I'll have to check my calendar. Why?"

"Ever done any technical stuff? Microphotography? Layouts?"

Rose opened her mouth, closed it again and shrugged. "Micro, not since college. I don't have the equipment. Technical layouts, yes, some."

"If I provide the equipment, will you do some work for me? Or rather, for Castle Industries?"

"Work for you? What sort of work?" Rose hedged, while her mind chewed on this suspiciously fortuitous turn of events. This, she was sure, was exactly what Titan had hoped for when he engineered her "accident."

"Castle's technical literature—manuals, catalogs and so forth—are due for updating. We'd be looking for a good commercial photographer soon anyway. It might as well be you, if you're qualified."

"Oh, I'm qualified," Rose said hurriedly, remembering just in time that Rose St. James would be tickled to death at such a job offer, and with no reservations.

Jade cocked an eyebrow at her and stooped to pick up her sodden cameras and the case of ruined film. "I assume you can pass a security clearance check?"

"I don't know why I shouldn't," she said lightly, and then, belatedly remembering her vow to remove herself from this case at the first opportunity, "But I'll have to check my schedule first. I'll let you know later."

"Of course." Jade's Australian accent had become very pronounced. He patted his hip pocket absently. "Come back to the house and let me get you a phone number to call when you've made up your mind."

A little later Rose sat in her modest Nissan in the huge curved driveway of the Castle estate, fingering a small white card embossed with a shiny black rook. Her cameras were leaking water all over the floor in the back of the car, and Jade Castle was leaning on the window. His face was very near.

"Please call," he said with an odd intensity, holding her eyes with his. "Give me a chance to make amends." When she didn't answer, his mouth lifted in one of his crooked smiles. "In case you think this is charity, I really do need you, Rose."

Her lips parted, an unconscious reaction to the small jolt of recognition, but he had captured her eyes with his, and she couldn't for the moment think where she'd heard those words before.

"Oh, and by the way, love," he drawled, touching her nose with a forefinger. Something hard and bleak in his eyes tugged at her; she felt trapped, incapable of pulling away. "I haven't always had 'plenty of money.'" Rose's pulse began to beat in a slow, painful cadence. In that soft, drawling voice he went on, "I've known what it's like to have *nothing*. Nothing but the breath in my body, and no guarantees that the next breath might not be my last."

And then, unexpectedly—but somehow inevitably—he lowered his head and kissed her.

Chapter 4

The first thought to break clear of the turbulence in her mind was that she had been wrong to think he had no softness in him....

He looked as hard and unyielding as the pendant he wore, but his lips were warm silk, and incredibly gentle. And if he'd meant the kiss to be a brief, farewell kind of thing, it double-crossed him and developed a will of its own. His lips didn't pull away, but lingered to play with hers in a series of tender, butterfly caresses. She sat very still, with her eyes closed and her lips slightly parted, awed by the sensation. Her lips began to move with his, touching as his touched, exploring as his explored. She tilted her head slightly to his without thinking, and felt his fingers touch her throat, warm on the side of her neck, and then lift along her jawline in gentle appeal.

His tongue touched her with such delicacy that it seemed a gift rather than an intrusion. Her mouth softened in response and formed a rapt smile.

His fingers moved, burrowing upward into her hair. A prickling, shimmering current spread through her, settling in her hands and feet like pins and needles. Unexpectedly, and for the first time in her memory, she began to tremble. As if he were reading her response, his tongue entered her mouth in a gentle but utterly devastating invasion. And then withdrew.

Rose sat still, dazed and shaking with deep-down tremors. It was a moment or two before she could open her eyes. She found that his were still very close to her, and for once she could see into the shadows. After a moment's silent communion they crinkled with his smile. His hand still rested on her neck; he tightened it briefly, giving her head a little shake.

"Well, Rose," he said, barely whispering, "you do realize that's something that can never happen again."

Shock made a cold starburst inside her chest. Unable to speak, she licked her lips instead and found the taste of him still on her mouth. His gaze slid downward to watch the movement of her tongue, and his thumb moved across her lips, wiping the moisture from them.

"The *first* kiss," Jade said softly, recapturing her eyes, "can only happen once." He straightened abruptly, with a gesture of farewell. "Drive safely, Rose."

Drive safely? Impossible, under the circumstances. Rose left the estate and drove through the maze of Bel Air streets to Sunset Boulevard on automatic pilot, too shaken to think. Her legs were weak, her coordination jerky. She felt a strange and alien urge to cry.

At Sunset she turned west, looking for a gas station. She had to go down to Wilshire to find one, but coping with Westwood traffic was therapy, of a sort. At least it forced her to concentrate on the business of staying alive.

By the time she had located a station with a pay phone, bought a soft drink from a vending machine, and sorted out change and her calling card, she was almost calm.

The call-code sequence Michaels had given her was a relatively simple one, but even so it took Rose several minutes to work through the shunts and relays designed to prevent a phone number. from being traced to its source. The connection opened to listening silence after three rings.

"Hello, Titan," Rose said evenly. "Jordan Rose calling."

"Hello, Rose." Titan's voice sounded detestably cheerful. "How'd it go?"

"Swimmingly," Rose said tartly. "You'll be pleased to know that your gambit was a big success. Your pawn has been offered a position in the opponent's camp."

"Offered?" Titan focused unerringly on the operative word. "I take it you haven't accepted."

"No." Rose took a deep breath. "I haven't."

"Why not?"

"I . . . can't."

"Come on now, Rose, you know you'll have to do better than that." Titan's voice was very soft; it shivered over her skin like a knife's edge.

The phone felt slippery in her hand. Resisting an urge to wipe her hands on her skirt, she gripped the receiver tightly and frowned at the Sunday traffic. She'd have to tell Titan the truth. He insisted on it—*always.*

And where in the world had she heard *that* just recently?

"It would be unwise," she said, making her voice professionally emotionless. "There is an objectivity problem."

"Oh?" Titan's voice was, if possible, even softer.

Rose closed her eyes. "Yes. It seems that I may be . . . emotionally susceptible to the suspect."

"Rose," Titan said, "this isn't like you."

"I know." She sighed, and then, with a soft ironic laugh, said, "There's no accounting for chemistry."

"What was that?"

"Nothing. But you can see why I can't accept the assignment. I'm sorry." She was surprised to find that she *was* sorry. Everything about Jade Castle fascinated her. She would have given a lot to solve his mysteries, to find out if he had other hidden signs of softness.

But she knew, if anyone did, how dangerous it could be when emotions interfered with an operation.

"I'd like you to take the assignment anyway," Titan said after a moment's consideration.

"What?" She couldn't believe she'd heard him right. With a sardonic laugh she added, "This isn't like you, Titan."

There was no answering chuckle. "I need information—concrete data. If you have—" now he did chuckle—"an 'emotional susceptibility' to Castle, it could be to your advantage."

Anger locked her jaw and put ice in her voice. "There's a name for what you're asking me to do, you know that, Titan? And a very special name for you for asking, too."

This time, infuriatingly, he did respond with amusement. "Take the job, Rose," he said with arrogant finality and broke the connection.

Rose stood for a long time without moving, gripping the phone until her hand felt numb. She wondered, not for the first time, whether she hated Titan. Was it even possible to hate a man she'd never seen?

He'd been such a big part of her life for so long. During her days with the Bureau he'd been the single most important factor in her existence. The order and shape of her days had been determined by that implacable voice on the telephone. There were times when she'd resented him, times when she'd felt as if she were no more than a puppet, and he the master who controlled her strings. But those same strings had been her lifeline, at times, and her salvation....

How many times had she speculated about Titan? Who was he? What did he look like? Why was his identity such a closely guarded secret? During the early years she'd actually tried to find out, but despite all her skills she'd never come close to solving the mystery. She'd concluded that he must be someone famous, or at least well-known, with another life, another identity to protect. She'd invented fantasy backgrounds for him, faces to go with the voice—handsome faces when things were good between them, hideous, even deformed faces when she wondered if she hated him.

And then Thad Moses had joined the Bureau, and for a brief time reality had superceded fantasy. What irony it was that her old nemesis and that particular stirring of the senses she'd last felt with Thad Moses should both reenter her life at the same time....

A polite cough brought Rose back to the here and now. With murmured apologies to the middle-aged woman waiting to use the pay phone, Rose gathered up her things and went back to her car. In a few minutes she was on the San Diego Freeway, not heading south, toward Venice and home, but north, out of the city, into the heat-shimmering vastnesses of the Mojave Desert.

In the days before freeways, when getting from here to there was part of the adventure and driving was a form a recreation, travelers had dared not venture into the desert without canteens filled with water, enough for the car radiator as well as themselves. To be stranded by even minor car trouble in the desert without water could be fatal.

Blacktopped roads linked small dusty towns together, but the miles between were lonely ones. To fill the long, empty gaps between towns, small outposts appeared, perched on the arrow-straight asphalt like dusty old crows on a telephone wire. Some sported signs that said succinctly, *GAS . . . EAT.* Others made do with a dusty Coca Cola sign in the window and the self-explanatory gas pump out in front. Some remained little more than shacks, seemingly barely able to stand against the relentless thermal winds; others grew, added garages and motel rooms, acquired competition across the road, and eventually turned into towns themselves.

The people who manned these outposts were a special breed—loners, most of them, fiercely independent and indifferent to the changes going on in the world beyond the desert. When the freeways came and passed their outposts by, some moved on, but others stayed and didn't even seem to notice.

It was to one of these outposts that Rose drove that Sunday afternoon. She parked her car in the only shade for miles around, a huge clump of centuries-old Joshua trees. A displaced roadrunner started up, trotted a few yards, then stopped to look back, disheartened at the lack of sport.

Rose had been here before, but it had been a while, and it occurred to her that there was something symbolic about this relic of the age of the Model T squatting only a few miles from the glittering white air strip that had become the favored landing site for NASA's space shuttle.

The place appeared deserted. The tall cylindrical gasoline pump hadn't held a drop of gas in decades, and the rusty ice chest in front of the store window hadn't been connected to a source of power for nearly that long. Tumbleweeds stirred among the car bodies that clustered around the stone and wood building like chicks around a molting hen. Rose's footsteps crunched loudly on fine gravel as she crossed the emptiness between the store and the road.

But in the garage in the back of the store a pair of feet encased in tennis shoes, attached to legs wearing oil-stained Levi's, protruded from under a stripped-down car body. Rose tucked her skirt under her bottom and gingerly squatted on her heels.

"Cracky," she called, "is that you?"

"Who wants to know?" The voice was an old man's voice, a croak as dry and harsh as the landscape.

"Come on out of there. It's me, Rose."

The angular body that followed the legs out from under the car wasn't an old man's body. But the face, even split wide open in a welcoming grin, was an old man's face. According to his Bureau file, Leif Cracken was no more than thirty-eight. He looked sixty. He'd come home from Vietnam after surviving six years of torture and starvation in a North Vietnamese prison to find that his parents had both died and the young bride he'd left behind seven years before had a three-year-old son. He hadn't blamed her, really, but there wasn't a place for him in her life anymore, so he joined the Bureau. And as it had for others, Rose included, the Bureau became his family.

Rose had worked with Cracken on several assignments, but she wasn't with him in Central America when he was taken hostage by guerrilla forces. Ten months later he'd walked out of the jungle with fourteen broken bones—mostly ribs and fingers—and a ruined larynx. His body healed, after a fashion, but his mind said, "That's enough." The Bureau had retired him on full disability, and Cracken had gone searching for a place without jungles. A place where he could see what was coming a long time before it got there. He lived alone, and with what was left of his hands he built hot rods. He'd been left with just a thumb and half a forefinger on his left hand, but his right was whole except for the tips of his ring and little fingers. For Cracken it was enough.

"Rose," he rasped, getting to his feet with a young man's agility. "Hey, long time no see!"

Rose laughed and reached out to touch the gray beard that almost reached his collar button. "What's all this? You're too skinny for Santa Claus."

"Ah, hell." Cracken grinned and patted the wavy growth. "Got tired of people asking about the damn scars."

He was in a rational mood today, thank God. Rose had sat with him on more than one occasion while he'd wrestled with his demons, but today...today she needed help with some demons of her own, and Cracken was the one person she could trust who might also understand.

She linked her arm through his and said briskly, "Well, buy me a drink and get me out of this heat before I mummify. What way is this to treat an old friend?"

"Cracky," Rose said sometime later, frowning at the interlocking moisture rings she was making with her Coke can on the red Formica tabletop, "did you ever feel like you were being manipulated?"

Cracken didn't answer. He went on staring at the magazine pictures of James Dean on the wall behind her head. The paper made a faint rustling sound in the breeze from a small oscillating fan.

"I feel," Rose went on, "like I'm involved in some sort of elaborate game—chess, maybe."

"So what else is new?" Cracken rasped. "That's all it's ever been, babe. A great big chess game."

"Yeah, I know. But this time...this time I don't think I'm one of the players, Cracky. I'm beginning to think I'm nothing but a pawn."

Cracken dragged his aged blue eyes to Rose's face. "Rosie, babe, don't you know that's all you ever were? All any of us were. Are. Just pawns in somebody else's game." He tipped back his head and drank from his own can, then touched his mouth with the back of his good hand. "So, whose game is it this time?"

"Titan's," Rose said moodily. "Who else?"

Cracken's eyes narrowed in surprise. "Titan? How'd you manage to get mixed up with him again? I thought you were all through with that stuff."

"He found me. I sure didn't go looking for him!"

Cracken began to nod. "What's he got you into this time? A hunting expedition?"

Rose shook her head. "No, just fishing, so far. A man named Jade Castle of Castle Industries. Know him?"

Cracken's shoulders rose an inch and then settled. He drank again. "Well, he makes a pretty damn good grease cutter, I know that much."

"Among other things," Rose said dryly. "Chemical weapons, for starters." She had no qualms about leaking classified information. Telling Cracken was like whispering into the desert wind. "An exclusive contract arrangement with the Pentagon. Only for some reason, someone at Castle decided to go nonexclusive."

"Ah," Cracken said. His nodding had become repetitious, almost rhythmic, as if he'd forgotten to turn off the switch.

"Yes. So naturally this has caused the Bureau to take an interest in Castle's affairs."

Cracken stopped nodding abruptly. His eyes moved until they were focused on her face, and he said very quietly, "Go on."

"The weapons are being rerouted by computer, using top secret access codes, which points to someone at or very near the top."

"Castle himself?"

"That's one theory."

Cracken's mouth lifted in a wry grin. "But you don't like that one."

Rose shifted in her chair and released a small snort. "Cracky, I don't know what's happened to me. Have I slipped so badly? Have I been away from it too long? Logic says one thing, but my instincts tell me another."

"Nothin' wrong with your instincts, babe. Never was."

"No..." Rose settled back with a sigh. "The trouble is, Jade Castle is a mystery all by himself. In a way that muddies things—do you know what I mean? And then..." She laced her fingers around her can and frowned at them. "I've got a feeling I'm being kept in the dark. And manipulated. I never did like to work in the dark, Cracky. Titan knows that. But he's not being straight with me; I'd swear it."

Cracken muttered something under his breath, but when Rose said, "What?" he shook his head.

"He knows more about this than he's telling me," she went on when he remained obstinately silent. "And there are things..." Cracken didn't prompt her when she lapsed into thoughtful silence; it wasn't his way. After a few minutes Rose suddenly leaned forward.

"Cracky, do you know who Titan is?"

His reply was a cackle of laughter, a rustling sound like sand blowing against adobe walls. "Nobody knows who Titan is, babe. Nobody."

Disappointed, but not surprised, Rose persisted, "Would you tell me if you knew?"

After a moment Cracken nodded. His eyes were flat, like polished blue stones. "In a minute, babe. In a minute. I don't owe nobody. And I'll tell you something now, free of charge. You look out for that Titan. Don't you trust him. Because you're damn right he's not being straight with you."

Rose felt her body grow cold and still. With studied calm she asked, "Cracky, what do you know?"

"I know that whatever game you're in, it ain't the Bureau's."

Even more softly Rose repeated, "Cracky, what do you know? Tell me."

"I know you've been out of touch." Cracken tilted back his head to drain his soft drink, revealing for a moment the livid rope scars that had destroyed his larynx. Then, with a violent sound he crushed the can and dropped it back on the table. Watching it rock he whispered slowly, "Or you'd know that Titan left the Bureau almost two years ago—not long after you did."

The room was filled with tiny sounds: a tinny clanking from the rocking can; the soft whoosh of the fan; the rustling of James Dean's images on the walls. But inside Rose there was a great stillness. She didn't question Cracken's statement. For him to make it, it had to be true.

Cracken, watching her, said, "You're going to play the game out anyway, aren't you?"

Without the slightest shred of humor, Rose smiled. "Oh yes . . ."

Cracken had begun to nod again. "You can't get out of it, you know. Never. They won't let you."

Aching at the bleakness in his face and the emptiness in his eyes, Rose swallowed and murmured, "The Bureau?"

"The *life*," Cracken said vaguely, still nodding. "You can't leave it alone. . . ."

Rose stood up abruptly, then bent impulsively to kiss her old friend's leathery cheek. For a moment she held him close, stroking his hair, his beard. Then she whispered, "It's all right. I'll be all right. I'll be careful. Thanks, Cracky. And take care of yourself."

Outside she lifted her face to the wind, facing into it as she pulled the clips from her hair. The wind clawed through it, sucked the moisture from her skin, her lips, her eyes.

You can't leave the life.

Cracken was right. Once an agent, always an agent. She'd only thought she'd put it all behind her when she left the Bureau. She hadn't even realized that her life was stale and flat—until now, for the first time in two years, she felt alive again! Her blood was surging through her veins; adrenaline was flowing; all her senses were fine-tuned and sharp. Who had she thought she was kidding? All that jogging—what had she been keeping herself fit for, if not this?

She sure hadn't fooled Titan. Titan had known what Cracken knew: that she would be unable to resist the bugles.

Titan. So it was his game. His and his alone. The Bureau might fit into the puzzle somewhere, but she didn't know how or where. Just as she didn't know where *she* fit. Or Jade Castle. But she knew one thing for certain: if it was the last thing she ever did, she was going to find out.

The primary production facility of Castle Industries sprawled across a mesa overlooking the Pacific Ocean. The corporate headquarters backed up to the precipice, so close that from the executive suite a glass elevator could ferry passengers down the cliff face to a semiprivate cove below. Jade had often overheard employees joking that when the "Big One"—California's cataclysmic earthquake—came, the corporate big shots would be the first to slide into the Pacific Ocean. Like most Californians, they joked about it, but didn't worry much.

The west wall of Jade's office was glass. The view from his desk consisted of sky and sea and the distant horizon, and sometimes when fog and darkness blurred that dividing line, it was hard to tell where one left off and the other began. Some people found it monotonous, but Jade never tired of it.

Right now, though, he had his back to the view. He'd arranged himself that way on purpose. His intercom had just announced his newest employee, and he wanted to see her face, her eyes, before she had a chance to read his.

As he waited for the knock on the door he was surprised by an unfamiliar feeling in his belly. He thought in amazement. Butterflies?

The expected knock sounded, and Jade called quietly, "Come in," steeling himself for his first look at her since he'd kissed her Saturday morning. That had been another surprise. He hadn't known he was going to do that at that particular moment. He'd accepted the fact that he would do it eventually, but had meant to pick a more auspicious time and place. He'd been bemused to discover that in some things, you don't always do the choosing.

Somewhat irrelevantly he wondered what she would be wearing this morning. Something absolutely correct for the role she was playing, he could count on that. He wondered about her hair, whether she would take pains to make it appear severe and frumpish, as she had on Saturday. It would be interesting to see whether vanity would win out over professionalism. If he were a betting man, he would put every dime he had on the latter.

When she pushed open the door and walked into the room he didn't know whether to be disappointed or not; the crooked grin he wore was full of sincere admiration. His fortune was safe—professionalism had won, hands down. Not for the first time he wondered how in the world so beautiful a woman could contrive to make herself look so...insignificant.

"Hello, Rose," he said. "I'm glad you're here."

But she wasn't looking at him, and she didn't return his greeting. She had stopped just inside the door, momentarily stunned by the panorama that had suddenly opened up before her. Jade knew the feeling. Coming into his office was like walking out on a precipice and stepping unexpectedly into thin air—and then, instead of plummeting downward, finding that you were soaring.

"It's like flying," Rose said softly as she walked across to stand before the window. "Like being a part of it—the sky, the sea."

"Yes," Jade said, and waited, sensing that she would say more if he left her alone.

She didn't say anything for a long time. Instead she reached out and placed her hand on the window, palm flat and fingers spread. The expression on her face was rapt and wistful. Jade saw the glow in her eyes, the almost childlike parting of her lips, and felt a kind of hunger he'd only known a long, long time ago and to which he had never been able to put a name. It was both hunger and thirst, loneliness and longing. It was being cold and lost and scared, and hearing music and laughter in the distance.

He touched the pendant that lay against his chest and, remembering to keep Australia in his voice, said softly. "I take it you like the sea."

She looked at him then and smiled. "I guess it must come from growing up so far from any ocean. As a child, you see, I had only books and imagination. But I used to look out my window and dream of the sea, and of sailing away to wonderful and exciting places." She shrugged and laughed a little self-consciously. "Silly, I know."

"Not at all. Tell me," he asked, watching her closely, "when you grew up, did you find your dream?"

Her eyes locked with his, and he saw his own longings mirrored in hers. "No," she said slowly. "I went to the strange and exciting places, but..."

"But?"

She shrugged and looked away. "There was nothing there for me after all."

"So you're still looking?"

Her voice was barely audible. "Perhaps."

"And tell me, Rose, do you still dream?" He'd moved close enough to touch her, and he did. He hadn't meant to, not so soon. But her eyes were so luminous they pulled at him. He felt the velvet texture of her cheek with his fingertips, the ridge of her jaw, and the vibrant, pulsing column of her neck.

Her mouth moved, a tiny involuntary spasm of emotional distress that gave him another in a series of surprises. *Vulnerability?* In this woman? He wouldn't have thought it possible, but nobody was that good an actress.

And then he stopped, mentally shaking his head with both admiration and chagrin. Oh, yes she *was* that good. After all, it was what made her so capable at what she did. It was why he was counting on her.

The one thing he hadn't counted on was the strength of the attraction between them. It was a physical thing, an almost tangible force that went beyond her acting skills and transcended her cover. She might remind him at times of water sprites and moonbeams, spitting kittens and homeless waifs, but first and always he was aware of her as a woman. And never more strongly than at this moment.

He wasn't sure yet just what he was going to do about it, but he did know one thing: if either of them thought they were going to be able to manage this on a strict employer-employee basis, they were kidding themselves.

Rose saw Jade's mouth tighten at the same moment his fingers moved in her hair, rubbing gently, sensually, at the base of her skull. His touch mesmerized her even as she wondered what had passed through his mind and taken the softness away with it. She closed her eyes to hide her brief spasm of panic.

Dear God, she was thinking, what am I going to do? I can't go through with this, but I don't want to give it up. All he has to do is touch me, and all I can think about is when will he touch me again . . . ?

She knew that she was very close to doing something she'd never done before in all her years with the Bureau—prostituting herself in the line of duty. Her body and her femininity were her best tools, of course, and in the course of her assignments she'd used them both in many ways. But never that way. And there had been times when her job might have been easier, and far less dangerous, if her personal code of ethics had been less strict.

But now...now she seemed to have no defenses against this man. He'd caught her with her shields down. She'd never felt such a strong reaction to a man. Never. Suddenly, perhaps for the first time in her adult life, Rose was afraid.

Chapter 5

She cleared her throat and said, "What?" because she'd forgotten the question. It seemed a year since either of them had spoken.

Very softly Jade repeated it. "Do you still dream, Rose?"

Seconds passed, counted in the slow, steady cadence of her pulse. Under his hand her throat felt tight and sore. Then she murmured, "Dreams are for children," and pulled herself away from his touch.

Jade's hand dropped. He said "Rose..." just as she turned from the window and began, "Mr. Castle, I—"

"*Jade,*" he said harshly, interrupting her. "Don't you think you could call me Jade?"

Their positions had changed; now the light from the window was on *his* face. In the deep indigo depths of his eyes Rose saw anger, frustration, and something else she didn't dare put a name to. Fighting for calm, she said, "It hardly seems appropriate. You're my employer."

He brushed that aside with an impatient, almost angry gesture. "A technicality."

"You've hired me to do a job for you, Mr. Castle," Rose said pointedly. "That makes you my employer." She was sparring with him now, and in doing so, relieving some of the tension between them. She was also finding that sparring with him was exciting in a different way.

Jade crossed his arms and gazed implacably down at her. "I hire a good many people to do things for me, Rose. Some of them, depending on what we've shared beyond that, call me Jade. I'd like you to be one of them."

Rose responded with a lift of the chin that was an automatic reaction to the studied arrogance in his manner and said frostily, "Oh?" She wondered briefly whether the businesslike Miss St. James would take that tone of voice, then thought, Oh, the hell with it! After all, she *was* Rose St. James, and arrogance had always made her hackles rise. In fact, at this moment Jade Castle was reminding her an awful lot of someone else she knew—the most insufferably arrogant man she'd ever had to deal with, and the last person she wanted to think about now.

"And just what have we shared, Mr. Castle? As I recall, you *took* something from me, and without asking."

His laugh was sardonic. "What did I take from you? You mean the kiss? I rather thought I was giving you something—something, as I recall, that you accepted pretty readily. And, come to think of it, as long as you're keeping score, you accepted a few other things from me."

"Other things?"

"Yes. A rose, for starters. But since you insist on a full accounting, let's go back to the beginning, shall we?" He began to tick off points on his fingers while Rose fumed. "For openers, I'll remind you that you entered my estate under false pretenses—"

"False—"

"—Claiming to be a member of the press. A transgression, by the way, that I graciously overlooked. I then took you on a privately conducted tour of the party, during which you enjoyed the services of my gypsy fortune-teller and drank my wine. And, of course, there's the little matter of your unauthorized dip in my pool."

"Unauthorized!"

"Remember who pulled you out, Rose?" he asked softly. His eyes were darker than indigo. Rose gazed into them, remembering, and closed her mouth on her protest. "That's right. I might even have saved your life. At the very least I carried you soaking wet and shivering in my arms, love. You bathed in my tub and slept in my pajamas. I gave you my hospitality, one rose, and one very lovely kiss."

"My cameras," Rose managed to whisper.

"I've replaced your cameras. You'll find them down in your laboratory. And I've given you a job to make up for the loss of your photographs. It seems to me, love, that this accounting shows I have a balance due me. And I'm calling in your account right now."

"Oh?" Rose choked, struggling to get a grip on her anger. My God, she was thinking, does *every* man I'm forced to deal with have to be like this? "And what do you think I owe you?"

There was a little silence, and then, "Just call me Jade."

She noticed that his body had relaxed, and that his eyes were blue again. The arrogance was gone, and with it

went most of her anger. Feeling oddly weak she repeated, "Just call you 'Jade?' That's all?"

He shrugged. "That's all. And then we're even—for
now."

"All right," she said, proud of the cool control in her
voice. "If that's the way you want it." But she was
thinking. Point to you, Jade Castle. She'd lost in a battle of wills to a stronger player, and learned an important lesson cheaply enough: she was no match for this
particular opponent in a head-to-head confrontation.

But it seemed that he wasn't going to let her go so
cheaply after all. "Say it now," Jade insisted. "So you
won't forget it."

"Say it now? Your name?" Why did it suddenly seem
like the most difficult thing she'd ever been asked to do?

"Yes." His voice was soft, seductive. "I want to hear
you say it."

This was so ridiculous. And childish. But for some
reason it seemed terribly important to both of them. God
only knew what their reasons were, but to Rose, saying
his name represented a surrender far greater than the
point of this one small skirmish. She'd tried so hard to
steel herself against him, to deny the chemistry between
them. Calling him "Mr. Castle" had been one more attempt to keep him at a distance. To yield on this point,
she felt, would be to accept the inevitable.

He was waiting, silent and implacable. Rose licked her
lips and took a deep breath. "All right," she said, and
gave a little laugh. "Jade..."

She hadn't meant it to come out like that. She'd meant
to just *say* it: Jade. But it had come out on a gentle exhalation, like a sigh.

His mouth lifted in a smile, and Rose discovered a new
softness in his eyes. All at once she felt drained, relieved

that the ridiculous struggle was over. The pull of his eyes
was overpowering. She knew that if he moved his arms,
if he opened up to her even slightly, she would go to him
like iron to a magnet. And with her bastions already destroyed and her walls breached. No wonder she was
afraid.

She was saved by a small whirlwind as the door behind her erupted inward and Tessa breezed into the room.
A profound emotion washed through Rose, leaving her
feeling hollow and empty; she would never know whether
it was relief or disappointment.

"Hel-*lo*, love!" Tessa Freedom croaked, sweeping past
Rose to kiss Jade ecstatically on the lips. "Wonderful,
isn't it? The money is just *pouring* in!" She whirled on
Rose. "Oh, let's see, the photographer, isn't it? The one
who fell in the pond! I'm sorry; I'm terrible with names."

"Which is why she calls everybody 'love'," Jade explained in a matter-of-fact aside to no one in particular.

"Rose St. James," Rose supplied, trying not to stare.
This was Tessa Freedom in full plumage, and the effect
was dynamite. Today her hair was mostly white, with
only a few streaks of pink. A fuchsia scarf was tied
around it Indian-style, with a large butterfly bow just
above one ear. Hanging from the other ear was what appeared to be a small stained glass window. But it wasn't
her clothes and hair that made her so overwhelming. The
energy and sheer power of personality that could reach
out to an audience of ninety thousand in a huge stadium
and make each person there feel as if she had touched
him was simply too much to contain in one ordinary-
sized room. It was like bottling lightning.

Tessa had already turned the force of her personality
back on Jade. "Well, love, are you all ready to go? I'm

so excited about this. Wasn't the concert lovely? One of my best, I think, but then—"

"Tessa," Jade said patiently, smiling the way a boy smiles at an embarrassingly effusive baby sister, "you *are* going to tell me where it is I'm supposed to be going I hope?"

"Oh! Well, to get the *money*, of course. The Coliseum commission is turning over the check this morning—the concert proceeds, you know—and then *we* are turning it all over to what's-their-names—the feed-the-millions people. Full media coverage. Why do you think I'm in full regalia so early in the day? Jade, you didn't *forget*? No, you didn't; you never forget anything. You are going to try to get out of it again; I *know* it. Now listen."

Jade lifted his shoulders and gave Rose a look of helpless appeal that was almost comic. Rose shrugged back and then deliberately shifted her gaze, disassociating herself from the ensuing argument. It didn't concern her, and while it raged she could use the time to unobtrusively check out the office for pieces to the puzzle that was Jade Castle.

Jade's office appeared to be as barren of clues as his study and bedroom—except for one thing. On the wall directly behind his desk was a photograph of a boat, a large framed blowup of a snapshot, it appeared. Rose knew nothing about boats, but imagined it was a yacht, sleek and powerful, dazzling white against the ultramarine sea and cobalt sky. Jade's boat? Probably. Why else would he keep a framed snapshot in such a prominent place? It occurred to her the boat might be where he kept the telltale pieces of himself, the pieces that could tell her about Jade Castle, the man.

She tried, **without** appearing obvious, to make out the name on the stern, but it was partially obscured by spray, and all she could determine was that it began with a "T."

"Rose, I'm sorry." Jade was touching her arm, and the regret in his voice sounded sincere. "I'm afraid I'm not going to be able to show you around after all. I'm not sure how long this business is going to take. I'll have my secretary take you on the tour, and then she can show you your lab and introduce you to the staff you'll be working with. Okay with you?"

Rose murmured, "Of course."

Jade pressed a button on his desk, and almost immediately the attractive gray-haired woman Rose had spoken to in the outer office came into the room. Rose took note of the fact that Tessa Freedom received a stare of frosty resentment from the woman, something to do, no doubt, with the way Tessa had burst into Jade's inner sanctum unannounced. It occurred to Rose that it would be wise to tread carefully with Jade's secretary. She obviously had a well-developed mother-hen complex where her boss was concerned.

"Rose, this is Dorie Payton; I guess you've already met. Dorie, will you show Rose around then take her down to the photo lab? Dorie knows more about Castle Industries than I do, anyway," Jade explained, giving Dorie's shoulders a squeeze that she endured with unruffled patience, like a mother accepting a kiss from a grubby child.

And does she know as much about the *head* of Castle Industries? Rose wondered as she murmured, "I'm so glad to meet you." She noticed as she shook hands that the woman had very nice brown eyes, compassionate eyes, surrounded by smile lines. But Rose knew too well that eyes are not always windows of the soul. She thought, I wonder if she has access to top secret computer codes?

In any case, Dorie Payton would be a valuable person to cultivate.

That she could also be a difficult person to cultivate became apparent as she was showing Rose through the miles of corridors and multileveled buildings of the huge production plant. She seemed the quintessential executive secretary: efficient, courteous, and discreet. If it hadn't been for those lines around her eyes and the revealing look Rose had seen her give Tessa, she might have wondered whether the woman had any personal feelings at all.

It was nearly noon by the time the tour ended in the technical arts department. Rose's head was swimming, her stomach growling and she was feeling overwhelmed and discouraged. Dorie introduced her to a small army of technical writers, graphics artists and designers, and layout technicians, then left to resume her own interrupted duties. One brief glimpse of the department responsible for turning out all the support literature, catalogues and brochures for Castle's products was an eye-opener for Rose. She'd had no idea of the sheer volume of printed material that accompanied such highly technical products.

But that one glimpse was all she had time for before she was swept away to the company cafeteria for lunch. She ate on an open patio overlooking the Pacific Ocean, with a large, friendly group of her new colleagues, and in an atmosphere of such sunny normality that it was impossible to think of mysteries and puzzles and dangerous games.

She didn't have time to think of those things as she spent the afternoon immersed in her other vocation,

either. She was a little awed to discover a completely au-
tomated photolab, as well as a fully equipped darkroom
and studio. She also found, on a small desk in a corner
of the studio, exact duplicates of her ruined cameras and
a beautiful leather case filled with fresh film, filters and
lenses. Beside the case, in a crystal vase, was one perfect, half-opened rosebud.

She put out a hand to touch the pink-blushed petals,
then jerked it back and turned away. She didn't look at
the flower again as she plunged into the job of learning
her way around the lab and the new equipment, but she
could see it there anyway, mocking her with its beauty. As
beautiful as it was, that rose was becoming a symbol to
her—a symbol of dark secrets, uncertainties and unanswered questions.

In spite of the rose and what it stood for, or perhaps
because of it, Rose threw herself into her work with such
determination that it was nearly six o'clock when she finally emerged from the darkroom. The art department
was silent and deserted.

It occurred to her that other departments would be
deserted, as well, and that it might be a good time for her
to do some exploring on her own. A moment's consideration convinced her that it would be a waste of time. It
would do her no good to check out the computer lab; she
knew absolutely nothing about computers. And it had
already been established that the weapons transfer had
been accomplished through the use of top secret codes
accessible only to top Castle executives—the very top.
No, Titan was right. Jade Castle himself was the key, no
matter how much she might want to deny that fact. And
the obvious place to start was still Jade's office.

The outer office was open, but Dorie Payton had gone.
Rose expected to find the door to Jade's private suite

locked, which wouldn't have presented an insurmountable problem; she was adept at picking locks with makeshift tools. But it wouldn't be necessary this time. That door, too, was open.

Which could only mean that Jade was still in his office. That realization sent Rose's pulse rate into high gear, and for a moment she seriously considered turning tail and running. It was incredible that she could stand there with ice water in her veins contemplating burglary, then come unglued at the prospect of saying an innocent goodnight to her new employer. What would Titan say?

She gave a snort of self-disgust as she pushed open the door to Jade's office. Maybe she ought to tell Titan exactly how she felt. Maybe if he knew how badly she'd slipped since her Bureau days he would take her off this idiotic assignment.

Jade's office was empty. That fact did nothing to still the kettledrum in Rose's chest, though, because it had occurred to her to wonder if the empty office was a trap. Had she been set up? Of course. She'd forgotten that the whole plant, and especially this office, would probably be under constant security surveillance. And so, for the benefit of whoever might be observing her, she took a deep, calming breath and stepped hesitantly into the room.

"Mr. Castle? Jade?" she called softly. "Are you in here?" He wasn't; she knew that. Displaying what she hoped would look to anyone watching on the monitors like normal curiosity, she moved around the office, glancing casually at the expensive but featureless books and knickknacks. Still casually, she leaned close to examine the photograph of the yacht. There was a man on the deck who *might* have been Jade. *Damn!* If she could only make out that name...

She moved on, idly trailing her fingers over the smooth surface of Jade's desk, and crossed to the window. It provided a different picture now, with the sun at its afternoon angle. It was an ever-changing canvas, never the same twice.

A tiny movement drew her gaze downward to the sandy cove at the foot of the cliff. She felt her breath like a foreign substance in her chest, something hard and hurting just under her breasts. Jade was there, walking on the sand. His light fawn-colored jacket hung from one hooked finger over his shoulder, and his shirt sleeves were rolled to his elbows. As he moved slowly down the beach toward the water, his head lifted to the wind, he looked, Rose couldn't help but think, as if he were drawing sustenance from the wind, renewing himself. He stood for a long time gazing out to sea; it seemed a very private communion, and she almost turned quietly to leave without disturbing him. But then he shifted his shoulders and turned and looked up at the window, almost as if he'd known she would be there.

She saw him lift his hand, wave, and then point to the elevator. She nodded, and her hand went to the call-button, compelled by forces beyond her control. As she stood in the glass cube and watched the sand and the sea and Jade rise slowly to meet her, she had the feeling that she'd stepped across a boundary, or over a precipice. And it was too soon to tell whether she would find herself soaring, or hurtling down onto the rocks.

Jade was waiting for her on the platform, and he offered a hand to help her down steps that were made treacherous by a thin covering of sand. Once on the beach she took two tentative steps and then, using Jade's arm to steady herself, bent to slip the straps of her sandals over her heels.

"There," she said, glancing up at Jade, using the action to cover her breathlessness. "That's better."

His smile was crooked, his eyes shadowed, but his face seemed smoother, somehow, younger. She wondered if perhaps in some way the sea and the wind did nourish and renew him, though she knew that his appearance of casualness could be deceptive. She noticed that though they were walking in deep sand, Jade kept his shoes on. She tried to imagine him without shoes, walking barefoot in the sand, free and uninhibited, but the image eluded her completely.

"This is lovely," she said when they had reached the packed moist sand near the water's edge. "Is it yours? Private property?"

"Not technically. It's not fenced off or posted; it can be reached at anytime except the highest tide by anyone walking along the beach. But because of the cliffs the nearest beach access is a mile or two away in either direction." Jade smiled down at her. "I don't have many visitors. Invited or otherwise."

"I think I'm honored," Rose murmured. There was tension in her, like the humming of a high voltage power line, the kind of tension she used to feel when she knew she was walking into a dangerous situation. And that puzzled her. Surely she wasn't in any danger here, now, with this man.

"You must really love the sea to have had that window installed, and all this." She gestured with her arm, taking in the semicircular cove and the elevator. "It's a kind of sanctuary for you, isn't it?"

"Perceptive of you," he murmured in his dry way. And then, looking off toward the sun-shot horizon, "Yes, I suppose I do have an affinity for the sea."

"That picture, the one behind your desk," Rose ventured. "Is it your boat?"

She could see his smile form before he turned his head to bestow it on her briefly. And then, in an oddly flat, dismissive tone he said, "Yes. It's my boat."

For some reason it suddenly seemed unwise to pursue that subject. So instead, striving for lightness, Rose asked, "Well, what's the reason for *your* love affair with the sea? I've told you why I'm so fascinated with it."

He was silent for so long, gazing out toward the gilded horizon, that she didn't think he would answer. When he did, his voice was remote, as if he weren't talking to her at all.

"The first time I saw the ocean I mistook it for heaven." He laughed softly, but there was pain in the sound. Rose held her breath, wise enough not to interrupt him with questions, and after a while he went on. "It was from an airplane. I woke up in an airplane. The sun was setting, and the water looked like liquid gold, the way it does now. There were a few clouds, and they were gold, too, and pink. I thought I had died." He looked at Rose and shrugged, smiling with a ruefulness that touched her heart. "Well, what can I say? I was only about six or seven, and I'd never seen the ocean, or been in an airplane, and the only notion of heaven I had was from the painting behind the altar of a church I used to sleep in."

He was silent again, letting the words he'd spoken lie there exposed and tantalizing, like pieces of eight in the sand.

Rose stirred and moved closer to him. Her mind was whirling, a maelstrom of questions, but all she dared to ask was, "Did you grow up landlocked, then, like I did?"

"No." He shook his head, and the last of his smile faded, leaving his eyes bleak. "I grew up in Singapore."

"Singapore. But that's—"

"A seaport. I know." His voice was hard. "I may even have seen the harbor, the ships—I don't remember—but from the perspective of a child, one mean street looks pretty much like another."

Rose found that she was hugging herself. She felt chilled, and not from the wind off the ocean. *Mean streets.* She put that together with what he'd said just before he kissed her—about knowing what it was like to have nothing—and said haltingly, in disbelief, "You grew up in the streets of Singapore? You don't mean... *alone?*"

He turned to her and nodded, gripping her with haunted eyes. "That's right."

"Tell me," she whispered with a kind of awe. "Please."

He shrugged and looked over her head. "I have no idea who my parents were, or why I was abandoned. And I never will. My earliest memories are of being hungry...and scared, of course. Singapore being where it is, I wasn't often cold, but when I was, I could usually find a safe place—like that church. A priest there gave me food and told me about heaven, but when he tried to put me in an orphanage, I ran away. I didn't understand that he was trying to help. I was an animal, and I trusted no one."

It was a recital, flat and toneless. Rose swallowed and asked very softly, "How did you survive?"

"I almost didn't." His laugh was brittle. "I must have run into someone bigger, tougher. I don't remember much about what happened—probably a quarrel over food or space. I woke up in that airplane—or, as I was sure at the time, in heaven."

His eyes came back to her, clear of shadows. His laughter was ironic, but without the edge of hardness. "As it turned out, I was a long way from heaven. My rescuers were smugglers. Drugs, guns, you name it—if it was profitable they ran it. Though I think they'd probably have preferred to call themselves adventurers, or soldiers of fortune. They told me later that when they found me in that alley I was naked and had something clutched in my fist. They had to pry my fingers off it to see what it was."

He touched his chest, and Rose's eyes followed the gesture as she breathed, "The pendant." It was so incredible. She wasn't gullible; she didn't know why she believed it, but she did.

"Yep. So if you've been wondering whether I got my name from the pendant, or vice versa, now you know. Of course..." He turned, taking her with him with a touch on her arm, and began walking slowly along the beach. "I didn't take the name then, only much later, when I found a need for one. My smuggler friends just called me 'Kid'"

He seemed relaxed now, almost cheerful, as if having gotten past those initial fragmentary revelations, the rest didn't matter. Rose walked along beside him, digging her toes in the cool, wet sand and trying desperately to formulate questions out of the whirlpool in her mind. But all she could think, with shocked irrelevance was, No wonder he doesn't take off his shoes.

Remembering the scantiness of the Bureau's dossier, and the aura of isolation she'd sensed in this man from the first, it occurred to her that she might be the first person he'd ever told this story to. That thought kept her humbled and silent. After a while Jade touched her shoulder and said, "You're very quiet, Rose. Have I shocked you?"

"Of course. You know you have." She pulled away from him, wondering why she suddenly felt angry. He'd *meant* to shock her. And she didn't want to believe the incredible tale. All her training would tell her—certainly Titan would tell her—that she was a fool to believe it.

But Titan had told her to listen to her instincts, and her instincts were telling her it was true. The memories had come as if they were being dragged from a box so rusty it wouldn't open more than a crack. She sensed the man's pain, and his loneliness.

She kept her back to him, hugging herself against the cold wind. Damn Titan. She blamed him for this. Just go and meet the man, he'd said. She had done so and found herself battling a physical attraction so powerful it was like grasping a live wire. Take the job anyway, Titan had said. And so she had, against all her better judgment, and now she found herself fighting a greater battle, one she already knew she was losing.

"Rose...?"

She could feel him there, his body hard and unyielding at her back. She tried to harden her own body against the pull of his. But in her mind the distant crying of the gulls had become the whimpers of a frightened child. The cold, damp wind penetrated deep into her core and became a loneliness so acute it was physical pain.

"Rose."

She jerked herself angrily from his touch, but his hands captured her face and held it. She closed her eyes and felt his thumbs brush against her cheeks.

"Rose?" There was wonder in the way he said her name. "Are you crying?"

"Of course not," she said indignantly. "It's from the surf."

"Oh yeah? Let's see...."

She felt his breath on her face, and then his mouth. It moved across one cheek and then the other, and then his voice came softly, "Well, it is saltwater, but so are tears. Don't cry for me, Rose. I'm a survivor." And then he kissed her, and she tasted her own tears on his lips.

Her mouth was already soft and trembling. He gently moved her head from side to side, while he tasted the salt-sweet textures of her. He felt her breath, released in the softest of sighs, felt her hands touch his elbows, then the sides of his body. A swell of hunger and longing began deep inside him, surging through his muscles and throbbing in his veins. With a sigh of his own he released her face and pulled her against him. He wanted to crush her to his body, but knowing how hungry he was, he made a special effort to hold her with restraint. His body quivered with the tension of his self-control. And with that same reserve he took her mouth, dipping gently with his tongue.

He felt her hands on his back, stroking him, and knew that nothing had ever felt so good. With his own hands he explored the contours of her back, marveling at the taut resilience of her muscles, the smallness of her waist. With his mouth he fondled and caressed her lips, learning their shape and flavor. With great care he began to discover the different textures of her: the velvety smoothness of her cheek, the vibrance and vulnerability of her throat, the fragility of an eyelid. And all the while as he held her against him and felt the tremors in her body, he was thinking, My God, she's incredible... incredible.

Even while his need for her was blossoming inside him, he was reminding himself that it wasn't real, that *she* wasn't real. She was the Jordan Rose, one of the very best in a profession that demanded complete mastery of the arts of deception. And he was surprised at the pain that came with that reminder.

He pulled away from her, a sardonic little smile on his lips. He couldn't help it. He saw her lips part and her eyes widen slightly with the shock of his rejection, and he could have sworn that in her eyes he saw uncertainty, vulnerability and the unmistakable sheen of tears. And then he thought, No. Don't kid yourself. He couldn't let himself forget for a moment who and what she was. The physical response was real enough, but as for the rest . . . She was a consummate actress, playing a role, and that was all.

"Well," he said, taking a deep breath as he dropped his arm across her shoulders and began walking again with her in the cradle of his arm. "That was another first." He was surprised to hear gravel in his voice. He cleared it carefully. "The first time I ever kissed you on this beach. I can't wait to find out what other firsts we have to look forward to, can you?"

He felt the tremor that rippled through her body and wished he could believe it. He almost—*almost*—did.

Chapter 6

Her telephone was ringing. Rose heard it as she was crossing the wooden footbridge. She knew it was hers because her neighbors' houses were spilling light and voices out onto the oily black ripples of the canal; there was no reason for them to let a phone ring unanswered. Still, she didn't increase her pace. There was only one person who would let a telephone ring with such persistence and patience, and he was the last person she felt like talking to just now.

It was a fair distance from upper Malibu to Venice. Rose had had time to pass through several emotional stages as she drove through the sunset on the Pacific Coast Highway. She hadn't even been able to put a name to some of them. The most recent and clearly defined had been anger, but that had passed, too, and now she just felt tired, dispirited and unusually lonely.

Aloneness had always been a fact of her existence. She had been a solitary child by choice, escaping from the forced togetherness of institutional life into books and playacting. She'd joined the Bureau when she was barely out of her teens, and then isolation had become a necessity. Most of the time she had worked alone, so far underground that she dared trust no one. The relationships she formed there were transitory and sometimes treacherous. Her fellow agents were like her: solitary, self-contained men and women walled off from each other by the ingrained habits of suspicion and subterfuge. There was easy camaraderie and light, casual friendship, but for the most part emotions were kept guarded and protected...inviolate.

Which made the trust she'd given Thad Moses such a miracle. And the betrayal of that trust so shattering...

It had been barely two years—not nearly long enough. The shock and pain had faded to fuzzy, unfocused grays, but it didn't take much to jar the memories into sharp detail again, in stark and living colors.

Beirut...a city gone mad. A place where reality was indistinguishable from nightmare, and morning never came.

She and Thad had lived in the nightmare for months, posing as man and wife while they worked underground to locate several missing hostages. It had begun as another assignment, grown into a precious interlude, and then exploded in nightmare. Rose could still close her eyes and see it all, seared indelibly on the backs of her eyelids: the delicately choreographed exchange underway, all going without a hitch; the dun-colored hills; brown men; and the cold olive gray of guns; the heat and glare; and the smell of diesel fuel from the idling trucks. And then, from out of nowhere, the planes... The convoy carrying the Palestinian prisoners exploding in pillars of black, oily smoke and geysers of orange flame...

The terrorists turning in rage on their stunned hostages...

And Thad Moses, the only person besides herself who could possibly have known the exact time and place of the exchange. Thad Moses, shot in the struggle to save the hostages, dying, turning upon her a look of ...*what*? How many times since had she tried to understand that look? Guilt, certainly; regret, maybe. And his words: "I'm sorry, Rose."

She'd asked why. He'd coughed and said simply, "Orders." In disbelief she'd cried, *"itan's?"* And he'd moved his head from side to side and said, "No..."

He'd died then, and it had been a while before she'd known for certain that Thad Moses's first allegiance hadn't been to the Bureau, or even to the United States. And certainly not to her.

How could she not have suspected that Thad Moses was a double agent? She, who had been so close to him, she, whose job it had been to know. She ought to have known. She would have known—if she hadn't been too close. If she hadn't let her emotions become involved. Her emotions had blinded her to the truth.

Which was why Titan had to be crazy to ask her to do this. *Crazy!* Her instincts were worthless when her emotions were involved. He knew that very well, and yet he'd insisted she stay with the assignment.

Assignment. That was a laugh. Funny, too, how habit made her keep referring to this game in Bureau terms, when, according to Leif Cracken, it wasn't the Bureau's game at all. It was Titan's game.

Rose picked up the receiver, cutting off the racket in mid-ring, and said flatly, "Yes?"

She was somewhat surprised when, instead of his usual smug greeting, Titan snapped with equal brevity, "Report."

She closed her eyes in exasperation and shifted the phone while she disposed of her purse and car keys and settled herself on the arm of the couch. And all the while she could hear Titan's impatience like an almost audible hum on the other end of the line. She smiled to herself in grim triumph when at last he was compelled to repeat, "Rose? Report, please."

"That's the magic word," she remarked mildly, unduly happy with the small victory, and added blithely over Titan's snort, "Nothing to report, *sir*."

There was another silence, and then, "Knock it off, Rose. Sarcasm has never been your best weapon."

Rose took a deep breath and counted slowly to five. Titan's voice was brittle; he was on edge about something. Almost angry, she would have thought, except she couldn't imagine what she might have done to make him so. In an ever-so-slightly conciliatory tone she said, "Look, Titan, I just got home; it's been a long day. Give me a break, okay? And a minute or two to catch my breath. In case you didn't know it," she lied, "I had to run for the phone from the other side of the canal." It had occurred to her that it would be unwise to rile Titan. The only way she was ever going to find out what game he was playing was to play along with it.

She could hear Titan take a deep breath, audibly controlling himself. In a curiously toneless voice he asked, "Make any progress with Castle?"

A knot began to throb in the pit of Rose's stomach. "A little," she said evasively. "Nothing concrete."

There was a little silence. "Any problems with your... what did you call it? Your 'emotional susceptibility'?"

Cold anger swept over her, lifting the fine hairs on the back of her neck. How dare he? How dare he throw her own words back at her in that mocking tone? What a stupid phrase it was anyway, inadequate to describe the effect Jade Castle had on her. And she would be damned if she would tell Titan about that!

That incredible, searing heat that suffused her skin where Jade touched it. That insistent throbbing in her belly. That fire deep in the core of her body. The longing to touch him, cling to him, taste him.

No! She would die before she would tell Titan about that. Or how desperately she wanted to feel that lean, rawhide-tough body hard against her, while Jade's hands—his unexpectedly, wonderfully gentle hands—caressed her neck, her breasts, her belly and all her secret places.

"Under control," she snapped into the phone.

"Using it to your advantage, I take it?" Titan's voice was cold, almost a sneer.

"Of course." What was the matter with him?

There was silence again. After a moment Titan said with unveiled disbelief, "And you still maintain you have nothing at all to report?"

"Voyeurism, Titan? Shame on you."

"Don't hold out on me, Rose." There was a dangerous edge to his voice now, and Rose took a deep breath and flexed the fingers that had been gripping the receiver. She couldn't afford to antagonize him, not at this stage of the game. And he knew her too well.

"Nothing concrete," she revised. "I do have one lead, but I'd like to check it out before I—"

"Lead?" Titan pounced. "What is it?"

"I think he may have a boat." Rose surrendered the tidbit with reluctance.

"A boat?" The voice on the other end of the line was suddenly alert.

"Yes. As in yacht. I'm going to check it out tomorrow when I go for my morning run. If I find anything, I assure you that you'll be the first to know."

"Sarcasm, as I've said, is not one of your greatest strengths, Rose."

"Sorry," she said glibly, and then, with a sudden inspired thought, "Oh, one more thing. Will you please check the Bureau's computer files for anything on Tessa Freedom?" There, let him chew on that one. She hoped he'd choke. She knew he no longer had access to Bureau files; she wanted to hear how he would wriggle out of that one!

"Tessa Freedom?" With great relish Rose heard unfamiliar surprise and consternation in the familiar voice. "Any particular reason?"

"Oh, just a hunch."

"I'll see what I can do," Titan said abruptly, and rang off, leaving Rose smiling at an empty receiver.

Where Titan was concerned, the smallest victory was sweet.

"She is good," Michaels said with frank admiration when Titan told him about the boat. "I would have thought—"

"Head her off," Titan interjected crisply.

"What?"

"Tomorrow morning. Get the limo. Intercept her. Stall her. I don't care what you do, but don't let her find that boat."

"But I thought—"

"Not yet." Titan stood abruptly, turning his back on Michaels's puzzled frown. "Not yet." He rubbed a hand across his mouth, muting the near-desperation in his next words. "I want—*need*—more time."

Rose had never known the morning fog to hang on so long into August. Not that she minded; she liked fog, and it made it pleasantly cool for her morning run.

She stopped as usual on the footbridge to throw a handful of oats to the ducks, and then thought unexpectedly, as she watched them squabbling and diving in the murky brown water, Maybe I should get a boat. A little rowboat. Almost everyone who lived on the canal had some sort of boat. She could tie it up to the wooden jetty just outside her front gate, and whenever she wanted to be alone she could drift away on the canal, without a thought or a care in the world.

Instead of turning right at the Grand Canal and making her way down Venice to Ocean Front, Rose turned left, toward the Marina. The harbormaster's office, she supposed, would most likely be down near the entrance channel, and if it wasn't, no doubt there would be someone around whom she could ask.

Rose liked running in fog, liked the moistness of it against her cheeks, the way it muffled all sound, except, for some reason, the sharp-edged screeching of the gulls. Out there beyond the condos and townhouses the Pacific would be quietly undulating in slippery pewter swells, while the gulls wheeled and cried, still distraught over the predawn departure of the sportfishing boats. In a little while they would settle on rocks and pilings to await the fishermen's return, meanwhile ignoring the comings and goings of the pretty white-sailed playthings of Southern California's privileged.

She didn't see or hear the limousine until it turned ponderously in front of her at the Washington Street intersection, blocking her progress. The power door locks disengaged with a loud click, a less-than-subtle invitation. A grimace of vexation twisted Rose's mouth, and for a moment she went on jogging in place while she considered her alternatives. She could refuse to get in; the flow of traffic would force the car to move on, and she could continue on her way. She could turn around and go back the way she had come; she knew shortcuts that would frustrate vehicular pursuit. But as much as she resented being summarily waylaid like this, she knew that the alternatives were both childish and pointless. Titan wouldn't do this unless he had information that he couldn't give her over the phone. Curiosity and plain common sense told her to stop fuming, accept the inevitable and get into the car.

The limousine's interior was warm after the early-morning chill, and smelled of leather and another, more elusive and disturbing essence. A tantalizing familiar fragrance, clean and unmistakably masculine. She inhaled deeply, trying to grasp memories that shivered across her mind and then hovered hauntingly out of reach. As she settled into the soft seat she caught herself rubbing absently at her arms, distracted to discover that her entire body had broken out in tingling gooseflesh.

The intercom came to life. "Good morning, Rose. This is Michaels. Sorry to interrupt your run." The pleasant voice paused politely for Rose's snort, and then went on, "The envelope contains the dossier you requested on Tessa Freedom. Titan thought you would want it as soon as possible."

Frowning, Rose picked up the manila envelope from the seat beside her and opened it. She was both disappointed and puzzled. How had Titan managed to come up with a dossier on the rock singer so quickly without access to the Bureau's computer files? And if he did have access to Bureau files, was Cracken wrong? Was Titan still part of the Bureau, perhaps unofficially? Or had Titan found a way to tap into the Bureau's resources unauthorized? Either way, his own resources had proven more than equal to her request for information, so her little ploy had failed. Too bad. She made a face and laid the envelope back on the seat.

"Thanks a lot," she said neutrally. "Tell Titan I appreciate it, won't you? And now, if you'll just let me off on the marina..."

"Uh, sorry, Rose." Michaels's voice actually sounded regretful. "Titan wants you to read the file now and comment. We'll just drive around a bit while you read. Take your time."

"Comment? *Now?*" Rose glanced at her watch, realized she wasn't wearing one, and threw up her hands in exasperation. "Mind telling me why?"

Michaels coughed. "Well, you threw us a curve, asking for a dossier on Tessa Freedom. Naturally, Titan is, uh, curious. Specifically, he would like to know whether you have reason to suspect Ms. Freedom's involvement in the weapons transfer, and whether information contained in that file confirms those suspicions."

"I see." Nice going, Rose, she was thinking. Hoist on your own petard—whatever that is. Served her right for trying to get the best of Titan; it had never worked yet.

A glance out the window told her that they were cruising north on Pacific, away from the marina. Damn. By the time she'd digested the file and concocted something plausible enough to satisfy Titan's curiosity, it would be time to go to work. She would probably even be late, depending on traffic. Oh well, it was her own fault. She'd better get to it. Her search for Jade Castle's yacht would have to wait for another day.

A little later—though it seemed like several hours— Rose looked up from the print-out pages in her lap and wondered when it had gotten so cold in the car. Or perhaps the cold was just inside her.

Funny, life's little coincidences. Fate's little jokes. If she hadn't been ticked off at Titan, she would never have asked for a computer check on a flamboyant but empty-headed rock singer with weird hair and improbable made-up name. And she would never have discovered that Tessa Freedom's real name was even more improbable: Francesca Maria y Orlando Santana de la Cruz.

Or that, like her close friend Jade Castle, she wasn't American-born. That Tessa/Francesca had begun life in, of all places, Costa Brava. Rose had spent too many years with the Bureau to believe in coincidence.

At that moment Rose fully realized just how much she had wanted to believe that Jade Castle was an innocent victim of coincidence. At that moment, when everything she uncovered made it clear he was neither innocent nor a victim.

"Has Titan read this?" she asked stiffly, knowing the answer.

"Of course," Michaels confirmed.

"Well, then, he already knows what my comments would be. It's very obvious. Let me out here, please."

"We're miles from your place," Michaels objected, sounding distressed. "I'll take you—"

"I said, let me out of this car." Rose felt pain in her jaws and made a conscious effort to unclench her teeth.

"Or, I swear, you can tell Titan to find himself another bird-dog."

"Please," Michaels said unhappily, then stopped. Rose heard him clear his throat. "Rose...can I ask you a rather personal question?"

Caught off guard, Rose blinked and said, "Of course."

"Why do you hate Titan so?"

"Hate Titan?" She sat abruptly back against the seat cushions. "I don't hate Titan."

Did she? There were times when she felt as if she did, times when he infuriated her beyond bearing, times when she thought she could cheerfully strangle him. But hate him? What about the times when his quiet strength and intelligence and, yes, even his arrogance had been her only lifeline, her anchor to reality? Even, in a strange way, her comfort... But if she didn't hate Titan, how *did* she feel about him?

The intercom was silent, waiting. Rose put her head back against the seat and said softly, "I don't hate him, Michaels. Maybe I...resent him."

Michaels said carefully, "I'm not sure I understand."

With a sigh and a chuckle she said, "I'm not sure I do, either. But try to understand what it's like having your life directed by someone you've never seen. Being accountable to someone you aren't allowed to see, or know anything whatsoever about. Michaels, have *you* ever seen him?"

There was a cautious pause, and then a murmured affirmative.

"Well, I've known him for almost *ten years*, and I know nothing at all about him—not how old he is, or what he looks like—nothing. And he knows everything there is to know about me. Everything. Michaels, you'd know—he *has* seen me, hasn't he?''

"Oh yes," Michaels breathed emphatically.

Rose was silent, digesting the revealing inflection in Michaels's voice, wondering if it really meant what she thought it did, and wondering why the thought of Titan's admiration of her as a woman should give her such a warm and unexpected glow. After a moment she cleared her throat and said, "Well, then. There you are. He's omnipotent. He's God. And yet I know darn well he's *not* God; he's just a *man*. He brushes his teeth and puts on his pants one leg at a time, just like anybody else. He laughs and *feels*, just like I do. And I'm not allowed to see that part of him. So I resent him, damn it. Do you understand?''

"Yes," Michaels said quietly. "I think I do."

Rose sighed again and sat forward to put her hand on the door latch. "Please let me out, Michaels. It's only a couple of miles. I really do need a chance to clear my head and try to think."

The limousine slid smoothly to the empty curb and stopped. The power locks clunked. Rose stepped out into the brightening morning and watched the car pull away like a lone gray phantom.

As she jogged home through the shabby streets of Venice, she knew that in spite of what she'd told Michaels, it was useless to try to think. She felt—she *knew*—that it was all there in front of her, only she couldn't see it. She was too close. She felt crowded, hemmed in on all sides by a forest of great tree trunks, so that she couldn't see where she was going. If only she could get out of the forest, stand back a little ...

But "if onlys" were pointless, right in there with wishes. She would just have to keep looking for puzzle pieces until she found the key, and until then, all she could do was go on playing things Titan's way.

All the way up the Pacific Coast Highway that morning, Rose's mind played games with her. For some reason it insisted on placing Jade Castle and Titan side by side and comparing them with each other. There were some similarities, as she'd already observed. They were both arrogant as hell, that was for sure. Both were powerful. Both men had an aura of isolation about them. Jade because of his past, possibly, and Titan because of his inaccessibility. Both—an odd coincidence—had given her the same rose....

The truth was that she didn't know very much about either man, though she thought she was beginning to learn a little about Jade Castle. At least Jade had a face. She could read his expressions, look into his eyes. And he had a body, a body she could touch.

A body.... A powerful sensual memory struck her like an unexpected blow to the stomach, making her feel almost physically sick. And awed. And scared. She took a deep breath, flexed her fingers on the steering wheel and murmured, ''Oh boy.''

Feebly, she added, ''Get a grip on yourself, Rose.'' She knew that if she weren't careful this particular ''chemical'' reaction could explode in her face.

She was half an hour late for work, which got her a few glances and a brief but pregnant silence as she walked through the technical arts department. No one dared say anything, obviously the word was that she was directly accountable only to Mr. Castle himself. But Rose's professional pride was at stake. At the moment photography might be just her cover, but it also happened to be the way she made her living these days, and the glances and silences pricked her ego. So, to make up for the lost time, she made a point of not only working through lunch, but stayed a half-hour past quitting time as well.

And then, for no other reason than that she couldn't help herself, instead of going to the parking lot and home, she made her way through the complex of buildings to the corporate offices.

There wasn't any justification for it, no excuse at all. There was nothing more to be gleaned from Jade's office, no missing puzzle pieces to be found there. To be honest, her only reason was a desire that had been with her all night and all day, a desire that was well on its way to becoming a compulsion: she just wanted to see Jade again.

To Rose's consternation Dorie Payton was still in her office, tidying up. Hastily concocting a story to account for her visit and hoping it wouldn't sound too implausible, Rose said breathlessly, "Oh, am I too late? Has Mr. Castle gone home? He asked me to stop by after work, but I'm afraid I lost track of time. I do that sometimes, working in the darkroom. I hope it wasn't anything important."

To her absolute astonishment Jade's secretary said with her usual composure, "Mr. Castle is expecting you. I believe he's down on the beach. You are welcome to join him there, or wait for him in his office. Good night, Ms. St. James."

The words themselves were concise, spare to the point of coldness. But Dorie Payton was the sort of person who could manage to convey a lot with subtle inflections, expressions and postures. To Rose, who was trained to pick up and decipher such nonverbal signals, the reading was one of cautious approval. Which was a surprise, considering Dorie's attitude toward Tessa Freedom!

Tessa. The name was like a squall blowing up on the horizon.

Impulsively, Rose turned in the doorway to Jade's office and said, "Dorie, would you consider joining me for lunch tomorrow?"

Again to her surprise, the older woman flashed a brief but warm smile, deepening the creases around her eyes. "How nice. I'd like that. Shall we meet in the cafeteria at, say, twelve-fifteen?"

The date confirmed, Jade's secretary efficiently gathered up her purse and keys and, with a wave and another smile, departed.

Rose waited a few moments and then, feeling like an actress making an opening-night entrance, pushed open the doors to the inner office. This time, with her heart racing out of control inside her chest, she went straight to the window. And this time, when she stepped over the precipice, she knew beyond a shadow of a doubt that she was soaring.

Oh dear God, she thought in helpless wonder. I'm in love with him!

And then: Titan, I hope you're satisfied.

She couldn't see Jade on the beach. The tide was low, and a line of footprints trailed across the still wet sand to the north and disappeared around the point of the cove. Rose pushed the elevator call-button and then stood fidgeting like a schoolgirl waiting for her first date. All the way down the cliff in that glass cocoon she listened to her heart playing the song over and over, like a record stuck in a groove: I'm in love with him ... in love with him.

The elevator hit bottom with a tiny thud, jarring her to full awareness of her situation. She'd done the unthinkable. She'd fallen in love with the suspect. And Titan was to blame. No, she was to blame for not being strong enough to stand up to Titan. For not being strong enough this very minute to push the button that would carry her up and away from Jade Castle, away from mysteries and games—forever.

Because, God help her, at the moment she didn't care that Jade Castle was her target, that he was very probably a traitor to his country, a man without scruples. She didn't even care that the hardness and isolation, the mean streets of his childhood, had probably left such deep scars on his soul that he wouldn't have the capacity to love her back. Right now she just wanted to see him...touch him...hold him.

Without stopping to take off her shoes, she stepped from the elevator onto the platform and almost ran to the steps. The hard sole of one wedge-heeled sandal met sand-covered concrete and, with a sound like the ripping of fabric, slid out from under her.

Rose's reflexes, while perhaps not as finely tuned as in her Bureau days, were still pretty sharp. If she had allowed her body to succumb to the consequences of gravity she would very likely have sustained considerable damage to her posterior, her spine and possibly the back of her head. In her instinctive effort to avoid those consequences she twisted her body and flailed her arms, for all the world like someone doing their best to learn to fly. Of course, in the end gravity inevitably won, and she came down heavily and awkwardly on her left foot. Her ankle collapsed, and she pitched face forward down the last two steps onto the sand. She broke her fall with her hands and then lay absolutely still for a few moments, dazed and blinking.

Her first thought was, Boy, I must have looked ridiculous. I hope no one saw me!

And her second thought, as she pulled herself slowly and painfully to a sitting position and began to take inventory, was, I think I've really done it this time.

In all her years with the Bureau, with all the countless times her life had been on the line, she had never suffered even a minor injury. Even in Beirut she had emerged from the fiasco unscathed—physically. After all that, it was the height of irony that she should hurt herself running to meet the man she loved.

She didn't know how badly she was hurt. Her ankle throbbed, her palms stung, and every muscle in her body felt wrenched and sore. She wasn't sure whether her ankle would support her, but she was still too shaken to try to get up and find out. What she really wanted, more than anything in the world, was to hang on to someone strong and sob like a child.

And yet, perversely, when strong hands did touch her, she flinched and cried out, "No!"

"Yes," Jade answered, a guttural sound, gravelly with emotion. "For God's sake, Rose. Don't be an idiot!"

Chastened by the hardness in his voice, all desire to weep gone, she leaned back on her hands, wincing at the pain in her palms. She couldn't explain that his touch was like a brand, and her recoil instinctive, because of the jolt of electricity it sent knifing through her.

"Where are you hurt?" The words sounded as if they were being bitten off at the source. But even as he spoke his hands were moving down her arms to her wrists, drawing her hands forward gently but inexorably, turning them palm-up. His eyes took in the scrapes and then lifted to hers. She drew in her breath sharply at the look.

"It's nothing," she whispered. "But I think . . . my ankle . . ."

His thumbs were moving absentmindedly, stroking the hollows of her palms. He went on looking down at her hands—a long, intent gaze, as if he were reluctant to release them. And then, quickly, as if the gesture embarrassed him, he kissed one palm and placed her hands carefully in her lap.

"I saw you fall," he grunted as he shifted position. "If it's just your ankle you're damn lucky!"

Rose groaned aloud and closed her eyes.

His response was immediate. "Am I hurting you?"

She gave a high, desperate laugh. "No, far from it." How could she tell him that she didn't feel pain anywhere anymore? That all she could feel was a sharp-edged inner trembling, and a kind of excitement that was almost fear? Trying to hide the precariousness of her emotions, she said, laughing unsteadily, "I'm just embarrassed."

There was no answering smile to soften the hard edges of Jade's features. He murmured, "Damn," and leaned a forearm across a flexed knee. "I don't think it's broken—sprained maybe. Can you put any weight on it?"

"I don't know."

He took her by the elbows and drew her carefully to her feet, then supported her while she tested the injured ankle. The pain she'd forgotten shot up her leg and turned muscles and tendons to jelly.

"Ooops," she gasped as Jade caught her and lifted her into his arms.

For one contrary moment, because it was what she wanted so badly, she stiffened. And then she gave a sign and relaxed against him. Her arms crept around him and she turned her face into the curve of his neck.

"When I spoke of 'firsts,' Rose, you know this wasn't what I had in mind." Jade's voice was a dry rumble. The irony in it tugged at her memory, but the catastrophic effect he had on her senses had turned her mind to mush. She couldn't think, didn't even want to think.

"This isn't a first," she murmured, and found that it was the most natural thing in the world to lay her lips against his neck.

"No," he agreed. She felt his cheek on the top of her head and wondered at the tremor that rippled through him.

She gave a sigh to ease her own inner tensions and whispered daringly, "The last time you carried me, you took me to your bedroom. Are you going to do that now?"

"Yes," he whispered back. "I am. God help me. Rose are you sure that's what you want?"

"No," she answered, and laughed unsteadily. "I didn't expect to feel this way about you. I don't know why I do. I don't know you at all. And I certainly didn't expect you to feel this way about me. I'm not—"

"Rose..." Her name was barely a sigh, telling her that he was done with words. He found her mouth as surely and gently as before, but this time he mastered her, plunging deep with his tongue and then withdrawing, in a slowly swelling rhythm so evocative of sexual possession that it ultimately took control of her mind, her body, her senses. Pain was forgotten. His mouth became her only reality.

She didn't know when he began to walk with her up those treacherous steps to the elevator. The lurch in her stomach from the rising elevator was only one more giddy sensation in the body she had already lost control of.

When the kiss ended they were standing in the middle of Jade's office. Rose moaned and hid her moist and swollen lips in the hollow of his neck. When he started across the office to the outer doors she murmured an inarticulate question, an unmistakable protest.

"Not here," Jade said gutturally, turning slightly to glance over her head toward the sand-covered couch. "Not the first time."

"You have a thing about firsts, haven't you?" Rose said softly, feeling a lump form in her chest. It wouldn't be a first for her—not quite. She didn't know whether she felt relieved, or sad.

Chapter 7

The doctor had been and gone. Rose had objected to the house call until Jade reminded her that he was still her employer, that she had been injured on Castle property, and that there were such technicalities as liability insurance and lawsuits to think about.

To Jade's relief the injury to her ankle had been diagnosed as only a minor sprain. She had been told to stay off of it for a few days and rest it, but the swelling had already subsided. At the moment she was in his bathroom soaking her wrenched muscles in his huge sunken tub—except for her ankle, which was propped on pillows and icebags. He'd seen to the preparations, then removed himself to give her privacy. He was fully aware that, to her, he was still a stranger.

So now here he was in his study, sipping straight bourbon and pacing like a bridegroom on his wedding night. And, like most bridegrooms, wondering what the hell he was doing there at all.

In a way he wished he'd taken her there on the beach, when the thunder in his blood and the fire in his loins were drowning out the warning sirens in his head. He had to be out of his mind. He *was* out of his mind—with wanting her. The trouble was that he didn't want to "take" her, not on the beach, or in his office, or anywhere. He wanted to make love with her, and that had him feeling surprised and confused. Wanting her, *that* he could understand. It was a feeling he'd grown accustomed to. What he wasn't prepared for were the other feelings. The feelings that made his hands become gentle when he touched her. The vulnerability—his own, and hers—and the tenderness.

He'd come to terms with the fact that in all probability her "feelings" were no more than a first-class job of acting. He wanted her badly enough that he was willing to take whatever she was willing to give. And when he was away from her, he could convince himself that it was enough. But when he was with her, he didn't want to *take* anything at all from her. He wanted to *give* her himself, all he was able to give. And in return he wanted her to give all of herself—willingly—to him.

Ah, hell. Jade rolled bourbon on his tongue and stopped pacing to stare into the amber depths of his glass. That was probably too much to ask of anyone. He doubted whether very many married couples, loving couples, ever achieved it, much less two people who couldn't even be called a couple. His mouth twisted. Just two people with chemistry.

With a soft snort Jade set his glass down on his desk. He wasn't one to knock chemistry. Or underrate it, either. Maybe it would be enough. It would have to be.

With a swift, almost angry gesture, he picked up the glass, drained it and turned to the bedroom door.

* * *

Rose was discovering that there are times when it is very easy not to think. Lying in Jade's bathtub, surrounded by polished black tile and white plush carpeting, submerged to her chin in bubbles, she drifted in a somnolent, steamy haze. Now and then reason would hover on the misty perimeters of her consciousness, but it wasn't hard to steer away from it.

Luxury... Like an obscure, exotic drug, it had cast its spell on her. If she had allowed herself to think, she would have thought that she'd never known luxury like this before in her life. Orphans don't get many luxuries. Not the sullen, intractable, rebellious and uncommunicative ones, anyway. The ones labeled "unadoptable."

And, of course, neither do secret agents.

But Rose wasn't thinking. She was looking through an atrium filled with lush ferns and exotic flowers out over the diamond-dust sparkle of a Los Angeles night, but she wasn't seeing it. Her mind was a blank. In fact, she had no mind. Only a body...

She shifted in the water, made restless suddenly by vague discomforts in her breasts, belly and thighs. The water soothed her with its warm, liquid caress. A small disturbance, the slightest of breezes, stirred the rising steam in graceful eddys, chilling the moisture on her exposed skin. She shivered and saw the tips of her breasts peek through the soap bubbles, like pink rosebuds in the snow. Primitive awareness moved through her like a current of electricity, roughening her skin with goosebumps and drawing her nipples so taut they ached. She lifted her gaze unerringly to the spot where Jade stood just inside the door.

His eyes were indigo shadows, smoky and unreadable. She searched his face, looking for softness, but found none. Inexplicably she began to tremble. And then she reminded herself, It's in his hands. The softness is in his hands.

But that was thinking, and she wouldn't allow herself to think.

From beneath eyelids already heavy with a strange, sweet lassitude, she watched him come toward her. When he sat on the edge of the bath she let her lids drift down. With her eyes closed she couldn't see the hardness in his face, the secrets in his eyes. There was only the incredible gentleness of his hands.

His hands touched her forehead first. He brushed the steam-dampened tendrils of hair on her temples with his fingertips, smoothing them back, moving past her hairline to gently massage her scalp. Slowly his hands settled on her face, framing it. His thumbs stroked across her eyebrows, then rested for a moment on the delicate, fluttering skin of her closed lids. Her lips curved and parted in sweet anticipation.

He wouldn't be hurried. He traced the outer rims of her ears, the fine lines of her jaw, the downy curve of her cheek. He softly stroked the silky underside of her chin, while her lips grew swollen and hungry for his touch. When at last she felt his thumb brush the tingling fullness of her lower lip, she caught it between her teeth with a quick, impatient movement, nipping the fleshy part to chide him for denying her, for making her wait. Then, to ask for pardon, she drew it between her lips to lave it with her tongue. In response he gently pulled his thumb free and drew it across her lips, glazing them with her own essence. As her lips cooled and tingled she turned her head, searching, and found the warm hollow of the palm of his hand. His hand made love to her mouth in a caress so sensual and erotic that when at last he pulled it away her blood was thundering through her body, and her breathing was quick and anguished.

For a long moment he let his hand rest on her throat, measuring the cadence of her pulse. With an effort she opened her eyes and looked into his face. Eyes the deep blue-gray of storm clouds locked with hers and held them, while his hand slid down the column of her throat to her chest. Casually, almost negligently, he nudged the layer of bubbles that covered her breasts. The fragile barrier dissipated like ocean foam. Then, and only then, did he pull his gaze from hers and allow himself to examine what his hand had revealed.

Rose kept her own eyes on his face, watching his profile while he watched his hand skim the surface of the water and lightly brush the rosebud tips of her nipples. She saw the tension of passion in his jaw, the faint movement throbbing in his temple. She sighed and arched her back, bringing her breast into his hand. Not especially generous to begin with, her breasts seemed small and weightless in the water. His hand completely covered one, then gently molded and reshaped it, bringing the pouting crest of it clear of the water. Beside her his body flexed and tightened as he bent down to take her nipple into his mouth.

As he did the black jade pendant swung forward, slipping from his open shirtfront to lie cradled in the hollow just above her collarbone. Sensation shot through her, hot and sweet. She gave a soft gasp and lifted her hand to touch his head, then remembered that her hand was wet, and instead let it hover without touching him while she drifted, helpless, on waves of desire.

The gentle pressure on her nipple intensified and became rhythmic. The simple process of breathing became painful. She felt an urge to whimper. She wanted to em-

brace him, to pull his head against her heart, to hold onto
him. The water, which had been so soothing and caressing, became instead an impediment to her desires.

As if sensing her frustrations, or perhaps feeling the
same ones himself, Jade suddenly released her breast and,
catching her hand in his, stood up. Holding her eyes with
a dark and somber gaze, he held out his other hand.
Trustingly, Rose lifted her hand from the water and
placed it in his. With great care but no apparent effort,
Jade drew her out of the water and then lifted her into his
arms. As if she were something fragile and precious, he
set her feet on the furry white carpet, testing her ability
to stand upright before he leaned away from her to reach
for a towel.

Neither of them spoke. It wasn't so much that no
words were necessary—although they weren't—it was
more a mutual avoidance of words. Words and conscious thought would make them strangers; their bodies
called to each other through lines of communication as
old as mankind. They moved together in perfect har-
mony, initiating, anticipating, responding, like dancers
who had been rehearsing together for years.

He stood facing her and wrapped the towel around her,
then began to dry her, inch by inch, in slow, feathering
strokes. The towel was so thick and soft it felt like fur
against her skin. His eyes, following the movements of
the towel, caressed her body with indigo velvet. She began to shiver, but not with cold.

His hands guided the towel further forward over her
shoulders, across her collarbones to the hollow at the
base of her throat. Lightly he feathered the towel over the
crests of her breasts, then moved on. Gliding, petting
strokes drank moisture from her ribs and the fragile skin
on the undersides of her arms. He treated her wrists,

hands and fingers as if they were precision instruments and left them sensitized, longing to touch and to hold. When he dropped to his knees before her, it felt so good to let her tingling hands come to rest on his shoulders.

The towel slipped to her waist. Jade drew its ends around her hips and across the delicately draped bones of her pelvis to meet over the soft dark mound at the juncture of her thighs. His head came forward, and with his mouth he tasted the drops of water that had pooled in the small hollow of her navel, bringing a tiny surprised gasp from her. The towel moved slowly downward to her feet, then upward, inch by inexorable inch, along the insides of her legs. When it reached the place where her thighs touched, softness became pressure, gentle but insistent, until she parted her legs to allow him access to her body's most secret places.

Her legs melted and all but buckled; only her hands on his shoulders kept her from falling. The towel slithered down her legs to lie in a pool around her feet. Jade's arms came around her hips. And then, unexpectedly, he laid his head against her belly and enfolded her tightly in a hard, almost desperate embrace. She felt vibrations deep within his body and could only wonder at the powerful emotions that could make such a hard, controlled man tremble.

It was her undoing.

Until now it had been a feast for the senses, a banquet, languorous and erotic, each course meant to be savored unhurriedly. Her emotions, like her thoughts, had been kept buried and inviolate. But that telltale little tremor, that evidence of *his* emotions, was like a match to a fuse. Her emotions exploded through her, as unstoppable as a geyser, and erupted in a sound that was very nearly a sob. She clasped his head to her body and held on for dear life. Great shudders rocked her.

Then Jade was on his feet, his arms around her, crushing the breath from her, and it wasn't enough. His hands were tangled in her hair, his mouth was bruising her, his tongue was filling her mouth, and it wasn't enough. Rose abandoned all hope of sanity and control. Her hands raked at the fabric of his shirt, furious with that barrier. She kneaded the muscles beneath with an urgency and impatience that finally communicated themselves to him, even through the red fog of his passion. He tore his mouth from hers and, gripping her shoulders so hard it hurt, held her from him.

For a few moments they stared at each other, breathing like prize-fighters between rounds. And then Jade spoke for the first time. His voice sounded rusty and unused. *"Touch me."* And then, in a whisper, "Easy, love..."

She understood. He was trying to restore order and regain his own self-control. She nodded and swallowed. Her hands still rested on his shoulders; now she let them slide down his shirt front to the top button, but they were shaking too much to be of any use. In a gesture of unexpected tenderness Jade clasped her hands in his and lifted them to his mouth, holding one against his jaw while he kissed and soothed the other. When their trembling had stilled he carried them back to his chest and tucked them inside the open neck of his shirt.

It occurred to Rose that he wasn't in any hurry to undress. And as she stood there naked, lightly pressed against his hard, fully clothed male body, with her hands inside his shirt, she decided that she wasn't in any hurry, either. There was something incredibly exciting, unbelievably erotic, about her nakedness and his lack of it.

She felt vulnerable and, in a very primitive way, utterly feminine.

So instead of struggling urgently with his buttons she stood on tiptoe to press her mouth, hot and open, to the indentation in the center of his chest, straining the limits of her own control as far as she could before finally releasing that first button.

Her hands moved downward over the hard swell of his chest. She felt the changing textures, the slight roughness of hair around his nipples. She brushed them with her palms and felt them become pebbly with the stimulation of her touch. The next button gave way to her questing fingers. As she let her mouth slide lower on his chest she encountered an alien hardness—though the jade was so smooth and warm it felt almost like flesh, a part of him. She touched it with her lips.

Jade's hands tightened on her waist. He lowered his head to intercept her mouth with a hot, drugging kiss. Rose sighed deep in her throat. Her fingers dealt quickly with the remaining buttons, and she tugged his shirttails free. When she slipped her arms around him inside the shirt and let her breasts flatten against his body, he began to stroke her back, slowly, sensuously, from her shoulders to the inward curve of her waist. Then lower, grasping her buttocks to pull her hard into his lower body. Suddenly she didn't want to play games anymore. She wanted it *all*. She wanted his skin caressing hers. She wanted the full weight of his body crushing hers. She wanted to feel his strength and his passion, filling her.

She swayed her hips, moving her body sinuously against him. And then for the first time, she spoke. "Jade." Just his name, and nothing more.

And he answered, "Yes . . . *yes*, love."

The bed was huge and empty, except for the pillows at its head. Jade had swept everything else onto the floor. He laid her on the smooth sheet and stood over her, scorching her for a long, silent moment with his eyes. Slowly he drew his fingertips over her body from her belly to her throat, then brushed her cheek with the backs of his fingers. For some inexplicable reason the gesture made her throat ache.

With burning eyes she watched him as he dropped his white shirt onto the floor. And then, sensing somehow that he would want a measure of privacy, she shifted her gaze to her own body. The sheets were dark—deep brown or indigo, perhaps; she couldn't tell what color in the near darkness. Against that background her body looked pale and fragile, almost translucent. She looked up to find that Jade had finished undressing and was moving toward her with that wild grace she'd noticed the first time she saw him. He had reminded her then of a tiger, prowling the forests of the night. And suddenly, just for a moment, she felt afraid.

Jade seemed to understand. He lay down beside her and gathered her close, just holding her and petting her with long, reassuring strokes. His lips touched gentle kisses on her temple, her eyelid, her nose, her mouth. And then, with a hand placed firmly in the small of her back, he pulled her against him, making her feel his need of her, giving her the chance to accustom herself to his body.

And as always, when she allowed her sense of touch to supersede all others, her fear melted away like frost in sunshine. She relaxed in Jade's arms, snuggling first, and then matching him caress for caress, exploring the hard, masculine lines of his body with her hands. When he lay back and pulled her over him she moved languorously, fitting herself to him, glorying in the silky whisper of skin on skin. A sound escaped her, a throaty little chuckle, a feminine sound of joy and pleasure.

Jade's answering chuckle sounded delighted, and surprised. His hands slid over her buttocks to the backs of her thighs, parting them. Beneath her she felt the muscles of his torso gather and tighten as he lifted his head and shoulders to claim her mouth. Their relative positions were meaningless; he dominated her with the sheer strength and power of his embrace.

When at last he rolled her onto her back she felt heavy and honeyed, drugged with desire. Through half-closed eyes she watched him raise himself to kneel between her thighs. His hands, his marvelous hands, rested on her ribs, defined and molded her breasts, then moved inch by inch down her torso to nearly span her waist. She arched into his hands like a cat being petted. When his hands reached her hips his thumbs rotated downward, following the satin hollows inside her pelvic bones. With her thighs in his gentle grasp he exerted a slow, inexorable pressure, until her body and all its secrets lay open to him.

She could not have been more vulnerable, yet where was her fear now? Her breathing was quick and shallow, her heartbeat a trip-hammer, but she wasn't afraid.

In a stupor of desire she watched him fit himself to her feminine softness, not entering her, but only replacing the pressure of his hands with the weight of his body. His hands retraced their path upward over her body, and again she arched in involuntary response. His hands lifted and covered her breasts, brushed the erect and tender tips, then moved down her sides before slipping along the undersides of her arms. Very gently he raised her arms overhead and pinned them to the pillows.

Her fingers fanned wide to lace with his. The pressure on the lower part of her body increased...and increased. She expected pain, even braced for it; her body was unaccustomed to such intrusions. But there was no pain, only searing heat that slowly filled her. Her mouth opened in a silent gasp. Jade leaned forward to cover her mouth with his, entering her with his tongue and going deep, filling her mouth as he filled her body.

Rose moaned and arched upward, pressing her breasts against his chest. The jade pendant slithered over her breast and came to rest in the hollow of her throat. It felt like a cool, chaste kiss on her fevered skin.

Their bodies were tuned to the same music; they moved together like old lovers, in a slow and graceful dance. And after the music had reached its crescendo and the last sweet chords had died, they fell asleep with their bodies still entwined, so quickly that Rose didn't have time to wonder at the silent tears that slipped coldly into her hair.

She woke alone. Jade had covered her with a sheet and a light blanket, and left the bathroom light on so that she wouldn't be disoriented if she woke. And then he had left her.

Rose struggled to a sitting position in the middle of the great wide bed, frowning. Jade's clothes were gone, too. So he had dressed and left his bedroom. Why?

She wondered what time it was. Was it just that he preferred not to sleep with her, or something else entirely? Something more sinister.

Her watch. It would be there right beside the bed on the night table, where she'd left it when she undressed for her bath. Jerkily, twanging with the adrenaline surge of abrupt awakening, she sprawled across the bed to reach for it. She squinted at it in the dim light and gave a soft snort. Twelve-ten. A.M. or P.M., for Pete's sake! She had no idea how long she'd slept, or even whether it was day or night.

Completely unmindful of her nakedness, she scrambled off the bed and cautiously moved a fold of the heavy draperies back from the window. Still night, thank God. She'd slept only a short time, then, which made Jade's disappearance even more puzzling—and suspicious.

For just a moment she leaned against the wall and closed her eyes, and let herself remember all the magic and beauty of the dance they'd shared. She was staggered by a wave of pain so awful that she thought she might become violently sick. She leaned into the pain, and after a moment, it numbed a little and became manageable.

Once again she'd been betrayed by her own emotions. She'd known how dangerous it was to allow her emotions to interfere with an assignment; there were no excuses. She'd been seduced, lulled to sleep—literally— by the sweetness, the gentleness, of a man she'd once thought devoid of softness.

She dressed quickly, clamping her jaw grimly against the pain of her wrenched ankle and abused muscles. It had been a dream, that was all. A luxurious, erotic dream. This was reality, hard and bitter. She wasn't meant to know such things as love and light, warmth and beauty. This was where she belonged: in the cold, unpredictable world of intrigue and mystery and dangerous games.

She opened the door and stood on the step for a moment, peering into the shadowy courtyard, breathing deeply of the night air. It was heavy with the scent of jasmine, a perfume evocative of soft tropical nights. But

TAKE 4 FREE BOOKS
WHEN YOU PEEL OFF THE BOUQUET
AND SEND IT ON THE POSTPAID CARD

❤ Silhouette Intimate Moments®

Catherine Coulter's AFTER-SHOCKS. When Dr. Elliot Mallory met Georgina, everything between them seemed so right. Yet, Georgina was just beginning a promising career, and a life with him would cheat her out of so many things. Still, Elliot could not seem to let her go.

Nora Roberts' DUAL IMAGE. Actress Ariel Kirkwood wanted desperately to play the scheming wife in Booth De Witt's new play. As Ariel the actress, she awoke the ghosts of Booth's past. As Ariel the woman, she awoke Booth's long-repressed emotions . . . and tempted him to love again.

Diana Holdsworth's SHINING MO-MENT. Derek had been smuggled out of Russia as a child. Now, with the help of an acting troupe and its lovely leading lady, Kate, he had a chance to go back and rescue his father. And when he fell in love with Kate, he knew he might never be able to tell her.

Barbara Faith's ISLANDS IN TUR-QUOISE. When Marisa saved Michael's life during a raging storm, it gave her a chance to save her own life, too. Yet, she felt she had to return to a husband who did not love her. Which is better, a love without a future or a future without love?

OPEN YOUR DOOR to these exciting, love-filled, full-length novels. They are yours *absolutely FREE* along with your Folding Umbrella and Mystery Gift.

AT-HOME DELIVERY. After you receive your 4 FREE books, we'll send you 4 more Silhouette Intimate Moments novels each and every month to examine FREE for fifteen days. If you decide to keep them, pay just $9.00 (a $10.00 value) — with no additional charges for home delivery. If not completely satisfied, just drop us a note and we'll cancel your subscription, no questions asked. **EXTRA BONUS:** You'll also receive the Silhouette Books Newsletter FREE with every book shipment. Every issue is filled with interviews, news about upcoming books, recipes from your favorite authors, and more.

Rose wasn't distracted. Somewhere out there in the shadows, Jade Castle was abroad on business so secret and urgent, or so personal and private, that it had taken him from a bed still warm from their lovemaking. She meant to find out what that business was. She was tired of mysteries, sick to death of being a pawn in someone else's game.

As she stepped outside the courtyard door she half expected the dogs to intercept her, but they were no-where about. So either they didn't question her right to be there, or they were off somewhere with Jade. Either way, no one bothered her as she crept around the main house, using a half-crouch that made it hard to favor her sore ankle. She didn't try the doors and windows—they were probably wired electronically—just looked and lis-tened for signs that someone was up and around. All seemed dark and still until she reached the side of the south wing that faced the pool and the rose gardens. Here a solitary light burned in a ground-floor window, just a faint glimmer that might have been mistaken for re-flected moonlight, except that it flickered in an erratic pattern.

With her heart pounding, Rose crept closer, easing si-lently through shrubbery that scratched and prickled until she was crouched on one knee directly underneath the window. Odd sounds reached her, electronic music as erratic as the light pulses. With practiced stealth she raised herself to peer over the edge of the stone sill. And then, feeling foolish, she straightened and released a long-held breath.

Tran, the housekeeper's son, sat hunched over a so-phisticated-looking computer console. His fingers flew over the keyboard. His brow was creased with concen-tration and tension. On the screen brightly colored space vehicles were firing missiles at each other while dodging busily among hurtling asteroids and exploding planets. All this mayhem was punctuated with electronic beeps and explosions and musical phrases.

Video games. Rose sagged against the cold stone wall and shook with silent, rueful laughter. Video games. How mysterious. How sinister. How ridiculous.

A moment later she nearly jumped through the window as a cold canine nose poked itself inquisitively into her hand.

Chapter 8

As he stood in the copse of birch and juniper, Jade had watched Rose come around the house, moving slowly and cautiously, like a doe sensing danger. When the dogs would have gone joyfully to greet her, he called them softly to heel. He wasn't surprised that she'd followed him, just sorry she'd had to awaken alone. Under those circumstances most women would feel betrayed, abandoned, but he could never be sure what Rose felt.

That was the trouble, of course. With Rose, he could never be sure of anything.

He'd already called himself seven different kinds of fool as he'd stood looking down at her while she slept. Sleeping, unguarded like that, with all her pretenses and camouflage stripped away, she had been a breathtaking, heart-tugging mixture of voluptuousness and innocence. He saw innocence in the childlike curl of the hand that pillowed her cheek, in her softly parted lips and the dark crescent sweep of lashes. He found a voluptuousness that was unsuspected in one so slender, so gracefully built. Even at that moment, so soon after making love to her, the sight of her lying there lush and naked in his bed had made his loins stir with new life.

Fool, he told himself now for the hundredth time. Desire her, then, if you can't help yourself, but don't let your emotions get tangled up with your lust.

With a swift, violent motion he pushed himself away from the tree at his back and made his way toward the house. He moved silently and easily, at home in the darkness. Maybe, he thought in a rare moment of whimsy, in a former life he'd been a tiger, or a panther, a solitary night hunter. And then he snorted. More likely it was his lifelong insomnia that had made the nighttime his home territory.

A few feet from where Rose stood he stopped and released the dogs with a gesture. A moment later he heard her startled gasp.

Keeping his voice cool and dry, he inquired, "Lost, love?"

"Jade?" Was it guilt or merely relief that made her voice breathless? Her shadow had separated itself from the shrubbery near the wall, and she was moving toward him. One of the dogs—Clyde, probably—was trotting beside her, nudging her leg adoringly. "Jade, I woke up and found you gone."

"I know. I'm sorry," he said softly. "I couldn't sleep. I often walk at night. I didn't mean to alarm you."

"I wasn't. Not really. I just wanted—" She stopped. Words were meaningless. Tension crackled across the space between them. He could see her cross her arms, hugging herself as if trying to hold herself together. Something caught at Jade's throat, a strangeness, an awkwardness that made it hard to speak. They had been more at ease in each other's company, words had come easier, the first time they stood face to face. But the closer he came to her physically, the farther he seemed to be from her. The thought filled him with an especially bleak kind of loneliness.

"I was looking for you," Rose was saying. "I saw that light, and I thought—but it's only Tran, I think."

Jade gave a dry laugh. "Playing video games on my computer, no doubt. Actually, I believe the kid's quite a whiz. Takes classes in high school. Does his homework on my equipment. It's quite all right."

Glib phrases . . . small talk between strangers. Incredible, after what they'd just shared.

Jade dropped his arm across Rose's shoulders and turned with her to stroll into the gardens, casually, like friendly acquaintances. "He seems to have a real knack for it. I sure don't. How's your ankle?"

"Better." Was that her voice? That breathless croak?

"You're still limping." He stopped and turned her toward him. "You shouldn't be walking around on it. I'll carry you."

"No." There was an odd urgency, almost panic, in her voice. But the denial had come too late. Her hand had already touched his arm; his hands were on her waist. The pretense of casualness crumpled and fell away. Their bodies were fine-tuned to each other's wavelength, sensitized, programmed to instant response. Almost before he knew what he was doing his arms were full of her, and he found her mouth as easily and naturally as if it had been a part of himself. He kissed her deeply, and she responded with an urgency that fanned the banked fires in him. Her hands were on his neck, reaching up to the back of his head; her tongue was in his mouth, hot and vibrant. He groaned softly deep in his throat and pressed

her lower body hard against his. He felt her breasts grow taut against his chest, felt her tremble, and knew that her arousal had been as immediate and as violent as his.

She suddenly tore her mouth from his and clung to him. "Oh, God," she whispered, breathing the words against the base of his throat.

"Rose..." He wrapped his arms around her, holding her so tightly he half expected to feel her ribs crack. "Rose," he heard himself say, "stay with me."

Rose heard more than the words; she heard the loneliness behind them. The loneliness and the plea. Pain knifed through her, hot, searing pain. The same pain that had overwhelmed her earlier that night, when she had felt him tremble. This is how it must feel, she thought, to be hit by a bullet.

What was it about vulnerability in a strong man that was so devastating to female emotions?

"I will," she whispered thickly. "Tonight..."

"No." The words were warm in her hair. "I mean *stay* with me. Here. Come live with me."

And be my love. Rose jerked away from him, angry all at once. It was her only defense. "I can't," she said, forcing the words past jaws that felt as if they'd rusted shut.

"Why not?" He'd gone very still, like a wary animal.

"Because..." She made an impatient gesture with her hand and then wrapped her arms across her body, hugging herself tightly. "I don't know you, Jade. We're strangers."

"I'm offering you the chance to remedy that." His voice was very quiet. "If you discovered anything you couldn't live with, you'd be free to leave."

How odd, Rose thought. He said nothing about getting to know me.

Maybe, she thought, that's the way he wants it. Maybe he likes his women to be purely sex objects. Maybe he prefers his relationships simple and uncomplicated.

If that were true, why did the idea frighten her so? Wasn't that just exactly what the doctor had ordered? What Titan had ordered? Here the suspect was offering her, on a silver platter, the chance to discover his secrets without giving up any of her own. What more could she ask for? Why was she shaking with a fear so profound she felt as if she might fall apart?

She was afraid of knowing him. She was nothing but a bird-dog for a man she'd never seen, but whose ruthlessness she knew only too well, and this man was her quarry. She was already in love with him—it was too late to do anything about that. But to get to *know* him, as a man, a human being, and then to find that he was an enemy, someone she would have to help destroy...

It would destroy *her*.

"I think...I'm afraid of you, Jade Castle," Rose said clearly, lifting her head to stare bleakly out over the sparkling city. She was reaching deep within herself, drawing on her own true feelings, and wasn't even aware that she had slipped out of her role.

He prompted her cautiously. "Afraid? Why?"

She shrugged. "Maybe because I don't believe you have it in you to let anyone really know you. How can you?" She gave a harsh, painful laugh. "You don't even know who you are. You told me so yourself. You made up your name."

She heard his sharp intake of breath and closed her eyes, hating herself for attacking him at his most vulnerable point.

"I know who I *am*," he corrected her, his voice very Australian. "Just not where I originally sprang from. If that's important to you, I guess we have a problem. For the rest . . . tell me, love, what would you like to know?''

Gathering her courage, she whirled on him. ''What do I want to know? My God! Start with, who raised you? You tell me you survived the streets of Singapore at an age when most kids are watching cartoons. You grew up with smugglers, running drugs, guns, God knows what else! Whatever else you are now, I think you must be a very hard and ruthless man. You'd have to be to have survived at all, much less to have gotten where you are now. Tell me why I shouldn't be afraid of you!''

Instead of answering her with words, he slowly extended his hand and touched the side of her face, brushing his fingers up and down over her cheek, just in front of her ear. Encountering a strand of hair, he let it slide like liquid satin through his fingers, then tucked it tenderly behind her ear.

She closed her eyes and tried to remain perfectly rigid, but the compulsion to swallow was overpowering. Jade's fingers, following the lock of hair down the side of her neck, felt the telltale movement. He began to stroke up and down, up and down, right over the ache in her throat. Her breath sighed through her in an anguished whimper.

''Rose,'' Jade whispered at last, ''have I ever hurt you?'' His hand moved down the column of her neck. With his thumb he defined the hollow at its base, testing her pulse.

She shook her head and silently formed the word ''no.''

His hand moved slowly down her body and became a warm weight on her breast. His other hand brushed wisps of hair back from her forehead, then dropped downward to her other breast. He began a gentle rotation, sliding the thin material of her blouse over her tender, sensitized nipples until they shivered into hard buttons in the hollows of his palms.

"Are my hands hard?" There was gravel in his voice. "Ruthless?"

Rose swayed forward into his touch. No, she cried silently. Not hard. But ruthless? Oh yes, there was a kind of ruthlessness about his hands. She had no defense against them, and he knew it. They cast a spell on her. They could easily enslave her, rob her of her will. They gave him absolute power over her. Ruthless? Oh yes.

He caressed the sides of her breasts and the skin under her arms. He didn't have to pull her into his arms; she just went, without thought or plan. She felt the surge of power in his lean, hard body as his arms came around her. There was an answering surge in her, a shaft of desire, pure and hot. His hands tunneled through her hair, tilting her head back and turning her face up to meet his descending mouth.

She heard a sound, low and primitive, and wasn't even surprised to find that it had come from her own throat. She didn't care who this man was. What was in a name, anyway? She didn't care if he *was* dangerous, or ruthless. She didn't care who had taught him how to give pleasure to a woman. He owned her body and her soul, and she had no mind at all.

He released her lips only long enough to whisper against them, "Am I hurting you now?" His breath was hot in her mouth. She shook her head in frantic denial. "Am I giving you pleasure?"

Touching abandoned kisses over his lips and the corners of his mouth, she gasped, "Yes...yes."

"What would you like me to do, Rose? Tell me." His voice was soft, but it was also a command.

She whispered, "Please..." not knowing how to tell him with words what she wanted so desperately. But this time he wouldn't let her get away with body talk.

"Tell me," he demanded again, holding her head still with his hands.

Rose heard herself whimper, "Please... make love to me. Love me, Jade...."

A growl of purely masculine triumph rumbled through his chest and into her mouth. He kissed her long, hard, and so deeply that she felt consumed. Her legs lost the power to support her; she sobbed in relief when Jade lifted her into his arms.

This time their loving wasn't a dance for two. It was a claiming, and an unconditional surrender.

It was different, waking alone in Jade's bed for the second time. This time sunlight was oozing through cracks in the curtains, and the summer morning was alive with bird song and the rhythmic sibilance of sprinklers. And this time Jade's presence was still there with her. The pillow beside her bore the imprint of his head; the sheets were rumpled and warm, and smelled subtly and evocatively of his body. She felt stiff and lethargic, and disgustingly, incongruously *happy*.

The world of sinister shadows, of secrets and deceptions, mystery and intrigue, seemed far, far away.

It came back slowly, bit by bit, like a wild thing inching closer to the firelight.

The first to come were the questions Jade had left unanswered the night before—one question in particular. *Who taught you gentleness, Jade?* She didn't know, when she allowed that one question to settle on the perimeter of her consciousness, that all the others would creep in after it until she was surrounded once again.

Who taught you the ways that please a woman, Jade? Growing up with smugglers, a survivor of the streets, where did you learn that the combination of strength and gentleness is irresistible?

Because, oddly enough, while his lovemaking was devastatingly skilled, it didn't seem practiced. Given what she knew about Jade, as well as what her instincts told her, she rather imagined that he would be very selective when it came to choosing his lovers. He was a solitary man, intensely private, uncomfortable with intimacy. She was remembering things about him now: the way he'd kept his shoes on, even on the beach; the way he'd left her alone in the bathroom, not intruding on *her* privacy; the way he'd left his own undressing until the last possible moment. The way he'd left her bed before she could wake and catch him without defenses... And somehow she knew that when he did appear this morning he would be shaved and showered and fully and immaculately dressed, his armor intact.

No, Jade Castle didn't easily share himself with anyone. And yet he'd asked her to stay with him. The implications of that fact sat on her chest like a lead weight and ushered in another disturbing question.

What about Tessa?

If Rose had had any lingering doubts about those tabloid rumors, they had been dispelled by the invitation. The same instincts that told her Jade wouldn't share himself readily also told her that he wouldn't share himself with more than one person at a time. And yet... the relationship between Tessa and Jade seemed strong and deep. Deeper than mere friendship. What hold could Tessa possibly have on him? Odd, that such a strong and powerful man seemed unable to deny the giddy rock star's slightest whim.

"Morning, love."

The weight on Rose's chest shattered into sunbeams and drifted away. He looked simply wonderful. There were no shadows this morning. He looked scrubbed, civilized. The white shirt and dark slacks hid the rock-hard contours of his body, disguising the power in his arms and shoulders. His hair gleamed with mahogany lights, like watered silk. He was smiling that particularly endearing, lopsided smile of his, and when he leaned over to kiss her, he smelled of soap and after-shave.

He kissed her with lingering thoroughness, then pulled back just far enough to look into her eyes. For the first time in Rose's memory his eyes were a clear, unclouded blue.

"Glad you're awake. Hungry?"

"Mmm-hmm. Starved."

"Good." He straightened and said briskly. "I'll have Kim bring you a tray while you—"

"No!" Rose's voice emerged as a croak of embarrassment. She propped herself on her elbows, cleared her throat and repeated, "Oh, no... please don't."

He turned to look at her, one eyebrow raised in amusement. "Why not?"

She raked a hand through her hair, dragging the tousled mass back from her face. "Well, look at me. I mean, here I am...."

"In my bed," Jade finished, his eyes soft with understanding. "Embarrassing, isn't it, love?"

"Well, yes," Rose said, not returning his smile. "I guess it is, a bit."

"Aren't you forgetting something? If you're going to be staying here, Kim is going to have to find out eventually, you know." His chuckle was indulgent, tender. "I can't very well keep you hidden away here—'' he pointed toward the ceiling ''—like a princess in a tower.''

A bubble of laughter escaped her. When he looked questioningly at her, she just shook her head and said, ''Nothing.'' Someday she would tell him about *her* childhood, and her dreams of princesses and dragons.

Someday. If only she could believe that there would be a ''someday'' for them.

Jade bent to plant a quick kiss on her forehead. ''Okay, I'll bring the tray. No more excuses now. Get up and get dressed. We've got to—what is it, love?'' He paused at the stricken look on her face.

''It's Wednesday!''

''Yes, it certainly is.''

''No, I mean, it's a work day. You brought me here from your—from work. I don't—I can't—I don't have anything to wear to work! My shoes—and my car—''

Jade sat down on the edge of the bed and picked up her hands. He carried one to his mouth, turned it palm up and kissed it, then laid it on his knee. ''Rose,'' he said with a sigh that sounded more sad than vexed, ''does it bother you so much to be linked with me?''

''Of course it bothers me!'' She couldn't look at his face, so she stared down at her hand instead. Warmth from his leg was spreading through her fingers. They began to tingle, and she rubbed them experimentally over the fabric of his slacks. ''I have to work with those people, Jade. To have everyone know I'm...'' She waved a hand distractedly, at a loss for the word. ''With the *boss*. It just looks so... it makes me seem like a...''

''All right.'' He stood up abruptly, making her feel strangely at odds with herself, both relieved and sorry. ''I can see I'm crowding you. You need some time. I understand that.'' He stood for a moment, looking down at her. There were shadows in his face again; they had come like windblown clouds covering the sun. Then he leaned to kiss her, just a gentle promise. "Don't worry, love. I'll work something out. Back in a bit."

After Jade had gone, Rose lay still, wasting precious minutes while she swallowed repeatedly, struggling against a distressing urge to cry. Damn it, life was such a bitch. She hadn't wanted to fall in love with anyone, not even somebody safe and undemanding and domesticated, let alone a wild and untamable man like Jade Castle. Let alone a *suspect*. She hadn't wanted to get involved with any such things as suspects, mysteries, or games, or deceptions. Damn Titan for this. Damn him to hell.

What was she going to do? She wanted to stay with Jade—and she didn't. She was afraid to stay with him, but knew that she had to. Her assignment demanded it. *Titan* would demand it. But she already had one foot on a roller coaster bound for disaster, maybe both feet. Maybe it was already too late, and another step closer to full involvement with the man wouldn't make much difference.

After all, she'd already admitted that she loved him. There wasn't anything else to say.

By the time Jade returned with her breakfast tray she had showered and dressed in yesterday's rumpled clothes. Her hair, brushed and still damp, was hanging loose on her shoulders. Jade set the tray on the foot of the bed and dropped a set of keys on it, then pulled her into his arms. He kissed her, tangling his hands in her hair and completely undoing all her efforts to restrain its natural vitality. She'd begun to notice that he particularly liked to do that, to fill his hands with the weight of her hair. Somehow it made her feel wanton, abandoned.

"Jade," she said plaintively when he released her, licking her lips, "you taste like *coffee*."

"Don't worry; I brought you some. And other good things, as well. Come, sit down. And don't dawdle; we've got some logistics to work out if we're going to save your reputation."

Rose glanced at him, and then, satisfied that he wasn't really making fun of her, dutifully sat and sank her teeth into a slice of toast. "What're those?" she asked, indicating the keys.

"The keys to Kim's car. She won't be needing it today. You can take it to work. Stop by your place and change clothes first, if you need to. Nobody at Castle knows the car, so it won't be connected to me."

"But how—"

"I'll have my driver drop me off in the limo. That way I can bring Kim's car home. I have a duplicate key. You can take your own car home. Simple?"

"Simple," Rose breathed, gazing at him. "It would be nice—"

"What would?" he prompted when she broke off and turned her focused attention upon her scrambled eggs.

She shrugged and took a deep breath. In a low, muffled voice she finally said, "I just wish all my problems could be solved so easily."

She half expected him to say something full of masculine arrogance like, "They can be, if you just leave them to me." But instead he leveled a dark, brooding gaze at her, then leaned across to touch her lips with his.

"Yeah..." he whispered against her mouth. "I know what you mean."

Rose felt chilled. Once again, the sun had been obscured by clouds.

* * *

"Titan, Rose here." It had taken her a while to get through to him this morning, and she felt testy. Even more so than usual. And to make matters worse, the connection was full of static. She must have reached him on a mobile unit.

"Hello, Rose. How are you?" His voice was unusually soft, without its usual brittle edge. She thought it must be the distance and the static. Or maybe, she thought vindictively, he's not feeling well. It was hard for her to think of Titan as a frail mortal who might catch a cold, or the flu, suffer from ulcers or have a hangover.

After a moment of waiting silence Rose said, "Fine. I'm . . . fine. Just peachy." Lord, but she hated having to tell him where she'd spent the night! How long could she postpone it?

"Anything to report?" There was tension in the casual question.

Rose closed her eyes and gripped the telephone. Her face felt swollen with the sudden and unexpected pressure of tears. Last night she'd let herself be ruled by her emotions. She hadn't felt dishonest. She'd felt desired, even loved. The night was imprinted on her memory forever as a montage of sensory images: the soft colors and patterns made by two bodies gracefully entwined; satin textures and exquisite pressures; and sweet explosions. Telling Titan would be like turning on a whole bank of fluorescent lights. It would make everything seem clinical and ugly, merely a matter of business. And it would make her seem no better than a—

"I've just come from the Castle Estate," she blurted in a rush of high, brittle words that hurt her throat. "I spent the night there."

"Oh?"

"Is that all you have to say? *'Oh?'*" Rose gave a sharp laugh. "I thought you'd be tickled to death."

Perhaps it was only distance that made Titan's voice sound so remote. "And?"

Dear God, what did he want? Details? "I've been invited to stay," Rose said woodenly. "Indefinitely."

There was a long pause. "And what have you decided?"

"Decided? Me?" Her voice seemed to keep climbing the scale. "You mean I have a choice?"

"Rose..."

"Wasn't this what you wanted, Titan? Wasn't it what you had in mind when you picked me for this job in the first place? Didn't you engineer all this, Titan? Meet him, Rose...take the job, Rose...go to bed with him, Rose.... You're a regular *procurer*, you know that?"

Titan's voice was cold. "The decision to sleep with Castle was yours, Rose. The decision to stay with him must be yours as well."

Decision? Had there been a decision to go to bed with Jade? She couldn't remember one. Looking back, she could barely remember just how it had happened. She pressed a hand against her forehead, distraught and confused.

"Rose," Titan prompted more gently, "it really is up to you. Do you want to stay with Castle?"

Did she want to stay? The answer was 'yes.' And 'no.' Yes, she wanted desperately to stay with him, forever if possible, without secrets and complications. And no, she didn't want to stay, not as a pawn in Titan's miserable game.

She didn't want to be the instrument of Jade's destruction.

She took a deep breath, restoring herself to a kind of cold, deadly calm. "Tell me, Titan," she said curiously, with a muffled sniffle left over from her near-hysterics. "Doesn't it bother you at all, asking me to make love to a man for *your* purposes?"

"For God's sake, Rose."

His voice sounded raw and strained. Rose felt a surge of triumph. For once in her life she'd actually managed to get to him! That unexpected hint of vulnerability fueled her anger and fanned a tiny spark of cruelty she hadn't even known she possessed. With cool detachment she asked, "Have you ever loved a woman, Titan?"

It was an impertinent and thoroughly asinine question. Rose didn't really expect him to dignify it with an answer, and was surprised when, after a long pause, he growled, "Oh, yes."

And then, incomprehensibly, she was on the brink of tears again. In a choked whisper she asked him, "Would you have asked of her what you did of me, Titan?"

There was another pause, and then, with what sounded like a sigh, "Yes . . ."

Rose's laughter erupted, though it came out sounding more like a sob. "You really *are* a bastard, aren't you? You know, all those years with the Bureau, I used to wonder about you, who you were, what you were like. I even—never mind. The one fantasy I did cling to was that there was a real human being on the other end of the line, despite frequent evidence to the contrary, a living, breathing man with flaws and frailties and *feelings*, damn it. But you really *are* completely ruthless, aren't you? The game is everything to you; the end justifies the means. Don't you . . . have you ever cared about *anyone*?"

"I assure you that I am a man, and most certainly flawed." Titan's voice was hard and angry. "As for feelings..." Rose heard his breath hiss as he struggled for control. When he spoke again it was with a return to his customary detachment. "Contrary to your opinion, I do care, Rose. I care about you."

"*Me!* Boy, is that a joke!"

"Laugh if you must. But if you're over your temper tantrum for the time being, I suggest you continue your report. In a professional manner, please."

I hate him, Rose thought. I really do hate him.

She stared incredulously at the telephone and counted slowly to ten. And then to twenty.

"Rose? Do you have anything else?"

"No," she said at last, feeling very tired all of a sudden. "Not yet. I still think the boat may hold some answers. I'm going to look for it tomorrow. I'll let you know if anything comes of it. Oh!" She rubbed at her forehead, which had begun to throb. "One thing. Small, but maybe important."

"Yes?"

"There's a computer terminal on the estate. And at least one other person besides Jade who knows how to use it. His name is Tran. I don't know any other names. His mother is the housekeeper. As I said, I can't really see where he'd fit into the picture, but he is, I'm told, something of a computer whiz.... Titan?" she said when the line remained silent. "Are you there?"

"Yes," he said softly. "I'm here. I was just thinking." Suddenly, elaborately casual, he asked. "Do you still feel the same way about carrying weapons, Rose?"

"Yes, I do. Why on earth would you ask that now? I'm in no danger from Jade Castle!" Not that kind of danger, anyway. "Titan, do you know something you're not telling me?"

"Just that we're not dealing with one person here," he said evasively. "We're dealing with a complex international conspiracy. And you know as well as I do that where conspiracy is concerned, you never know who might be involved. We're also caught up in someone else's war, someone else's cause. I don't have to tell you—"

"No," Rose said tightly. "You don't." Someone else's war—*Thad's* war—had nearly cost her her life, and something maybe more important: her self-esteem. "All right, Titan, I'll give it some thought. And if things heat up I'll consider carrying something. Right now, I can't see a need for it."

"Don't wait until too late, Rose."

"If you're not careful, you're going to have me thinking you actually *care*!"

"Oh, I do care," Titan said softly. "Believe me."

The line clicked and went dead.

Michaels's silence was a polite query. Titan ignored it for a few moments while he tapped his fingers absent-mindedly on the cradled receiver.

"Well, she's going after the boat," he said finally. And then, under his breath, "*Damn.* I'd hoped she'd forgotten."

"From what you've told me, sir, and from what I've seen, I'd have thought that possibility very remote."

"Yes.... Did you get the boat moved?"

"Yes, sir. It's now moored at Channel Islands."

Titan's breath hissed through his teeth. "That's the next most logical place for her to look. Couldn't you do any better than that?"

"Well, I understood that you only required a little more time, sir. I didn't think you wanted a permanent hiding place." Michaels sounded abused.

"It's all right," Titan said tiredly. "I'm not sure all the time in the world would make any difference."

"What shall I—"

"Never mind. I'll see to it myself this morning. It's been a while since I took her out. Maybe the sea air will clear my head. I can't seem to think clearly these days. I trust you took care of the harbormaster at the marina?"

Michaels smiled blandly. "His loyalty and silence have been assured."

"And I trust you told no one where you were taking it?"

Michaels shifted uncomfortably. "I'm afraid that Tessa knows, sir."

"Tessa!"

"I'm sorry, sir, but I didn't think you'd—it just doesn't seem feasible that she'd be involved in this."

"Michaels," the man called Titan murmured, "I hope you're right. I *devoutly* hope you're right."

Chapter 9

I'm sorry, Mr. Castle isn't in. May I give him a message?" Over the phone Dorie Payton's voice was cool, pleasant and thoroughly professional.

Rose slowly extended a forefinger to touch the fully blown flower in the vase in front of her. At her touch, several petals detached themselves and settled onto the desktop. "I see," she murmured, glancing at the clock on the wall. "All right, just...tell him I called. This is Rose, Rose St. James."

"Oh, yes, Rose." Did the secretary's voice seem a little warmer? "I certainly will tell Mr. Castle as soon as I hear from him."

"Thank you. Oh," Rose added hurriedly, before Dorie could break the connection, "do we still have a date for lunch?"

"Why, yes, certainly. I'm looking forward to it."

"Oh good." Rose let her breath out in a long, silent sigh. "Then I'll meet you in the cafeteria at twelve-fifteen."

"Lovely," Dorie said. "And I will give Mr. Castle your message."

"Thank you," Rose whispered to the dead line, and slowly replaced the receiver in its cradle. She sat for a long time, frowning at the telephone and rubbing her forehead. Her mind was absolutely blank. After a while she stood up, plucked the spent blossom from its vase and dropped it into the trash can beside her desk. Then she went into the darkroom and closed the door firmly behind her.

The man called Titan parked the car in the public parking lot nearest the Channel Islands Marina's guest slips. It was a medium-priced American-made car, about two years old and of a nondescript tan color. There were hundreds of cars like it on the road, and probably several in this lot that were at least similar. He had used the car, or one just as anonymous, on several occasions. There was nothing about it that could be connected to him unless one had the resources to run a computer check on the license and registration, and follow that up with a class B national security code check.

He got out of the car, locked it and dropped the keys into his pants pocket. From his other pocket he took the key Michaels had given him, the key to the dock gate. It would not be necessary for him to announce his presence to the harbormaster.

His footsteps echoed on the wooden bridge that sloped gently down to the dock. Below him tiny black crabs scuttled into cracks between rocks whitewashed with gull droppings. Small schools of fingerlings zipped about in

the shallow water beneath a thin rainbow film of petro-
leum pollution.

The docks were quiet. It was a beautiful day, still
foggy, but it would burn off soon to a brilliant August
morning. Most of the visiting boats had departed hours
ago, at first light. The only living thing to take note of his
arrival was a large brown pelican, startled from its roost
beneath the stern of a ketch called "Manderly," out of
San Diego's Mission Bay.

The rather abrupt and noisy departure of the pelican
startled Titan. He chuckled at his own nervousness and
wondered about the state of his mental faculties. He had
no reason to be edgy, no reason at all to feel the ice water trickle of unease that was raising the fine hairs on his
skin. It was a peaceful, ordinary morning on the docks.
Seagulls were dipping and wheeling aimlessly; pelicans
were skimming over the gray water. The only sounds were
familiar harbor sounds: the soft clanking of boat rig-
ging; the muted hum of a diesel engine; the occasional cry
of a seabird.

There was no reason why he should be thinking of a
conversation held in a gypsy camp, about such things as
ESP and premonitions, and the irrational and wholly
primitive awareness of something amiss....

Rose was five minutes late for her luncheon date with
Dorie Payton. She'd lost track of time in the darkroom
and had to literally run through the sprawling maze of
buildings and corridors to the employees' cafeteria. She
arrived out of breath and untidy, not the most auspicious beginning to what Rose hoped would be an en-
lightening meeting. She was going to need every ounce of
poise and self-confidence she possessed to deal with Dorie, who was always so superbly in control.

If only she could concentrate! She was so distracted by this Jade-Titan dilemma that she couldn't think of anything else. Her emotions were getting in the way of her professionalism again. Surely, somewhere in the secret agent's manual, it must state emphatically: IMPORTANT—NO FEELINGS ALLOWED!

"I'm sorry," she said casually enough when she and Dorie were seated. They had been through the salad bar; now Rose was making a time-consuming and elaborate production out of doctoring her iced tea with lemon and artificial sweetener. "I hope I didn't miss your call. I've been in the darkroom most of the morning."

"Oh, that's quite all right." Dorie's face was serene. "You didn't miss a thing. Mr. Castle hasn't come in yet."

"I see," Rose murmured, wondering how to persist without betraying too much. And then she thought, Rose, you idiot. You're out of practice. That's exactly what you *must* do—betray yourself.

She frowned at her salad, poked aimlessly at it, and allowed strain and just a touch of embarrassment to edge her voice. "When do you expect him?"

Dorie's eyes seemed kind. "I really don't know. He didn't tell me when he'd be in. But that isn't at all unusual for Mr. Castle; he does sometimes go AWOL." Her mouth curved with an unexpected flash of humor. "We've all learned to live with it."

Rose's mind was skittering like a panic-stricken bird in a cage. AWOL? Doing what? She skewered a garbanzo bean with her fork and then laid it down untasted. "Mrs. Payton—Dorie—you really must think it strange...a minor employee like me making such a—pestering the president of the company like this. It's not what you think. I mean, I'm not... Did he tell you—do you know how he happened to hire me?"

The older woman shook her head and took a bite of her salad. "Just that you'd had an accident of some kind on his estate, something about your equipment being damaged."

"Yes." Rose leaned forward eagerly. "And he wanted to make it up to me, so he gave me this job. I can't believe it. I mean, most people in his position would have just hauled out the checkbook, or turned it over to a lawyer, or something. But Mr. Castle, well, I've never met anyone like him before."

Dorie just smiled and said nothing.

Rose dashed on. "It just floors me, you know? He's so important. He knows so many people, and here he is, personally taking the time to take care of my problem." She shook her head in wonder. Dorie was watching her closely, with a rather ambiguous smile on her lips and a look of assessment in her eyes. Rose thought, Easy Rose. Don't lay it on too thick. She's no fool.

She launched into an animated and amusing version of her "accident" on the night of the charity benefit party. While she chattered she studied her companion covertly, looking for a weak spot and trying desperately to think of some way to get her to talk.

The sign, when it came, was so small, so brief, that Rose almost missed it. She was describing the scene at the bonfire, and when she mentioned Tessa Freedom's torrid dance with Raoul, Dorie's mouth suddenly tightened in a tiny spasm of annoyance. Just that one involuntary slip, but Rose caught it and thought triumphantly, Of course! Tessa!

"Imagine me, meeting and talking to Tessa Freedom! I couldn't believe it! And then, to have her come walking right into Mr. Castle's office while I was there... Does she do that very often?"

Dorie muttered, "Oh, *Tessa!*" exasperatedly under her breath, and sighed. "Not often, thank goodness. Not anymore. Not since her career keeps her so busy. Thank goodness for her career; at least it keeps her out of Mr. Castle's hair!"

Rose looked carefully bewildered. "I don't understand. I thought—"

"Yes, I know what you probably thought, thanks to those awful scandal papers. And that's ridiculous, just ridiculous! For heaven's sake, the child is his *ward!*"

"Ward?" Rose had no trouble at all looking and sounding shocked. Whatever she'd expected, it hadn't been this. *"Child?"*

"Well, obviously she's not a child anymore, although sometimes she reminds me of one, the way she dresses. Just like a little girl getting into her mother's makeup. She always was a show-off, an incorrigible ham."

Dorie paused to sip iced tea, and Rose took the risk of prompting, "Tessa Freedom is Mr. Castle's *ward*?" It was such a mind-boggling concept; she just hoped she could get the whole story out of Dorie before the secretary remembered her habit of reticence.

"Well, not anymore, of course. She's of age. Let's see . . . she'd be twenty-four now. Mr. Castle became her guardian when she was fourteen. She was, as you might imagine, quite a handful in those days, too! He put her through school, until she dropped out to become a rock singer, and then he subsidized her career. He still feels completely responsible for her, I know. Spoils her shamefully. She's always had the run of this place, and the estate, not to mention the boat. Cars, clothes . . ."

"Boat?" Rose pounced, no longer caring whether she was disturbing Dorie's revelations. She needn't have worried anyway. Whatever Tessa might have done to antagonize her guardian's secretary in the past, she was obviously still an itch that had been long overdue for a good scratch.

"Mm, yes, Mr. Castle's yacht. That girl has had full use of it since her eighteenth birthday, and I can tell you, some of the things she's had going on..."

"Would that be the boat in the picture?" Rose asked, breaking into the beginnings of what looked like a tirade. "The one behind Mr. Castle's desk?"

Dorie blinked and appeared to collect herself. "Yes...yes, it is."

"Oh, she's a real beauty. Where is she moored?"

"Why, at a marina somewhere in Los Angeles. Do you sail?"

"I have, a little," Rose hedged. "But I love boats and the sea. How big is Mr. Castle's boat?"

But Dorie was already retreating behind her natural reserve, like a hen settling onto her nest. "I really couldn't say. If you ask Mr. Castle, I'm sure he'd be happy to tell you all about it."

"He's really into sailing, then?"

Dorie smiled and unbent a little. "I'm not sure what that means. But he is fond of the boat and spends as much time as he can aboard. If you really are interested, be sure to ask him when you see him. I'm quite sure he'd welcome a chance to talk about it."

"I will, I certainly will," Rose murmured with enthusiasm. But she was remembering standing with Jade on the little crescent beach at sunset, talking almost wistfully of the sea. And the toneless way he'd answered her tentative question. *"Yes. It's my boat."* As flat and final as a closing door.

* * *

The boat was moored alone near the end of the dock. The man called Titan paused on the dock to look at her. She was a beauty, a sleek fifty-five foot sloop with diesel engines, all natural teak and gleaming white paint. Her decks were cleared, her sails furled and tied; everything was still battened down and rigged for ocean sailing, probably from her recent run up the Santa Barbara Channel from Los Angeles.

He stepped up onto the deck. Something heavy within him lightened; something tight inside him eased. The boat was, had always been, his narcotic, his anesthetic. His antidote for pain and loneliness. He felt soothed by her beauty and elegance.

In that tranquil state he reached into his pocket and took out the key to the hatch. He took two steps and put out his hand to touch the varnished teak of the hatch cover, and slowly drew it back. Peace and tranquility exploded, prickling his skin like a thousand glass shards. Every nerve in his body cried out.

The hatch was open.

In spite of the adrenaline that had his whole body twanging, his mind was humming like a well-oiled engine. It told him that, excluding carelessness, there was no reason for the hatch to be open. And Michaels was not a careless man. Silently, and with full cognizance of danger, he leaned over to look into the cabin.

Something exploded behind his left ear. He felt himself falling down the companionway, felt himself hit the floor with his shoulder, and then the back of his head. He had a hazy impression of things being out of place, things that moved, and things that didn't. His mind tried briefly to continue humming like a well-oiled engine...and then sank gratefully into oblivion.

* * *

There were no phones ringing when Rose crossed the footbridge that night, nothing to disturb the peace of the summer evening. It was the dinner hour—still plenty of time left before sunset and nighttime's foggy chill. The air smelled of the canal, fresh-cut grass and someone's outdoor barbecue. The only sign of life was a lone mud hen, etching a rippled "Vee" on the opaque surface of the water.

Rose let herself into her house and dropped her keys beside the telephone. Then she sank down onto the couch and lifted the phone into her lap. The white card embossed with a black rook was already in her hand. She stared at it for a long time before she finally picked up the receiver and dialed the number on the card.

"Good evening, Castle residence."

"Hello...Kim?" Rose stopped to clear her throat. "This is Rose—Rose St. James. May I please speak to Mr. Castle?"

"Oh, yes, Miss St. James, so nice to hear your voice." On the telephone Kim's accent gave her voice a charming lilt. "I'm very sorry. Mr. Castle not at home right now. I give him a message?"

"No, just tell him I called. Oh, Kim, by the way, I wanted to thank you for lending me your car this morning. I hope it got back safely."

"Oh, yes, Miss St. James, nice of you to ask. And very happy to be of help. I'm sure car be fine. Mr. Castle bring it back soon. When he comes home, I tell him you called."

"Thank you," Rose whispered, and slowly lowered the receiver.

After staring at nothing for uncounted minutes, she dialed another number. Ordinarily the wait for the code sequence seemed interminable; tonight it was completed while she sat in a fog of perplexity. When the line opened to Michaels's polite inquiry, she was caught off guard.

"Michaels?" Confusion made her blunt. "What are *you* doing there? Where's Titan?"

"Hello, Rose." Michaels's voice was cool and unruffled. "Titan isn't available at the moment, I'm afraid. May I help you?"

"Well, Titan can bloody well *make* himself available," Rose snapped tensely. "I need to talk to him."

"I'm sorry." Michaels was sympathetic, but implacable. "He really can't be reached. When I hear from him, I'll tell him to get in touch with you at once. Is there anything important I should tell him for you?"

Rose took a deep breath, mentally counting. "Yes. Tell him—" Tell him what? That Jade Castle had dropped off the face of the earth immediately after asking her to move into his home and bed, and before waiting to hear her decision? And what reason did she have for presuming he'd dropped off the face of the earth? The fact that he'd chosen to take the day off? He was the president of his company, for Pete's sake! He could do as he damn well pleased. And if he chose to spend the day fishing, or sleeping, or...

Sailing.

"Tell Titan he can go to hell," she said into the telephone, without any particular emphasis, and quietly put down the receiver.

Jade had gone to his boat. She knew it, though she wasn't sure why he'd chosen to make himself scarce just when he'd asked her to make a decision about her future with him. Maybe he'd thought that if he took himself out of the picture she would be able to think more clearly. Maybe he was using a bit of psychology on her, too, showing her how much she would miss him when he wasn't around. Who knew how Jade Castle's mind worked? That was the problem. She didn't. She didn't know him at all!

There was only one thing she was sure of: she had to find that boat.

She sat for a long time, thinking. And then, as the house was growing dark, she picked up the phone again and dialed Information. Moments later she dialed the number she had just scribbled on the back of Jade's business card.

"Harbormaster," the terse male voice said.

"Well hello, love!" The voice that came out of Rose's mouth was raspy, passionate, a raw-throated croak. It was, in fact, an eerily accurate imitation of Tessa Freedom. "This is Tessa Free—"

"Tessa! How've you been, babe?" The harbormaster's voice had warmed about forty degrees. This was either going to be very easy, or very dangerous. On the one hand, if the man knew Tessa personally it would be easy to slip up somewhere and give herself away without realizing it. On the other hand, Rose had already received confirmation of one very important fact: Jade's boat either was now, or had been at some time, moored at this marina.

"Hey, long time no see," the harbormaster went on in a voice full of playful intimacy. "You're sure one busy lady these days. When you comin' down to see us? They sure do miss you down on C-Dock—miss those wild parties. Now that you're famous, I guess you're too good for old friends, huh?"

Rose grimaced and wondered just how well Tessa knew the harbormaster! "Well," she purred, sounding a little like a contented cat, "as a matter of fact, I was thinking about throwing one this weekend. Just for old-times' sake. You been takin' good care of my boat?''

"Like she was my own, babe, like she was my own—right up to the minute she set sail.''

"Sail!" Rose covered her squeak of dismay with a pouty moan. "Oh damn! Nobody told me. Now where am I going to have my party?''

The harbormaster's chuckle was so suggestive it made Rose's skin crawl. "Well, I tell you, babe, I could name you about a hundred fifty guys that'd just love to offer their boats, any time! You just say the word.''

Rose gave a husky little giggle and rasped, "Ooh, lovely." And then, almost as an afterthought, "You don't happen to know where they've taken her, do you? If it's not too far away, maybe they'll be back by this weekend.''

"Wish I could help you. All I know is, she cast off yesterday afternoon, and she ain't been back. Sorry, babe.''

"So am I, love,'' Rose sighed and hung up.

So Jade had had his boat moved. Innocent coincidence? Or had her interest in the boat prompted desperate action? In the former case, there was no telling where the boat might be—on its way to Tahiti, for all she knew. But if the latter, logic told Rose that the boat would probably just have been moved to a new mooring, someplace farther away from her own front yard.

In her mind's eye she mapped the California coast. It didn't take her long to figure out that the next most convenient small-boat harbor to both Castle's estate and Castle Industries had to be Channel Islands Harbor. And before that thought had even solidified in her mind, she had changed her clothes, picked up her car keys and purse, and was on her way out the door.

It occurred to her as she was speeding northward on Pacific Coast Highway that she really ought to have tried again to reach Titan.

And then she thought, with a rising swell of anger, Oh, the hell with Titan! Where had he been when she needed him? And anyway, it wouldn't be the first time she'd initiated action on her own when the circumstances demanded it.

She resolutely pushed aside the vague feelings of unease, the nagging thought that she was missing something obvious, the awareness that she had more pieces to the puzzle than she knew and just couldn't seem to fit them together. She was so tired of mysteries, tired of puzzles. She was more than ever convinced that the key to everything was on that yacht. Titan would approve—and she wouldn't sleep until she'd found it.

Not that she would have been likely to sleep anyway, not tonight. Last night she'd been with Jade, her mind empty and her body on fire. Tonight her mind was a maelstrom, her body cold, and she didn't even know where Jade had gone. Loneliness had never hurt so much before.

She missed Jade. Missed him so much!

If she let herself, she would remember everything, every tiny detail: the smell of his skin, the feel of the black pendant pressed between her cheek and his chest; the rasp of his chin on her temple; the warmth of his mouth, its flavor, and vibrance. His hands...

Oh, God, she thought with new desperation, wiping moisture from her cheeks, Don't let me feel! Please just let me think of mysteries and secrets and puzzles instead!

Finding a needle in a haystack was a simple enough process. One simply took it apart one wisp at a time.

Rose had to ask directions twice in order to find the pleasure-boat harbor at Channel Islands. The harbormaster's office was closed. After that it was a question of walking and talking and asking questions of everyone she met.

In spite of the hour the marina was lively. Boats were still coming in; it was a beautiful night for a romantic sail around the harbor, and a pleasant time for puttering and enjoying the easy camaraderie of the docks. Rose had no trouble getting people to talk to her. She was wearing white jeans and topsiders and a bright yellow windbreaker, and her hair hung dark and heavy on her shoulders. When she put a sparkle in her eyes and a lilt in her voice and asked, "Hi, anybody here know where I can find Jade Castle's boat?" she got more offers of help than she needed. Most of the offers were in the nature of alternatives to the missing Castle yacht, which Rose laughingly declined. A few sincere-sounding souls—all male—offered to help her look. But no one had heard of Jade Castle or his boat.

Finally a middle-aged woman with the weathered, rawboned look of an experienced seaman beckoned, and when Rose drew near, jerked her head toward the far end of the dock.

"See that guy in the blue pullover? The one sitting on the dock box beside that floating cocktail lounge over there?"

Rose looked and nodded.

"He's the one to talk to. He's the resident narc—knows all the comings and goings."

"Narc?"

"Federal narcotics agent. If this guy you're looking for was an old-timer, everybody here'd know him. Since we don't, he's got to be new. If he's new, Bob over there will know about it.''

"Thank you," Rose said with sincerity and moved off to talk to the narcotics agent.

"Bob" wasn't very helpful. He looked Rose up and down with a steely, professional eye, then shrugged. "Nobody new in the permanent moorings," he grunted, chomping steadily on a piece of chewing gum. "Have you tried the guest slips on the other side of the harbor?" He jerked his thumb at the lights across the water.

"Thanks." Rose sighed and went back to her car.

She found her way around to the other side of the harbor with very little trouble, skirting the New England-style whaling village with its specialty shops and seafood restaurants, and the commercial fishing docks, where the sea-urchin harvesters were just coming in with their catches. Once again she found a public parking lot, locked her car and began a systematic dock-by-dock search.

The problem was, of course, that she didn't know exactly what she was looking for. She had no name, no idea what size of boat she was looking for. She knew only what the boat looked like running with full sails in heavy seas. It was a little like trying to find a bird in its nest, when you had only seen it soaring free in the distant skies.

She found that the friendliness and openness of the permanent residents were missing in the guest slips. People didn't stay long enough to get to know each other and develop a mutual support system. There was a feeling of suspicion and transience here—like a motel, or a bus station.

One dock drew Rose's attention. It was a hive of activity; someone was apparently preparing to sail. The process interested Rose for two reasons: first, it seemed strange that a boat would be leaving so late in the evening, when everyone else was coming into harbor; and second, she had never seen a yacht prepare to sail. So she strolled down the dock, hands in the pockets of her windbreaker, to watch.

It was a beautiful boat, sleek, graceful, streamlined. Over fifty feet, Rose guessed, with a single mast, all white with natural wood trim. The hatch was open, and dark-haired, dark-skinned men were working silently, stowing boxes of provisions below, doing unidentifiable things that were presumably necessary preparations for departure. They cast dark glances at Rose, but didn't challenge her.

She squinted at the boat, trying to see it from a distance, through a mist of spray, with its sail full and white against a turquoise sky. The silhouette was right. She moved closer. There was no one on deck at the moment, so she edged farther along the slip, trying to see the name on the stern.

Her senses were working properly; her eyes relayed the black stenciled letters to her brain for recording and translation. But there was something wrong with her reflexes. She stood very still for a long time, staring at the words.

TITAN. Los Angeles, California.

And they meant nothing to her. Nothing at all.

It happened slowly. She thought first, Los Angeles. The registry is right. And then she whispered it out loud: *"Titan..."*

Her head was suddenly filled with noise, the deafening, numbing clatter of pieces falling into place. She shook her head, trying to clear it so she could think. She had to think.

She whispered, "No, it's impossible."

But was it?

Jade Castle was "missing"; Titan was suddenly "unavailable."

Rose mentioned her interest in Jade's boat; Titan's limousine intercepted her before she could get to the marina where the boat was moored.

The pieces tumbled in on her too rapidly to grasp, a montage of impressions and memories: an Australian accent that came and went; phrases; words; coincidences; flashes of inexplicable familiarity...

"Aren't you the least bit curious?"

A rose that was almost, but not quite, white, with a blush of pink where the petals curled...

When she whispered "No..." again it was a long, anguished moan of denial. Because she knew it *was* possible.

Belatedly her reflexes took charge. Adrenaline flooded her system. There was no one in sight, so she jumped lightly onto the deck and crouched beside the open hatch, listening. The TITAN heaved gently. There was no sound from below. In an instant Rose had swung her legs through the hatch and down the steep companionway steps, to drop with a muffled thump onto the cabin floor.

Once more she dropped into a listening crouch. The cabin seemed to be deserted for the moment. Moving cautiously, gracefully, silently as a cat, Rose moved into the passageway that led to the aft stateroom.

The door was shut. Rose paused to listen, then very slowly opened the door. A spasm she couldn't control slashed across her face, twisting her mouth.

The man lying on one of the narrow berths sat up slowly and painfully. "Good evening," she said in a voice she didn't recognize. "Titan, I presume?"

"Well, Jordan Rose," Jade Castle said softly. "What took you so long?"

Chapter 10

One side of his face appeared to be swollen and discolored. He was pale, and his jaws were shadowed with day-old stubble. His hair was disheveled, and he was holding his body at an odd angle, as if he were in pain. In fact, he looked frankly awful, and without intending to Rose found herself searching for the Jade she knew—the proud, solitary hunter, immaculate, powerful, always in control.

She found him at last in the eyes. His eyes burned at her out of the shadows with the unquenchable fire of a tiger in a trap. Rose felt as if the boat had suddenly heaved beneath her feet, and she put out a hand, groping for the wall of the passageway to steady herself.

"I don't suppose you took my advice about arming yourself?" The voice was familiar at least; dry and cool, and Australian.

Rose shook her head. "No, I didn't. Why do you ask?"

His body had gone strangely still. His eyes were like gunmetal. "Because," he said with a sigh, "you are about to regret it."

Before the words were out of his mouth Rose heard a scuffling sound behind her. Before she could react something hard jabbed her cruelly in the small of the back. The hand that she had braced against the side of the passage was caught in a steel grip and twisted back and up. Warm breath redolent of tobacco and garlic stirred through her hair. A guttural voice spoke quietly in Spanish.

Jade hadn't moved. Now he said calmly, "He says that if you do exactly as he tells you, he will not break your arm. I'd advise you to do as he says. Take it from me, you don't want to be stuck in one of these bunks with a broken arm!"

"How am I supposed to know what he wants me to do?" Rose gasped. "I don't speak Spanish."

"I know."

"Oh, right, I forgot," Rose said bitterly. "Of course you do, Titan."

"That's all right; I'm fluent in Spanish. Aren't you glad you have me here to translate?"

Rose didn't trust herself to do more than grunt. The grip on her arm tightened, impelling her forward into the cabin. A brutal shove slammed her face down onto the empty berth. She lay absolutely motionless while her wrists were pulled together behind her, and tightly and efficiently bound. A hand tangled in her hair and yanked her head upward. Rose heard Jade speak rapidly, but quietly, in Spanish, and after a moment her hair was released. The cabin door clicked shut.

In the silence Rose lay without moving, barely even breathing. After a few tense moments, Jade said urgently, "Rose. *Rose,* are you all right?"

She rolled her head slowly to one side and glared at him. The position made her head ache.

He was still sitting at that awkward angle, but now one side of his mouth had lifted in a wry grin. For the first time Rose realized that he was also bound. "I can't help you, love. I would if I could, but I'm afraid I was noisier and messier about coming aboard than you were. I've sustained a bit of damage. Lord, I'm sorry I ever brought you into this mess!"

She turned her face down to the mattress cover once more and closed her eyes, trying desperately to pull herself together. When she felt reasonably sure she wouldn't fall apart, she struggled into a sitting position. Then she carefully pulled her feet up under her, leaned back against the bulkhead and watched the man she had known for so long as "Titan" through half-closed eyes.

He endured the silent scrutiny for several minutes, then remarked, "I wish like hell you wouldn't do that."

"Do what?" Rose's voice was a rusty croak. She cleared it impatiently, angry with it for betraying her.

"Look at me like that."

She shifted slightly, settling herself. "I'm just trying to decide what I should call you."

He made a noise—a little snort of pain or vexation—and closed his eyes. He looked, Rose thought dispassionately, like death warmed over.

"What difference does it make?" he said, sounding unbearably weary all of a sudden. "Your name, my name. They don't mean anything anyway, do they? We made them up, Rose, you and I. They don't bind us. We change them at will, like shoes. How many names have *you* been called in your lifetime? Call me anything you like. Call me a damned SOB if it makes you feel better.''

"How do you do that?" Rose asked admiringly.

"Do what?"

"Turn that Aussie accent on and off like that. It's amazing. Amazing what an effective disguise it was.''

Jade laughed softly, without humor. "Oh, I guess I just have an ear for accents...languages. I heard so many of them in the streets of Singapore when I was a kid.''

"That part was true, then?''

"Rose, everything I told you was true.''

Her only reply to that was a high, sharp laugh. It covered the sudden spasm of pain that clutched at her insides until she wanted to writhe with it. "Well," she said brightly after shoring up her defenses with a deep breath, "what languages do you speak? Besides Spanish, of course. Maybe we can pass the time playing word games. We're both so good at games. I'm fluent in several languages myself, you know.''

"I know," Jade said softly. "You speak Russian, Greek, Hungarian and Arabic. And a smattering of French, though mine is better. I'm afraid the only two languages we have in common are English and—''

"Why?" The word erupted from her unawares, in a small painful explosion. "Why did you do this to me? Do you have any idea how ... how *violated* I feel?''

"Rose, I never meant to make you feel like that, believe me. I never wanted to give you anything but good things.''

"No...''

"I tried to give you joy. And pleasure." In his voice she heard all the sensual awareness of the night they'd shared, and warm memories reached out to envelop her.

She recoiled. "No! No, and you'll never make me feel anything again but *loathing*. You are unspeakable. And I swear to you, you'll never touch me again. Ever."

His laugh was dry and carried traces of his old arrogance. "Careful, Rose. This is a very small cabin. I hate to think what it would do to someone with your pride to have to eat your words." He chuckled, and she answered him with stony silence.

In that silence they both heard footsteps echo on the wooden dock. Rose stiffened, and Jade hissed a warning.

"I told them you wouldn't try to yell for help, or you'd be wearing a gag right now. For God's sake, don't make a liar out of me. It's only the Terristas coming back anyway."

"The what?"

"Terristas. It's what this particular brand of terrorists call themselves. Never mind. Just keep quiet. I think we're about ready to leave."

"Where—"

"Hush!"

The cabin lights went out. In the darkness Rose lay still and listened to unidentifiable bumps, scrapes, groans and soft calls in Spanish. From very near came the muffled explosion of a diesel engine. The noise settled into a steady, throbbing pulse, and the boat began to move. The sensation of motion didn't strike Rose as being particularly pleasant. A thought occurred to her.

She whispered hoarsely, "I've never been on a boat before. What if I get seasick?"

There was no answer. "Jade?" Her eyes were getting used to the dark, and there was a little light coming through the small porthole above the berths. Rose could see that he was slumped sideways, half reclining on his bunk. She hitched herself forward, lowered her feet over the side of her bunk and carefully stood up. At that moment the floor surged upward and she fell forward onto Jade's bunk, knocking him against the bulkhead.

The sound he made was terrible, a strangled groan of pure agony.

"Oh, God. Jade?" Appalled, she struggled to right herself, to take her weight off him without doing further damage. She could hear his breathing. It was ragged, but held under control. "You didn't tell me you were hurt!"

"I did, too. You just weren't listening."

"Well, I was distracted, for Pete's sake. Look, do you *want* to quarrel? Where are you hurt?"

"My shoulder. I landed on it when they hit me. Fell through the hatch. Lucky I didn't break my neck..."

"Is it...your shoulder isn't *broken*?"

"I don't think so. Just bruised. Hurts like hell, though, the way they've got me tied. I'm hoping once we're safely out of the harbor, I can convince them to untie me...us."

"God, I hope so. I've thought of something. Did you hear me say I've never been on a boat? I'm pretty sure I'm going to get seasick."

His chuckle was dry, but reassuring. "So much for positive thinking."

"Be as arrogant as you please, but just remember, you're stuck in here with me. If I get seasick it's not going to make *your* life a bed of roses!"

"What an apt phrase," Jade observed pleasantly. And then, after a moment, "I have a well-stocked medicine cabinet, including seasick pills, if they'll let us get to it. Chances are they'll be in need of a little something themselves soon. I don't think more than a couple of these guys are experienced sailors. I may have a few bargaining chips up my sleeve. Here, help me up."

"With what? My teeth?"

Jade gave a put-upon sigh. "Rose, you know I hate it when you get sarcastic. Just lean over closer so I can get some leverage. I won't violate you. There. Thank you."

"Don't mention it." Rose moved back to her own side of the cabin and sat down on her bunk. She was trembling. Oh, God, she thought, what am I going to do? I want so badly to hate him! But all she had to do was go near him, touch him, feel the heat from his body, and she was so unnerved her teeth were chattering.

"What sort of 'bargaining chips'?" she asked grudgingly to distract herself from her sudden, overwhelming awareness of him.

Jade's voice was smug. "I know where the medicine is: they don't. Sit tight. I have a feeling somebody will be along very shortly."

"Well, I hope so," Rose said in a small voice. "Is there a bathroom in here?"

Jade's chuckle was soft with sympathy. "Yes, there is. And on a boat it's referred to as 'the head.'"

"Oh," Rose said meekly. "I'll remember that." She shifted, trying to get comfortable. Her hands were beginning to go numb, and there were other vague but persistent complaints from other parts of her body. She shut her eyes, but that only seemed to isolate her with her discomforts, so she opened them again and strained to see Jade across the dark cabin. If she was uncomfortable, she could only imagine what *he* must be enduring. How she wished she didn't care!

"Hey," she whispered after a while, trying to distract herself again. "Are you still there?"

"Yes." But he sounded groggy.

"Who are they? Where are they going? Do you feel up to filling me in?" Funny. In the darkness like this, listening to his voice, she wasn't thinking of him as Jade. Now he was Titan. In a cool, professionally detached voice she added, "I really do think I ought to know what's going on here, don't you?"

She heard him stir, trying to rouse himself, and fought her empathetic feelings. He needed this mental activity as much as she did.

After a moment his voice came, flat and dry. "How much do you know about the situation in Costa Brava?"

"Just what you told me when you briefed me for this 'assignment.'"

"Okay. So you know that about ten years ago the ruling family was deposed by a leftist coup. Most of the family was executed, except for the ones who managed to get out ahead of time."

"Like Tessa," Rose murmured.

Jade's head moved. Rose could feel his eyes focus on her. "Yes," he said briefly. "Like Tessa. Anyway, after that it gets complicated. One revolution after another, various factions jockeying for power, and the superpowers, not to mention Cuba, putting their money on their own special favorites. Currently the government is rather tenuously in the hands of a group of nationalists. Costa Brava for the Costa Bravans; get rid of all outside political interference, both East and West. Radical idea, huh? Well, believe me, like most dedicated patriots, these guys are a serious bunch. They call themselves 'Terristas.' Roughly translated, it means Earth people. There's not much they won't do to get what they want—and what they want is to get both the leftists and the United States out of Costa Brava."

"And so," Rose said slowly, "they steal the chemical weaponry, use it on leftist strongholds, then let it 'leak' that the weapons come courtesy of Uncle Sam. They eliminate the leftists and discredit the United States at the same time.''

"And just possibly start a chain reaction that could result in World War III," Jade finished dryly.

Rose kept silent, wondering if he would go on. When he didn't, she realized that he was waiting for her inevitable question. She had to swallow before she could ask it, and when she did her voice sounded unfamiliar. "So...who did it? Who made those computer transfers?"

"Assuming I didn't, you mean." Jade's silent laughter ended in a sigh. "Oh, Rose, I said I wished I'd never brought you into this, and I do. Believe me. But it was probably the right move. You saw the little things I'd missed because I was standing too close. You kept feeding me pieces of information that had been there all the time. I just hadn't seen the obvious.''

"I know the feeling," Rose murmured, holding herself together again. *The feeling that you had the answer right there in your hand, if only...*

"Funny." He sounded tired. And sad. "I knew the minute you asked for her file that it had to be Tessa. And I should have known that from the beginning, with her background.''

"Tessa." Rose lay back and closed her eyes. "I knew it.''

"And I should have," Jade said flatly. "I should have, but I didn't. I didn't want to believe it of her. She was...fond of me; I know that. I couldn't understand..." He stopped to rub a hand over his eyes. "I've been in this business long enough to know that, with enough leverage, you can make anyone do anything.''

"Leverage?" Rose prompted.

"I told you that most of Tessa's family were killed during the coup that deposed them. Well, somehow these Terristas managed to convince Tess that her mother was still alive in Costa Brava. They told her she would be killed if she didn't cooperate. It was a cruel hoax, of course. The Bureau has absolute proof of their deaths. If she'd just come to me..."

"I wouldn't have thought she had the brains to pull off a computer break-in," Rose mused thoughtlessly, and then, realizing she was speaking of someone he was fond of, said quickly, "I'm sorry."

"Oh, you're quite right." Jade's smile was bitter. "Tessa's no computer wizard. She used Tran."

"Tran?"

"Yeah. That's one of the pieces you gave me the other night, when you caught him playing with my home terminal. It's tied in with the Castle system. And Tran is brilliant. And, of course, you've seen the way Tessa can wrap anything male around her little finger. She lived on that estate all through high school, you know. She and Tran practically grew up together. He's besotted with her, like everyone else his age and sex. He'd do anything for her, I'd imagine, though I doubt he really had any idea just what he was doing. He thought it was just a harmless game...a new challenge."

His voice trailed off. Rose lay quiet, listening to the throb of the diesel engine. Awareness came slowly, almost unnoticed at first, just a barely perceptible easing inside her. Warmth filled her. In different circumstances, she would have thought it was happiness. Jade was innocent! Innocent!

Innocent of selling out his country, maybe. But guilty of things she could never have imagined in a million years, things that didn't matter much in the general ebb and flow of the universe, maybe, but that felt like a holocaust inside her heart.

The motion of the boat had increased noticeably. Rose shifted uneasily and murmured, "I'm sorry about Tessa."

"So am I."

"I know she was your ward."

Jade's laugh was surprised. "Oh yeah? Where did you find that out?"

"Dorie told me."

"*Dorie* told you? How in the world did you crack her? I'd have bet my life on her. She's the most close-mouthed thing in the world where I'm concerned."

"It wasn't hard." Rose smiled thinly into the darkness. "She's also very protective of you. And she's not fond of Tessa, you know. I just... found her weak spot and pushed on it a little bit."

"Yeah, you're good at that." Jade's voice was beginning to slur again. Rose wondered if he were sleepy, or fighting unconsciousness. Belatedly she remembered the swelling and discoloration on the side of his face.

"You really are the best, Rose. I knew it."

Rose lay very still, with her eyes shut tight, feeling herself fill up with the pressure of unshed tears. The best... As Titan, he'd needed her—the best. He'd used her as a pawn in his game, to force his opponents into the open. That much she could understand, and forgive. But the rest...

Jade Castle—Titan—whoever you are! Why did you do this to me? Why?

"Okay," she said, her voice high and strained with suppressed anguish, "but now what's going on? Why is your boat being hijacked? Do you know? Where are we going?''

"I'm not sure," Jade said quickly. "But I think they mean to rendezvous with a Costa Bravan freighter out beyond the islands."

"Why?" Desperation colored her voice; it was beginning to frustrate her, and frighten her, too, having him so weak and helpless. She could have dealt with just about anything but this vulnerability. She needed him strong. She wanted him arrogant and insufferable. She needed *Titan,* her lifeline and her nemesis. She wanted, needed, him to be strong enough to stand up to the weight of her hatred.

But instead he was Jade. Jade, a man, her lover. A man with tiger eyes and gentle hands. A man who had once held her tightly, trembling with his need of her. A man who had made her feel, in spite of everything, loved.

Again she cried, "Why?" It was almost a sob.

She wasn't asking about the boat at all, but Jade didn't understand. With his last ounce of strength he answered her original question. "Didn't I tell you? There's been another computer theft. This time they got the formulas. The formulas for those chemical weapons..."

And then he drifted away, leaving Rose crying helplessly, unable even to wipe away the tears that streamed unchecked down the sides of her face and into her hair.

Jade was neither asleep nor unconscious. He drifted in a nightmarish world of pain and remorse, listening to the sounds of Rose's breathing. He knew that she was crying.

And suddenly every lonely and desolate time he'd ever known was there with him in that dark cabin, closing him in, weighing him down. He felt as he had felt—was it only last night?—with Rose. When he had lost control

and held her so tightly that he'd wondered if he'd hurt
her, because she'd responded with that desperate little
cry.

He wanted her. With everything in him, he wanted her.
But it wasn't as simple a thing as wanting any woman. He
wanted *her* . . . Rose. He wanted to know her, share himself with her; he wanted to learn from her all she could
teach him, and teach her all he knew. He wanted her
there, in all the settings of his life. He wanted her in his
arms, in his bed, in his gardens, sitting across the table
from him. He wanted her sharing his toothpaste, leaving
her clothes on his bathroom floor. He wanted her laughter to wake him in the morning. He wanted her to know
him so well that she could finish his sentences for him.

His body began to shake with silent, bitter laughter. It
was just as well she hated him. He would have suffocated her, crushed the life out of her with the burden of
his need. After all, she was . . . Rose. A wild thing, a fantasy creature. Sea foam. Moonbeams. And you can't
hold on to a moonbeam.

She would never, ever forgive him. He knew that. He
only hoped he could get them both out of this mess, so
he could set her free.

The motion of the boat told him that they had cleared
the harbor and were well out into the channel. It was a
calm night; they were still on engine power. Thank
goodness for the calm seas. Thank goodness they'd been
put in the aft stateroom. Even on a quiet sea there was a
lot of motion in the forward cabin. Poor Rose. If she
were going to be seasick, that forward cabin would have
finished her by now!

On the other hand, the quiet seas were also postpon-
ing the Terristas' agony and Jade's chance to bargain
their way out of these bonds. He just hoped the lack of

circulation wasn't doing permanent damage to Rose's hands. He'd managed to loosen his own enough to keep his hands from going completely numb, but he would never forgive himself if...

The cabin lights came on. In her berth Rose made a spasmodic movement, shrinking reflexively from the sudden brightness.

She lifted her head as the cabin door slowly opened. A dark, wiry man with a receding hairline and a large moustache stood for a moment in the doorway. He spared Rose only a glance, then whacked his hand rudely across Jade's legs and barked something in staccato Spanish.

Jade slowly opened his eyes, made a brief, guttural comment, and closed them again.

With casual savagery the Terrista struck Jade in the right shoulder with his fist. Jade's face became a mask of muddy gray, and Rose felt an impulse to throw up, which had nothing to do with the motion of the boat.

Jade slowly sat up and swung his legs to the floor. Rose felt tension in him, that same tension she'd sensed in him once before, and prayed silently, Don't be stupid, Jade, please!

She noticed that he was breathing with careful concentration, almost as if he were measuring his air intake in micrograms. He spoke in calm, reasonable tones, and then yawned, deliberately and with jaw-popping relish. The Terrista responded with another rapid-fire demand. Jade shrugged and murmured his reply. The exchange went back and forth, and then the Terrista gave a frustrated-sounding grunt and went out, shutting the cabin door behind him. A moment later he was back, carrying a wicked-looking knife. Behind him in the passageway, Rose could see the dark form of a second man holding a gun, a rifle or a semiautomatic, she couldn't be sure which.

The Terrista with the knife went straight to Jade's bunk. Rose's whole body went cold with a fear unlike anything she'd ever felt in her life. She braced herself for horror, but the hijacker only jerked Jade's hands roughly around and slashed angrily at the ropes on his wrists. When the man turned his attention to her, Rose didn't wait to be manhandled. She rolled herself into a sitting position and turned her back to give him access to her hands. For an interminable moment she felt his breath on her face and in her hair, and then she felt the pressure on her arms ease. They fell slack at her sides like dead weights. The numbness in her hands gave way to an excruciating, throbbing ache. While she sat with her head bowed and her eyes closed, fighting the pain, she heard Jade get up and walk out of the cabin with the hijackers. Out in the passageway she heard his voice—Titan's voice—in another quiet exchange with the two men. The cabin door clicked shut again, and Jade's voice—*Jade's* voice—whispered tersely, "Rose, are you all right?"

She managed a tight laugh. "Yes. It just hurts like hell."

"I know. Here, let me see." He sat beside her on the narrow bunk. She felt a spasm of something remarkably like nausea.

"Sorry," he said stiffly when she jerked away from his touch, and moved to his own berth.

When Rose could bring herself to look at him again, she saw that he was examining his own swollen hands. A large medicine chest sat unopened beside him. As if he felt her eyes on him, he lifted his head and leveled an indigo stare at her from out of deeply shadowed sockets. "The head's in there," he rasped briefly, jerking his head a fraction of an inch toward a narrow door to the left of the passageway door. "Running warm water on those hands might help restore the circulation, at least speed it up a little. Though it'll probably make them hurt worse, at least for a while."

Rose nodded and retired gratefully to the relative privacy of the head.

When she came out her hands were feeling functional, if a bit stiff. Jade was still sitting where she had left him, staring at his hands. He glanced up at her and murmured, "Better?"

Rose nodded. In the compactly efficient stainless steel cocoon she'd just left, she had discovered that the pain in her hands was nothing. It was finite, controllable. She had discovered that there is no pain on earth like having your heart torn in two.

"Good." It was Titan's voice again, cold and commanding. "In that case, do you think you could bring yourself to take a look at my head and shoulder?"

Though everything in her cried out in silent and futile rebellion, she nodded, swallowed and sat down on Jade's berth. She moved the medicine chest out of the way and gingerly hitched herself closer. Steeling herself, she took his head between her hands. All her self-control couldn't keep her from trembling.

"You're shaking," Jade observed flatly.

"Temporary weakness in the arms," Rose shot back grimly. "Turn more to the light, please. I can't see a thing." With one hand on the back of his neck and the other cradling his stubbled jaw, she tilted and turned his head so that she could see the angry welt behind and just above his left ear. The jagged cut had already swelled tightly shut.

She swallowed again; her throat was so dry it felt as if a piece of paper were caught in it. "What did they hit you with?"

"I'm not sure. Gun butt, probably. And then I hit the floor, too. Went headfirst down the companionway."

"Clumsy of you," Rose murmured, and he responded with a dry chuckle. Jade's chuckle. She glanced at his face. His eyes were closed. Short, thick, brown lashes touched the purplish smudges on his lower lids. Rose felt a sudden desire to smooth those bruised and tender places with her thumbs.

"There's a cut," she said harshly, taking her hands away and clasping them together in her lap. "It's already closed up. Do you want it left alone, or cleaned out?"

"Clean it." His voice was strained. It occurred to Rose to wonder, suddenly, if he were finding this as intolerable as she was.

"It'll probably start to bleed all over again."

"Clean it. Disinfect it. Patch it." His voice sounded like cloth tearing. "Is that the only damage?"

"Isn't it enough? You have bruises, probably a concussion—you know that."

"I know. I've been trying to stay awake. I could use a little help with that, you know."

"Aye-aye, sir! What would you like me to do?"

His mouth twisted. "Just...talk to me, Rose, that's all. Without the sarcasm, if you can manage it."

"Talk to you?" Her voice got away from her and climbed half an octave. "Now, what in the world would we have to talk about?"

"Rose."

"All right, let's see." She sat rigidly, her hands gripping the lid to the medicine chest. "Have I asked you why you did what you did? I think I did. You just didn't answer me. Want to try it now?" She began to dab—not gently—at the cut with a piece of gauze. "That ought to keep us both awake, if not entertained."

"Rose . . ." He winced and shook his head.

She barked, *"Hold still!"*

"Look, it's a long story."

"Look, we're not going anywhere! What a perfect chance for you to explain it all to me. I'll just work on you here while you talk. What could be a better setting for such a fascinating story? I'll bet it's a real doozy, too. I can't wait!"

"Rose." Her name was a whisper, both tormented and reproachful. "I've never lied to you."

"Just didn't tell me the truth," she said uncompromisingly.

In Titan's clipped tones Jade suddenly exploded. "Look, are you going to be quiet and let me answer your question?" Rose was glad of his anger; it made it easier for her to hold her own feelings at bay.

"The fact is, I came to you just as I said I did—because I needed you. I couldn't think of anyone else who could do the job."

"*What* job? You aren't even with the Bureau anymore!"

His body jerked with surprise. "And who told you that?"

"Cracken. Leif Cracken. Remember him?"

"Yeah . . . yeah, I do. So you still keep in touch? How is he?"

"Still fighting his own private wars. But he'll be okay. Cracky has his own ways of surviving."

"Yes," Jade said slowly. "We all do, don't we?" He took a deep breath. "No, I'm not with the Bureau. I retired not long after you did. And then, when—"

"Why? Why did you retire?"

His lips thinned in a chilly little smile. "Well, Rose, it just wasn't the same without you. *Ouch.*" He pulled away from the sting of the antiseptic Rose was dabbing on his scalp. "It's immaterial why I left. The point is, when this theft occurred, the Bureau assumed I'd turned renegade. It wouldn't be the first time. Remember Ed Pemberton?"

"Yes," Rose whispered, feeling chilled.

"Well, I guess maybe they figured they owed me one...or two. Either that or times have changed. They decided that before they neutralized me, they'd give me a chance to answer the charges. They sent Michaels. I asked for an impartial investigation. We agreed on you."

"I see," Rose said woodenly. "That doesn't explain why you elected to keep me in the dark, about who you were."

"Yes, I think it does." Jade's voice was very quiet. His eyes slid upward to meet hers. "We were hardly strangers, you and I. We'd known each other for years."

"You knew me! I never knew you. You never—"

"Regardless. It was a condition of the agreement that you remain unaware of exactly who you were investigating. Where Titan was concerned, you couldn't be unbiased. In fact, given the degree of antagonism and resentment, even hate—"

"I never *hated* you!"

"No? Well, in any case, I considered it in my own best interests, as well as the Bureau's wish, to keep from you as long as possible the identity of the man you were investigating. I'm sure you can see the logic in that."

"Yes." Rose's throat had closed. She could only whisper. "It's very logical. Which brings us to what happened next. Tell me, Titan, did you plan that? Had you always wanted it? Was it something you'd wondered about, fantasized about, going to bed with me? Was it some kind of... what? Revenge? A joke?"

It seemed as though he winced again, although Rose hadn't touched him. A powerful emotion vibrated through his body. "No, I didn't plan it, Rose. It was as unexpected for me as it was for you." He took a deep breath, opened his mouth, closed it again and gave a soft, rueful laugh. She would probably never know what struggle had been going on inside him, but it had just been resolved. He smiled and shook his head. His body relaxed. "Chemistry. It was just... chemistry. We both felt it from the first, Rose."

Pain bubbled inside her. She fought it, and the struggle made her voice hard. "You've bled all over your shirt. You'll have to take it off."

Silence crackled all around them. Jade's eyes caught hers again, and this time he didn't let them go. He lifted his good hand and slowly, one by one, undid his shirt buttons. Then, still holding her eyes with a relentless, smoky gaze, he pulled the shirt free of the waistband of his slacks. One eyebrow rose, and his face altered subtly—a silent request. Helplessly, unable to resist, Rose lifted her hands to ease the shirt over his shoulders.

She hadn't wanted to touch his body, but the warm satin of his skin was an irresistible magnet to her fingers. And when they touched him, they trembled.

There was a corresponding vibration in him, like an electric current running just under his skin. She felt an overpowering urge to lean hard into the vibration, to still its sensitizing purr with firm, soothing pressure. She wanted to run her open palms over the hard, hot contours of his body, knead the resilient muscles of his back and lay her mouth against his chest.

"A powerful thing, chemistry." It was Jade's voice, his passion-voice, thick and evocative. "My turn now, love. My turn to ask you. What was your reason? Why did you make love with me?"

Chapter 11

Rose snatched her hands and her eyes away from him as if both had been burned. She found herself staring instead at the black jade pendant, lying like a splash of india ink on his chest.

"Was it chemistry for you, too, Rose?" He was Titan now, relentless and uncompromising. "Or did you have another reason entirely? Shall we say, a higher motive?"

"A higher motive?" She licked her lips, genuinely confused. "I don't know what you mean."

"Oh no? What about altruism. Duty."

"Duty!"

"As Titan, I practically ordered you into Jade Castle's bed!"

"And I wondered about that." Rose gave a tortured little laugh. "You'd never gone so far before." Her mouth twisted. "I guess I know why now, don't I? I called you a procurer, but I guess that only applies when it's for somebody else, huh? I wonder if there's even a name for someone like you."

"So," Jade breathed, "it was chemistry for you, too."

"Of course. What else would it have been?" She gave a bitter shrug. "Contrary to what you seem to think, I don't use my body for gain. Not political, not financial—"

"Just . . . chemistry."

"Right. *Chemistry*."

His laugh was low, intimate. "Then what are we quarreling about? As long as we both agree... Amazing, isn't it, what you can do with a little chemistry, when it's mutual and you stop fighting it?"

Rose didn't answer. She was suddenly remembering the way he'd held her, so tightly that she had felt his inner tremors. She thought triumphantly, you liar! It was more than chemistry for you. I know it was. I know it! She wanted more than anything to hurl that at him, but she didn't dare. She was too vulnerable herself in that area, far more so than he was. She forced a smile and murmured, "Yeah, amazing."

And then, as the thought occurred to her, she said, "I have another question. Why did you ask me to stay with you? Was that just a case of temporary insanity due to an overdose of chemistry, or did you have . . . what did you call it? A higher motive? Duty . . . altruism . . . ?"

She'd gone too far. She didn't know the limits of Jade Castle's temper yet, but she knew exactly how far she could push Titan, and she knew immediately that she'd pushed him too far.

He'd gone very still; it was fascinating, in a way, to be able to see what she had only heard and felt before. His eyes flared, then became flat and opaque, as hard as the pendant he wore around his neck. She thought, too late, of who and what he was: an abandoned child; the survivor of mean streets; smugglers' ward; soldier of fortune; industrial buccaneer; master gamesman. A man whose entire life had been lived on the knife-edge of danger, a gambler whose chips were human lives. A ruthless man...a man without softness.

She thought, I don't know this man. I don't know what he's capable of. Did I only think I'd found softness and tenderness in him? Just because his hands can turn my whole body to liquid fire...

Her stomach knotted with something that was only partly fear. Part of it was a strange kind of excitement. In spite of all he'd done, and all that he was, he excited her. She felt fine-tuned; her whole being was humming with a peculiar kind of controlled energy. Was this what it took to make her feel alive, then? Was she attracted by that knife-edge, too? Whatever it was that drew her to this man with no name, it was frightening to realize that, in spite of everything, she *wanted* him.

If he had kissed her then, or touched her... But he had withdrawn, Titanlike, behind his anger. Holding his injured arm close to his body, he stood up, walked to the head and closed the door behind him with blunt finality.

Rose sat for what seemed like an hour, staring at nothing. And then, feeling cold and oddly lonely, she crawled over to her bunk and lay down with her face to the bulkhead. There was no sound from Jade, or from the Terristas. The engines throbbed steadily, and the TITAN rocked gently on a calm sea. The rocking was soothing. Rose forgot that she had ever worried about seasickness, and, after a while, she fell asleep.

Jade stood in the dark cabin staring down at the sleeping woman. Rose... She slept like a child, curled on her side, with one hand under her cheek. Her hair was a dark waterfall, cascading away from her face and over the edge of the bunk, leaving the lines of her ear and temple pristine and vulnerable. Moonlight, finding its way through the portholes above her berth, touched her face and turned it to porcelain.

How beautiful she looked, like a silk rose that could almost make you believe it was real, until you leaned close to sniff its fragrance.

As Titan he'd known the Jordan Rose for many years, but he knew now that he didn't know the real Rose at all. He knew her history, her vital statistics, all the data that could be contained in a computer's memory system. But he knew now that he'd never really known her. She'd never let her cover slip, not with him, or anyone else. As Jade, he'd made love to her body, possessed it fully, but he still didn't know her. She'd let him into her body with an eagerness and abandon that had stunned him, but shut him out of her heart and her soul.

Damn her! A great wave of anger flooded him and then receded, leaving a vast sadness in its place. He wanted the real Rose, a woman of warmth and substance. Why did he keep thinking that woman was there, inside someplace, when every time he reached for her, he touched only silk? Or moonbeams.

Maybe there was nothing there to grasp after all. And the sooner he accepted that, the better off he'd be.

Hardening his heart and his voice, he reached out and touched her shoulder. "Rose."

She woke instantly, quietly and completely. Her eyes opened, and she turned over and sat up in one graceful motion. "Yes? What is it?" And then, listening, "Oh, we've stopped."

"Yes."

"Where are we? Do you know?"

"Not precisely. They've dropped anchor. Judging by the motion of the boat—or lack of it—I'd say we're in the lee of one of the islands. It'll be light soon. I'll take a look through the porthole and see if I can get a better reckoning."

Rose was gazing steadily at him, but as usual he couldn't read anything in her dark eyes. When he paused, she murmured an abstract acknowledgment and said softly, "Are you okay?"

Her concern caught him off guard. His first impulse was to counter with something flippant and sarcastic, but he quelled it and gave her a grin instead. "Just dandy, thanks love," he said, reverting, as he always did when he felt uncertain of the situation, to Australian.

"Fair dinkum," Rose muttered obscurely.

"What?"

"Isn't that what they say in Australia? Fair dinkum? I have an ear for languages, too, you know." She yawned and hopped down off the bunk.

Jade didn't for one minute think she'd intended to land so close to him that her hair would slide across his bare arm; it was just that it was a very small cabin. But his physical responses didn't care about reasons. Reaction flooded through his body, making him burn and tingle with sexual awareness. He suddenly felt as if there weren't quite enough oxygen in the space they shared.

He heard the sharp whisper of her indrawn breath just before he touched her arm—to steady her, he told himself—and then found that he couldn't withdraw his hand. A current of communication arced between them, communication on a level so primitive it predated language. The current was direct, but fragile. Words would have broken it, but neither of them spoke.

Rose didn't even look at him, not at his face, or into his eyes. She stood very still, barely even breathing, with her gaze fastened on his pendant. Very slowly Jade lifted his other hand to her shoulder. With the lightest pressure he compelled her toward him.

The tension between them became intolerable. He could see the rise and fall of her chest, and it was as if she not only had to remember to take each breath, but was finding it a painful process. His own heart beat in thunderous slow motion. She came to him by degrees, resisting him, resisting herself. She kept her face averted, mesmerized by the black pendant upon his chest.

Jade felt her inner struggle and understood it, but he could no more stop himself from compelling her than she could resist the compulsion. His hand moved across her shoulder to her neck, then turned to tangle in the silky weight of her hair. He pulled gently, but insistently, forcing her head back, lifting her face to his. Her eyes were closed, her lips parted. Jade stared down at her for a long moment, then arched above her like a stallion, claiming her mouth and trapping a small desperate cry in her throat.

Raw emotion erupted in him, a kind of exultation, primitive and fierce. He forgot to be gentle and thrust deep into her with his tongue, pressing her with the full weight of his body hard against the bunk, overpowering her with the heat and strength of his passion. He felt an urge to take her swiftly, there on the spot, to mate her, to brand her with his body, a kind of primal claiming. She would be his, then. *His!* He had stopped thinking; he could only feel. And all he could feel was the surging power in his loins, the overwhelming drive to master, to possess. He felt no pain in his shoulder at all, not even when he slipped his hands under her shirt to span her waist and lift her onto the bunk.

Then, as he bore her down beneath him, with his hands on her waist, he felt her tremble.

Reason didn't return to him like a blinding light; it came slowly, like a small voice calling to him from a distance. He ignored it at first, but as it came closer it grew more insistent, until he had no choice but to listen. When he did, he began to feel other things: her trembling; how slender her waist was in his hands; the softness of her skin.

He moved his hands to her face, bracing himself on his elbows to ease his weight from her. He felt moisture on her face, felt her hands pressing hard into the muscles of his back; tasted the brassy tang of blood on her lips. With terrible remorse he thought, I've hurt her.

He began to soothe her, bathing her mouth with his tongue, stroking her damp forehead, murmuring wordless sounds of comfort. And then he eased himself away from her, swearing softly and feeling as if every muscle in his body hurt.

Rose lay still, trying to stop the shudders that were racking her. She felt bludgeoned, not from any external assault, but from her own inner turmoil. She was being ripped apart! How could she love him? How *could* she? And who did she love? Who was there to hate?

With a sudden, almost convulsive movement, she lifted both hands and covered her face.

Jade's voice was hoarse with emotion. "Rose, I'm sorry. I don't know what got into me. I've never...forced a woman in my life. Forgive me."

For a moment longer she lay still; then she wiped her cheeks with jerky movements, gave a long sniff and sat up. She drew her knees up, wrapped her arms around them and rested her cheek on them, turning her face to the bulkhead, away from Jade. Perversely, his regret was making her angry. It wasn't *him* she couldn't forgive. The truth was that he would have been a long way from forcing her—but she would never, ever tell him that.

The silence grew palpable, like a curtain between them. After a while Rose took a deep breath and turned to look at Jade. He was sitting on his bunk, his back against the bulkhead, arms folded across his chest, watching her with brooding intensity.

Rose felt a sudden, painful urge to laugh. She was remembering a psychology class she'd taken back in the early days of her Bureau training. They had done a section on nonverbal communication, body language. She and Jade both looked like demonstration models for protective rejection. There they both sat, isolated by walls of silence and distrust, fortified against each other. What a pair of emotional misfits!

The miracle, Rose supposed, was that they had ever managed to become lovers at all. How would two people from backgrounds as barren of love and affection as hers and Jade's had been ever know how to love anyway?

Rose would never know how long that wretched silence might have gone on. It was broken by a noise from beyond their crowded cocoon. The hijackers were stirring.

Both Rose and Jade started and glanced up at the ceiling. While Rose slowly flexed her legs, Jade twisted to look out the porthole above his bunk. Then he got up and leaned across Rose's bunk to peer out that side. After a moment he straightened with a little grunt of satisfaction.

"Well, that's what I thought. That's Santa Ynez Island out there—I'm pretty sure, anyway." He lifted a hand to his face and rubbed at his two-day stubble as if it had become an annoyance. Then he sat back down and fixed Rose with a direct blue glare. "Rose, do you think you can get past what just happened, everything that's happened, and try to remember that we were once a damn good team?"

"I can," Rose said crisply, "if you can."

One eyebrow lifted. "Think you can work with me now? Because we're going to need each other if we're going to get out of this mess."

Rose shrugged and murmured, "No problems here."

Jade's lips stretched in a thin but poignant smile. "We really were a good team, Rose. Remember?"

"Yes." She nodded, because there was suddenly a peculiar tightness in her throat.

"Remember Bucharest?"

"Yes." Rose gave a little snort of laughter. "The one and only time I ever blew my cover."

"I got you out of that one, didn't I? And out of Romania."

"The gypsies," Rose murmured, smiling. "I remember." Suddenly she remembered another gypsy caravan, more recent, and infinitely more sanitary, picturesque and enjoyable. He was smiling; she knew that he was thinking of it, too. And of a fortune-teller with a Bronx accent, and a shared glass of sweet Hungarian wine.

For a moment it was as if two separate pictures had merged and snapped into sharp focus, like the images in a pair of binoculars. Jade...Titan. The same man. One multidimensional man.

"I was in Vienna," he said softly, "when you came out. Waiting for you. You didn't know that."

"No." Rose closed her eyes and the images frag-
mented once again. The image of Jade, her lover, faded,
leaving only the voice that had been her friend and her
nemesis. Titan's voice, but different somehow. A gentler
Titan. A more human Titan. Titan without arrogance.

"I was there...in the hotel. Practically next door."

"Why, Titan?"

He rubbed his jaw and looked away from her with a
shrug. "I just wanted to see for myself that you were all
right. That was the closest we ever came to losing you—
until Beirut."

"Yes. Until Beirut..." She stirred restlessly. The image of Titan wavered, blurring and confusing the image
of Jade. She didn't close her eyes again; she wanted to see
his face when she asked him the question that had been
haunting her ever since her visit to Cracken.

"Why did you leave the Bureau?"

Jade shrugged again. "I was tired, I guess. Burned out.
It happens."

"It happened," Rose said tightly, "right after Beirut.
Cracky told me. I want to know, did it have anything to
do with...what happened? I need to know, Titan. For
God's sake, you owe me that much! Somebody owes me
something." She was crying silent tears that welled up
and poured warmly down her cheeks like healing rain.

Jade's eyes were closed, so he didn't know about the
tears. His voice sounded dispassionate. "I left after—and
because of—Beirut. I more or less blame myself for
that."

"Why?"

"Because I had my suspicions about Thad Moses. And
I sent him with you anyway. I'd been given reason to
suspect he might be doubling, and I ignored it."

"Why?"

He sighed and opened his eyes. There was a lopsided smile on his face; it saddened him and wrenched her heart. "I figured if he was a double agent, the best way to smoke him would be to team him with the Jordan Rose. You'd never failed me before. Rose, I'm sorry."

She sniffed and swiped at the moisture on her cheeks. "So am I," she muttered, and drew a deep breath, banishing ghosts. "Okay, tell me, what do we do now? How do we get out of this one? And just incidentally, do these guys intend to feed us? I'm starving to death."

"Odd you should mention food, love." Jade's smile had changed, had become something that would frighten small children. "As they say in the time-honored tradition of TV action dramas, 'I have a plan.'"

"Oh, goody," Rose murmured dryly.

Jade looked pained. "I really do hope you can control that sarcasm, Rose. This plan depends on precision and split-second timing. It requires nerves of steel and a certain amount of athletic prowess."

"Sounds more like James Bond's style than mine," Rose observed caustically.

"We make do with who and what we have at hand, love. First of all, when our friends chose this cabin to lock us in, they overlooked the fact that the engine room has a door—albeit a small one—opening into it. That's it right over there, between the head and the passageway doors. Now, the engine room also has a door to the passageway outside. That's a big plus for a couple of reasons, if you see what I mean."

Rose slowly nodded. "Gives us a way out . . ."

Jade chuckled. "I knew you'd appreciate that fact. Advantage number two, I keep wet suits in that locker below your berth. There should be one that will do for you."

"I'm beginning to get your drift. How many of the Terristas are there?"

"Five, I think. I'm not certain of their firepower, but you've seen a bit of it yourself. They aren't amateurs."

"Okay, so we hide in the engine room, they think we've escaped, and in the confusion we go over the side in wet suits and swim to the island. There are flaws in the plan, Titan."

"Oh, you bet." Jade's face was grim. "For one thing, that takes care of only half the problem. You're forgetting the most critical point."

"The formulas."

He nodded. "This boat is going to rendezvous with a freighter, and turn over some chemical formulas that could result in an East-West crisis right in our backyard. Not to mention a lot of unnecessary deaths. Those formulas belong to me. So does this boat. I mean to stop them. Rose, I need you. Are you with me?"

Rose, I need you. "Aren't I always?" she whispered.

Their eyes locked in a moment of rare understanding. Then Jade looked away toward the lightening ports. "We're riding at anchor," he murmured, thinking aloud. "Just off Santa Ynez. What do you know about these islands?"

"Nothing," Rose said. "Except for Catalina, of course. Aren't the others pretty much uninhabited?"

"Pretty much. This one definitely is, except for seals and birds. It's very picturesque, with some spectacular rock formations, but it's the farthest out from the mainland and therefore not as popular with divers as, say, Anacapa. Also, the weather hits harder out here; it's more exposed." He took a deep breath. "All of which means that if we have to swim for it, we could be pretty much on our own. You know that, don't you? It could be a while before we're rescued."

"What about Michaels? Won't he think something's up when you don't come back? He did know where you were going, I trust? Will he think *you've* gone off with the formulas?"

"Michaels," Jade said with a smile, "is convinced of my loyalty, even if his employers are not. However, he's also convinced of something else—my...attraction to you." He lifted an eyebrow and gave a shrug of irony. "If we both turn up missing, along with the boat, I'm afraid Michaels will just assume we've gone off together on a romantic cruise. No, I'm afraid the only hope we have of an immediate rescue, outside of pure luck, is Tessa."

"Tessa!"

"She knew where the boat was; Michaels told her. And she turned it over to the Terristas. If she finds out from Michaels that I went to the boat, she'll know they've got me." He smiled grimly. "I guess it just depends on whether my life weighs more heavily in the balance than her mother's."

"You're right," Rose said stonily. "We might be out here for a while. I guess I should find a way to swipe some provisions from the galley, then."

Jade nodded. His jaw was hard. "That would be helpful, but that's not the only thing I want you to do in the galley, love." He took a deep breath. "I want you to turn on the propane valve. Turn it on and leave it on."

"I don't understand. That sounds—"

"The timing has to be right, though. Exactly right, or we go up along with everything else."

"Jade, what are you thinking of doing?"

"I think you know," he said implacably. "The only thing we can do—blow up the boat."

Chapter 12

Turn it into a floating time bomb, actually,'' he went on matter-of-factly when Rose just stared at him.

She whispered, "You're not serious."

He shrugged. "Tell me another way. James Bond we're not. As you pointed out, violence has never been your forte, and, believe it or not, it's not mine, either."

"Blowing up a boat with several people on it is pretty violent, Jade!"

"Consider the alternatives, Rose." The set of his jaw was as ruthless as his voice was quiet.

She did, and after a moment, nodded. "All right. But you said at least a couple of these guys were experienced seamen. Won't they be careful about venting the bilges, or whatever it is they do?"

"Not with diesel engines. Unless they discover the propane leak, they won't have reason to ventilate. When they start up the engines to go meet that freighter they won't know what hit 'em."

Rose sat silent and cold, then asked, "What if they go under sail?"

"That's a possibility, of course, but my guess is they'll use engine power for the rendezvous. For speed and maneuverability, engines have it over sails. Easier to control in tight quarters. No, sooner or later during that transfer they're going to go to the engines. That part doesn't worry me." He took another deep breath and gave her a long, searching look. "The tricky part is making sure we don't go up with it. A lot depends on timing and guts, but we're going to need some luck, too. I can't give you guarantees, love; I can't even give you odds."

Rose felt a familiar and welcome calm settle over her like a blanket of fog, insulating her from the sharper edges of fear. She smiled. "Any odds at all are still better than zero. Let's go for it."

Jade hesitated, then nodded briskly. "Okay. A few preparations first. First of all, wet suits. I'm not sure how long we'll have to be in that water, but even in August it'll be cold. The suits will help a little. Now, the only problem is . . ." He had dropped on one knee before Rose's berth and was opening the locker. "The only problem is what to wear under them." He lifted one suit out of the locker and placed it on the berth, where it lay like a headless black dummy. "That's mine," he grunted, poking around in the locker. "And I think . . . yeah . . . here it is." He dragged out a second suit, smaller than the first, and held it out to Rose. "That's Tessa's. She may be a little bigger than you are; you might have room inside for a blanket, or even your clothes."

"Even my clothes?" Rose handled the stiff black thing gingerly. It reminded her of a suit of armor, and in her imagination suits of armor had always seemed ready to march around all by themselves. "What do you mean, 'even my clothes'? What am I supposed to wear under this thing?"

"A bathing suit." Jade's voice was muffled; he was still half inside the locker, stirring through odds and ends of swimming and diving gear. "Unfortunately, however..." He sat back on his heels and squinted up at her. "I don't have one for you. Forgive me, Rose, but what are you wearing under those clothes right now?"

Rose blinked and hugged the wet suit against her breasts. "Um, the usual stuff. Bra, panties." She felt undressed already.

"Hmmm." He frowned suddenly and dived back into the locker. A moment later he straightened, holding a pair of black swimming trunks, a nylon net bag and a small yellow plastic canteen. He tossed them on top of his wet suit and stood up. "I'll have to think of something," he muttered. "You'll freeze to death on that island." He gathered up both his gear and hers and thrust all of it into the head.

"Now," he said purposefully, with the air of having gotten a difficult job out of the way, "are we ready to see what our friends are up to out there?"

"Jade," Rose said, frowning as the realities of the operation began to sink in, "the odds are beginning to look pretty dismal to me all of a sudden. Even with the engine room as an escape hatch, five of these guys on a boat with one companionway seems—"

"Not five," Jade said grinning. "Not anymore. At least, I don't think so."

Rose stared at him. "Jade? What did you do?"

He shrugged, looking both grim and smug. "Oh... well. Remember the medicine chest and those chips I said I had? Well, I also had an ace or two up my sleeve. I don't know exactly how many of our friends were suffering from seasickness, of course, but if anybody took the pills I gave them, we won't have to worry about them—not for a while. Have you noticed how quiet it's been?''

"Jade..."

He grinned suddenly, irrepressibly. "I gave them sleeping pills."

Rose had to quell two simultaneous impulses: to laugh out loud, and to throw her arms around the unshaven, unkempt, dangerous-looking man in front of her. It was amazing. Here she was, in about as unpredictable and deadly a situation as she'd ever been in, and yet for the first time in days she felt like laughing.

Jade had gone to stand with his hands flat on the door panels, head down and listening intently. After a moment he began to pound on the door and shout angrily in Spanish.

Heavy thumps sounded overhead. A moment later the door burst open, and the wiry Terrista with the moustache leveled the barrel of a semiautomatic rifle at Jade's belt buckle.

Jade stepped back and raised his hands. His tone became placating. The hijacker relaxed a little, but remained wary. Rose thought he seemed frazzled, as if he hadn't slept. Jade kept talking to him, nodding from time to time and gesturing toward Rose. Finally the hijacker nodded abruptly, stood aside in the doorway and gestured with the rifle barrel.

Rose looked a question at Jade.

"Relax, love," he said cheerfully. "You've been granted permission to fix us starving menfolk some breakfast."

"Wonderful," she responded darkly.

"You *can* cook, I hope. That's one thing they seem to have left out of your dossier."

Rose threw him a deadly look and moved ahead of him into the passageway. As they went through the door and past the watchful Terrista, Jade put his hands on her shoulders and lowered his head, bringing his lips close to her ear.

"Watch me," he murmured, the words audible only to her. "Wait for my signal to turn on the gas."

The rifle-wielding hijacker directed Jade to the table in the main cabin, where he joined a surly-looking, heavy-set man who kept yawning and rubbing his face. Heavy snores were coming from the forward cabin. Rose caught a glimpse of a pair of legs clad in khaki pants and dirty white canvas shoes before the wiry man pulled the door shut with a snort of disgust. She glanced at Jade. He lifted his shoulders in a shrug of complete innocence.

Rose was left to find her own way around the galley. The alert Terrista perched himself uneasily on the edge of the table, where he could watch her every move without taking his weapon off of Jade. It occurred to Rose that the man was feeling edgy because he was dangerously shorthanded. It was a good sign.

The galley was well-stocked, both with provisions and equipment. It looked as if the hijackers were prepared to sail their captured prize all the way to Costa Brava, if they could. Transferring the stolen formulas to the freighter was a safety precaution, probably, in case the TITAN was reported missing and intercepted by the Coast Guard.

For the first time it occurred to Rose to wonder what the hijackers intended to do with their unexpected passengers. She'd been too preoccupied with more personal trials before; now she wondered if the hijackers might be awaiting instructions from the freighter.

Shaking off a chill, she located coffee, cans of fruit, fresh eggs, green onions and peppers, some hot sausages and a loaf of refrigerated bread dough. The main gas valve was overhead, directly above the stove. She turned it on, then experimentally tried one of the stove burners. It gave a reassuring hiss. Satisfied, Rose turned the valve off and set about organizing the meal.

As she worked, she kept glancing over to where Jade sat, engaged in what appeared to be friendly masculine conversation with his captors. He could almost have been one of them. He looked dangerous and scruffy enough, with his stubble and shaggy hair, his hard face and deep-shadowed eyes. But every now and then when she looked at him, he would happen to glance up and catch her eye, and the contact was like the reassuring touch of a lover's hand in the dark.

It felt good having him there; again she wondered why, under the circumstances, she wasn't more afraid. It also felt familiar. It came as a kind of revelation, that feeling, because she realized that he'd always been there for her in the dangerous times.

For the first time she realized that in a very real way she and Titan had been partners. His support and confidence had been a solid presence at her side; she'd reached out and held on to them often enough to know how real they were. And the cool, analytical mind, the mind of the master gamesman, the mind that could assess a situation and come up with a clear and workable plan of action—that mind had constantly interacted with hers, sometimes meshing, sometimes clashing, but always stimulating.

It was incredible. For so many years she'd struggled to give Titan a face, to give that presence form and substance; and she'd built up layers of anger and resentment because she couldn't. And now that he had a face, she was discovering how little difference it made. Titan had *always* had form and substance in her life.

Another thought, a logical successor to the previous one, overtook her like a runaway train. It shook her so badly that she dropped a pancake turner with a clatter that drew instant attention from the hijackers at the table.

Titan's face—and body—belonged to Jade Castle. She loved Jade. Jade and Titan were the same person. Ergo, she loved Titan! Had she always loved Titan? Impossible. She'd hated Titan at times. No, that wasn't true. As she'd told Michaels, she'd resented Titan. But why had she cared so much? Why had it mattered to the point of such consuming frustration whether or not Titan had a face?

Because she'd wanted something tangible—some*one* tangible—to hold. To touch. Someone to love. Because as wonderful and real as the meshing of minds had been between her and Titan, it had been incomplete. Just as the communion of bodies between her and Jade had been incomplete. Each one alone had left her feeling frustrated and lonely, because she needed both.

Rose looked across the galley to where Jade sat between two hijackers. At that moment he lifted his eyes to her and she thought in sudden exultation, Now I have both . . . in the same man! She couldn't believe the wonder of it, the miracle. This man, with all his secrets and mysteries and private, unreachable hells, was hers. And at this moment, when it seemed she might lose him, that was all that mattered. He was hers, and she would be damned if she was going to lose him now, when she was barely beginning to discover him! If he were a caged tiger, so be it; she was the tiger's mate. And as everyone knows, the female is deadlier.

Resolve settled over her. She prepared the meal and served it to Jade and their captors with spare, economical movements, conserving her resources for the ordeal ahead. She ate with mechanical efficiency, refueling, storing energy. Her mind was clear and uncluttered for the first time in days, focused with laserlike intensity on one goal: her survival, and Jade's.

The dishes had been cleared away. The men were hunched over steaming mugs of coffee, the heavyset one still looking like a surly bear, the wiry one with the rifle still cradled in his arms. Rose was cleaning the galley. She heard Jade cough, and was so attuned to him that she knew instantly that it was more than a cough. Glancing over at him, she saw him lift his eyes to the gas valve and nod almost imperceptibly. Smoothly, casually, Rose reached up to turn on the gas valve. Almost simultaneously she turned the oven knob to ON.

The gas made an audible hiss. Rose looked at Jade, frowned, and touched her ear. He nodded, said something to the hijackers, then reached to turn on the stereo behind him. Vivaldi surged into the cabin, masking both conversation and the sound of the escaping propane.

It was done. The irreversible countdown had begun.

The moment the door of their cabin prison had clicked shut behind the Terristas, Jade dived into the head and hauled out the wet suits. In another moment he had stripped down to his underwear and was gesturing for Rose to do the same. After only a slight hesitation she pulled her sweater off over her head and unzipped her jeans.

"Good idea, turning on the music," she commented in a breathless undertone as she kicked off her shoes and pushed the jeans down over her hips. "Covers any noise we make in here."

"Right," Jade grunted as, without batting an eye, he skinned off his briefs and reached for the bathing trunks. At that point Rose decided it was a good time to bend down and pull her pant legs over her feet. "But don't forget, it covers any noise *they* make, too. We can't keep track of their movements."

It seemed impossible that they'd ever been intimate. That night had happened in another lifetime, to two different people. Where was the man who wouldn't go barefoot, not even on a private beach? Where was the man who'd seemed so reluctant and reserved about undressing, even in intimacy?

But, of course, this wasn't intimacy. This was Titan, and this was business, nothing more. That was obvious, both in the efficiency of his own undressing, and in the way he treated her. Which didn't help her own shyness much. It was like undressing in front of a stranger.

As she stood in her bra and panties, trying not to shiver, trying to deny the way her nipples had risen instantly into telltale relief, Jade surveyed her with detachment and muttered, "That wet suit was custom-made for Tessa. I think she's probably a little more...I think you're going to have some extra room. Why don't you try leaving your shirt on underneath? And if there's any more room, see if my shirt will fit. Were you able to get any food?"

Rose clapped both hands over her mouth. "Damn. I forgot." She had been too preoccupied with inner discoveries.

"You were being closely watched. Just as well you didn't try." His mouth was grim. He patted the nylon bag at his waist. "We have the water bottle, anyway; we'll just have to pray for an early rescue. Come, love. Dress up. We haven't got much time."

"How much *do* we have?" Rose's question was muffled by the sweater she was pulling back over her head. "Were you able to find out when the rendezvous is supposed to take place?"

Jade shook his head. "Sometime today, that's all I know. I don't think they know, exactly. They have a man topside looking for that freighter. Which means—"

"That at any moment they could spot it and kick in those engines," Rose finished calmly, "and blow us all to kingdom come."

"Right," Jade grunted. "So let's get the hell off this boat. The sooner the better. Ready?"

"Ready. Give me your shirt."

He folded it and handed it to her, and she tucked it into the front of her wet suit. "There," she said, grinning breathlessly as she closed the fastening. "How do I look?"

"Lumpy," Jade said, grinning back.

"Think what I'd have looked like with a bunch of groceries in here." They were both easing the unbearable tension with light banter, trying not to think about the propane gas that was at that moment seeping into the TITAN's bilges, or the freighter that was plowing steadily toward its rendezvous.

"I guess in that case I'd have to say you looked delicious," Jade shot back, and then was silent, just looking at her. Rose held the look, feeling her body grow still. Her breath hung suspended. The moment stretched forever, while the world became silent around them. Then Jade lifted a thumb and said softly, "Let's go, love."

Nothing went as they'd planned.

Jade was on his knees, working to unlock the low door to the engine compartment. Suddenly the companion-way door burst open. Instinctively Rose moved to position her body between Jade and the intruder.

It was the big, surly hijacker, which was probably their salvation. He'd obviously had a bit of Jade's "seasick medicine," not enough to put him out, but enough to slow his reflexes.

As the Terrista stood swaying like an angry bull and peering groggily into the cabin, Rose took one step to the side. As if at a prearranged signal, Jade came up off the floor. All the weight of his body, propelled by every ounce of strength in his legs, was channeled through the fist he brought up under the hijacker's chin. It connected with a dull and sickening sound. The hijacker's head snapped backward, and his body went slack. Jade caught him before he fell and lowered him carefully to the floor between the two berths.

"Too bad it wasn't the one with the gun," he observed, glancing briefly and analytically at his knuckles before stepping over the hijacker's inert body to rejoin Rose at the door. "We could have solved this thing with a lot less mess if we could have gotten our hands on that automatic." He flashed Rose a smile, a brief show of teeth in his dark-stubbled face. "Well, that's one down, two out, and two to go."

"Those two," Rose pointed out, "are the lively ones. Where do you suppose they are now? Topside?"

"Must be, or they'd be in here on top of us by this time. Now, the question is, do we proceed as planned and bring them down here, or do we try to get past them up there?''

"Well," Rose muttered with an uneasy glance at the engine room door, "I don't know about you, but I don't relish the idea of cozying up to a time bomb any longer than I have to. If this thing blows, I'd sure rather take my chances—" she stabbed a finger emphatically at the ceiling "—up there."

"Well," Jade said, glancing upward, "all things considered, me, too. So let's do it."

Jade led the way down the passageway to the cockpit, with Rose close behind. Except for Vivaldi, the cockpit and main cabin were deserted. The pair of legs was still visible in the forward cabin.

"You're sure there are only two up there?" Rose asked in a whisper.

Jade shushed her with an urgent wave of his hand and cocked his head. "Listen," he murmured after a moment. "Two sets of snores. Okay, you go up the steps first and take a peek. If the coast is clear, dive for the side. Got it? Do not pass 'go.' Just get the hell off this boat and don't look back. I'll be right behind you; I guarantee it."

"But—"

"*Go.* Promise me. Swim as hard and as fast as you can. Get as far from the boat as you can."

Rose set her mouth and gave a tight little nod. Arguing was futile, and old habits died hard. Besides, she trusted him. She'd seen the way he handled himself in an unanticipated crisis.

Once more their gazes locked in a look of fearsome intensity. And then Rose took a deep breath and went, as silently as a curl of smoke, up the companionway steps.

In the hatch opening she stopped and peered cautiously around.

Both hijackers—the wiry one with the rifle, and another one Rose hadn't seen before—were in the stern, searching the horizon with binoculars; the wiry one was apparently pleading querulously for a look. It was now or never. There would never be a better moment.

She felt Jade's hand on her ankle, giving it a gentle squeeze of encouragement. She braced herself with both arms, then levered herself out of the hatch and onto the deck in one swift motion. Two quick running strides took her to the edge of the boat. She gathered herself and launched herself through the air in a clean, shallow dive. As she hit the water she heard a hoarse cry of alarm.

She knifed the surface of the water at a shallow angle, then swam underwater until her lungs protested. Even as she surfaced, gasping for breath and shaking stinging saltwater out of her eyes, she was trying desperately so see where Jade was, to see what was happening on the boat.

What she saw turned her body to ice. On deck Jade was locked in a desperate struggle with the smaller hijacker. The rifle was sandwiched between their bodies. The second hijacker was leaning over the deck railing, pointing toward Rose. She could hear him shouting in high, staccato Spanish that echoed across the restive water like ricocheting bullets. She heard an answering shout, a strained bellow from the man locked in lethal combat with Jade. In an instant response to that shout the second man turned from the rail and dived down the companionway. And just as instantly Rose knew what he meant to do.

He meant to come after her. He meant to chase her down. He meant to start up the engines!

And Jade was still on the boat. Stuck on the boat, engaged in a fight for his life and for possession of that damned rifle!

"Jade! Jump!" She tried to shout a warning, but she was too far away. The current was carrying her away from the boat. Away from Jade. She could only watch, helpless, with her whole being braced for the explosion she knew was imminent. Time stopped.

"Jade...!"

At the last second he seemed to hear her. With one great gathering of his strength he wrested the rifle from the hijacker and, swinging it by the barrel, knocked the man backward across the hatch cover. Jade seemed to hesitate for an eternity, then turned at last to the railing to launch himself over the side.

Rose saw him poised there, a black silhouette against the sky, a flawless outline of male beauty, arms outstretched, muscles tensed as if for flight. She would carry that vision of him for the rest of her life, etched on her memory like a bas-relief carved on black jade, as she would carry the horror of what happened next.

The world exploded in a blinding maelstrom of heat and light. A split second later came the thunder. Rose would never know whether Jade had already jumped; she only saw the blast catch him and hurl his body through the air like just another piece of debris. Then the concussion slammed into her like a giant fist, stunning her. For a few moments blackness descended, and when it lifted she had lost sight of Jade. Black oily smoke and a stench of diesel fuel hung over the water. Bits of debris rained down around her, hitting the water with an irregular pattering sound. A little way off one or two large pieces of debris still sprouted little flowers of flame.

There was nothing recognizable left of the TITAN. There was no sign of life. And no sign of Jade.

Rose began to swim like a crazy person toward the floating debris. She heard herself making frantic little whimpering noises and forced herself to stop that and to call his name instead.

He'll float, she kept telling herself over and over again. He's wearing the suit. He'll float.

"Jade! Jade, where are you? *Titan*—don't you dare leave me, damn you! *Jade!*"

And then, just when despair seemed about to overwhelm her, when it seemed as though the chilly waters of the Pacific offered the only possible antidote to her awful grief, she saw him. He was floating, but face down. With a cry of joy mixed with fear she swam to him and turned him over, clutching at his head, touching his face, searching his neck for a pulse.

And finding it. He was alive. Breathing? She couldn't tell. And it was such a long way to the island. She looked frantically for a piece of debris large enough to support his body while she gave him mouth-to-mouth resuscitation, but couldn't find one, so she did the best she could, treading water and riding with the swell.

It didn't take long. The blast must only have stunned him. There didn't seem to be water in his airways when, after only a few breaths from Rose, his body tensed and began to fight her. He coughed once and began breathing on his own, a hoarse, tortured sound that was music to Rose.

But he was still unconscious. Treading water and supporting Jade's head, Rose tried to take inventory. There didn't appear to be any major structural damage; he had all his arms and legs, and there didn't seem to be any bleeding. But the wet suit was badly torn, or maybe burned, and of course she didn't know about internal injuries, or concussion. On top of his previous head injury...

Fear gripped her again, almost paralyzing her. She fought it down, replacing it with grim determination. She wouldn't think about that. She would *not* lose him now, not when she'd just found him. If it took every ounce of strength and will she had in her, she would save this man... *her* man.

Her hands roamed his face, caressingly, not frantically, wiping away saltwater from his eyes and mouth, smoothing the creases in his cheeks and forehead.

"Jade Castle," she said aloud, with the rusty whisper that was all the voice she had left, "we're survivors. You are a survivor. If you survived Singapore, you can survive this! We are going to make it; do you understand me? We're going to make it. I'm not going to lose you now!"

It was a long way to the island. Taking Jade's head in a firm lifesaver's tow hold, Rose began to swim.

Chapter 13

It was the heaven dream again. Funny, he hadn't had it since he was a child.

He was drifting...weightless... And there was golden light with soft edges, and furry sounds, like music playing in a far-off room. And overhead, an angel's face...

But he hadn't dreamed that dream in years. He'd learned long ago that there was no such thing as heaven. Knowing that, he struggled to wake himself up.

And then he began to feel that he *was* awake, except that certain elements of his dream were still with him. There was light, but he recognized it now as sunlight filtered through haze. It felt warm on his face and warmer still on his chest and legs. There was a sound, one he couldn't identify. And there was a face, though not an angel's. It looked a lot like Rose...only different. Her eyes were closed, and the skin around them looked bruised. The rest of her face was chalk-white and wet, and her hair hung in dark strings onto her neck and shoulders. Her lips were moving. He realized that she was responsible for that sound he'd been hearing. And now he knew what it was.

Crying. She was crying. But that was impossible. Rose would never cry. Not the Jordan Rose...*his* Rose.

And she was saying words, too. His name. "Jade. Jade, please wake up. Please be all right. Please don't die. I *need* you. I love you...."

That was when he knew that he was still dreaming. With a deep sigh he gave up and settled comfortably back into oblivion.

Rose woke because she was hot. The sun was high and beating down on her black wet suit, turning the inside of it into a pressure cooker. Her first thought was that Jade would be hot, too; she had to get him out of his wet suit, or out of the sun.

Her second thought was that the weight of his head was gone from her stomach. She came fully awake in a panic, throwing out her arm, wildly searching. "Jade? *Jade!*"

"Easy, love; I'm right here."

Jade's voice, dry, full of irony, and full of Australia.

Rose sat up slowly, raking a hand through the sandy tangle of her hair. "Jade? Are you all right?"

"I think so—more or less." He was sitting a little way off, with his knees drawn up and his forearms resting on them, hands dangling. His hands, Rose noticed with a painful wrenching inside her, looked scorched and swollen.

"I can't believe you're...I thought... You were unconscious for so long."

"I've been awake for quite a while, actually. You're the one who's been unconscious."

"*I've* been—why didn't you wake me up?"

"Because you looked exhausted. Did you bring me here? What a question. Of course you must have. Did you?"

"Yes." She went on staring at him, a fierce, almost angry glare. "You weren't breathing when I first found you. And then you were out for so long. Are you sure you're all right?"

Jade touched his head and gave her his best lopsided grin. "Damaged, but still ticking."

"Well," Rose went on, scowling at him because she couldn't trust herself to do anything else, "you look awful!"

His chuckle was a tonic to her soul. "So do you, love. Like bloody hell."

After that they just gazed at each other in silence, finding nourishment in the sight of each other, not knowing how to move on.

And then, at precisely the same instant that Jade said, "The boat," Rose said, "Oh, Jade."

Jade yielded, and Rose whispered, "Oh, Jade . . . your beautiful boat. The TITAN. There's nothing left of it. Or if there was, it sank."

His shrug was offhand, but Rose saw pain in the brief spasm that crossed his face. "The hijackers?"

It was Rose's turn to shrug. She looked down at her hands and swallowed hard. "I assume they're gone, too. I didn't see any survivors, but then, I was busy looking for you." Five people. Gone in an instant.

"Rose," Jade said quietly, "I know that was hard. I'm sorry. But they'd have killed us, you know. And those formulas would have killed God knows how many others."

"I know." She shook herself and took a deep breath. "Speaking of those formulas..."

"Don't worry," Jade said grimly. "The first thing I intend to do when we get home is take those formulas out of the computer. From now on I think I'll depend on good old-fashioned safes and padlocks! I wasn't cut out for the computer age. I think I was born in the wrong century."

Rose smiled, too tired to join in his laughter. "Well, you do look more like a brigand or a pirate than a prosperous businessman. Or, for that matter, an international spy."

He shifted uncomfortably. "Oh, I was never that."

"Director of international spies, then. And master game player." Her voice was light, but she couldn't keep a slight edge out of it. So, the hurt, the betrayal, were still hovering out there, in spite of her newly discovered feelings.

Jade didn't miss the edge, either. His gaze turned somber, and shadows crept across his face. "Rose, please believe me. It was never a game. I was fighting for my life."

"Well," she said slowly, still staring hard at her hands, "I guess that does justify using...any means. I don't blame you. Really." She got up and walked a few steps away from him, turning her back to gaze out at the distant horizon.

It was hot on the little spit of sand she'd brought them to. Hot, and unprotected. She needed to get out of her wet suit before she cooked in it. She needed to spread her sweater and Jade's shirt out somewhere to dry. They would need them tonight, when it got cold, and the fog rolled in from the sea. She needed to rinse the sand out of her hair and the stink of diesel fuel from her hands. She needed to wash away the memories....

"Rose." With her peripheral vision she saw him lurch stiffly to his feet without using his hands, sway, then come close to her. When his hand brushed her shoulder she flinched. He jerked it away as if he'd touched a hot stove. "Rose, the water. Would you like a drink? You'll have to take it off me."

"Oh, thank you. I guess I am thirsty. But only a sip." She untied the nylon bag and took out the canteen, drank, then turned to him, brisk and controlled, "Hey, if you're as hot as I am, you're half-stewed already. I think we should get out of these suits, and off this sand-bar and into some shade, don't you?"

He hesitated, gazing sadly down at her, then nodded. His mouth slipped sideways. "Right, but I'm afraid you'll have to help me." He held up his hands and gave an apologetic smile.

Rose's mouth formed a silent "Oh" of dismay. His hands were skinned and blistered, front and back. She had to swallow hard before she could whisper, "Your hands...what happened?"

He shrugged and examined his injuries with detachment. "Don't know. Must have happened in the blast. These aren't the only places that got it, though the wet suit seems to have protected most of me."

"It's in shreds," Rose observed, frowning to cover her distress. "Here, let me help."

As she undid the front closing and carefuly peeled the ripped and tattered rubber from his body, she couldn't seem to keep her hands from exploring his hot, moist skin, discovering every small wound. She ached with every discovery. She eased the suit down his arms and over his injured hands as carefully as she could, cringing when he winced involuntarily in reaction to the pain. The suit fell easily away from his torso, less easily over his narrow hips, and had to be tugged and pulled down his legs. There were injuries on the unprotected parts of his calves and feet, like those on his hands, but he didn't seem to mind them as much.

Finally the suit lay in an untidy pile at his feet. He kicked the shredded rubber away, and Rose stood, bringing her eyes back to his chest. It was then that she made the most painful discovery. With a small, stricken cry she laid her hand flat against his chest.

"Jade, your pendant. It's gone."

His hand jerked, fluttered briefly across his naked chest, then fell away. "So it is," he said and, looking away toward the empty horizon, muttered something vague and barely intelligible about the unpredictability of explosions.

With sympathy swelling her throat Rose whispered, "Your boat and your pendant, both gone."

His smile was gentle. "Small losses, Rose. All things considered."

"Yes." But there was a stillness about his body, as if he were listening to the dying echoes of memories, of times and places that would never be again. Rose would have liked to put her arms around him and rest her cheek against the empty place where the black jade had lain for so long, but she felt closed off from him. It was solitude he needed, not sympathy, so she muttered, "I'd better get out of my suit, too, I guess." She swiftly turned away from him.

It was harder than she'd thought it would be, stripping to her underwear under wide-open skies in front of Jade. She kept telling herself that her bra and panties didn't show any more than a bikini would, but as every woman knows, a bikini is one thing and underwear is quite another. She also told herself that he had been her lover, for heaven's sake; he'd already seen her body in the most intimate way imaginable. All that reminder did was shiver her skin with awareness and cause her nipples to tighten. And when she felt Jade come to stand behind her, her spine contracted and her buttocks tightened in a natural and wholly involuntary reaction to his nearness.

Jade felt the tension in her and was filled with sympathy. It must be hard for her to have to expose herself to him like this, under the circumstances. He had an urge to put his arms around her and offer her shelter and comfort—just that and nothing more. But, of course, it would hardly do, when *he* was the one she needed shelter and comfort from!

He wondered, all at once and with a vast sense of loss, how he could have botched things so badly with her. It came, he supposed, in being taken by surprise.

Oh, he'd admired her for years, both as a woman and as an agent. He'd been more than a little awed by her talent as an actress, her poise under pressure, her quick, intuitive mind. They'd worked well as a team, in spite of that penchant she'd had for sarcasm and for occasional temper tantrums. Some of her outbursts, those directed at him personally, had been pretty childish, in fact, but that had been years ago, and she had been very young then.

He'd appreciated her beauty the way a connoisseur values a work of art, but it had worried him too, at first. Contrary to popular fiction, successful secret agents are rarely attractive and never memorable. But he had soon learned that in spite of her beauty she could be as diffi-

1. How do you rate _____
   (Please print book TITLE)

   1.6 ☐ excellent   .4 ☐ good   .2 ☐ not so good
   .5 ☐ very good   .3 ☐ fair   .1 ☐ poor

   JABCD

2. How likely are you to purchase another book:

   in this *series* ?   by this *author* ?
   2.1 ☐ definitely would purchase   3.1 ☐ definitely would purchase
   .2 ☐ probably would puchase   .2 ☐ probably would puchase
   .3 ☐ probably would not purchase   .3 ☐ probably would not purchase
   .4 ☐ definitely would not purchase   .4 ☐ definitely would not purchase

3. How does this book compare with similar books you usually read?

   4.1 ☐ far better than others   .2 ☐ better than others   .3 ☐ about the
   .4 ☐ not as good   .5 ☐ definitely not as good   same

4. Please check the statements you feel best describe this book.

   5. ☐ Easy to read   6. ☐ Too much violence/anger
   7. ☐ Realistic conflict   8. ☐ Wholesome/not too sexy
   9. ☐ Too sexy   10. ☐ Interesting characters
   11. ☐ Original plot   12. ☐ Especially romantic
   13. ☐ Not enough humor   14. ☐ Difficult to read
   15. ☐ Didn't like the subject   16. ☐ Good humor in story
   17. ☐ Too predictable   18. ☐ Not enough description of setting
   19. ☐ Believable characters   20. ☐ Fast paced
   21. ☐ Couldn't put the book down   22. ☐ Heroine too juvenile/weak/silly
   23. ☐ Made me feel good   24. ☐ Too many foreign/unfamiliar words
   25. ☐ Hero too dominating   26. ☐ Too wholesome/not sexy enough
   27. ☐ Not enough romance   28. ☐ Liked the setting
   29. ☐ Ideal hero   30. ☐ Heroine too independent
   31. ☐ Slow moving   32. ☐ Unrealistic conflict
   33. ☐ Not enough suspense   34. ☐ Sensuous/not too sexy
   35. ☐ Liked the subject   36. ☐ Too much description of setting

5. What *most* prompted you to buy this book?

   37. ☐ Read others in series   38. ☐ Title   39. ☐ Cover art
   40. ☐ Friend's recommendation   41. ☐ Author   42. ☐ In-store display
   43. ☐ TV, radio or magazine ad   44. ☐ Price   45. ☐ Story outline
   46. ☐ Ad inside other books   47. ☐ Other _____ (please specify)

6. Please indicate how many romance paperbacks you read in a month.

   48.1 ☐ 1 to 4   .2 ☐ 5 to 10   .3 ☐ 11 to 15   .4 ☐ more than 15

7. Please indicate your sex and age group.

   49.1 ☐ Male   50.1 ☐ under 15   .3 ☐ 25-34   .5 ☐ 50-64
   .2 ☐ Female   .2 ☐ 15-24   .4 ☐ 35-49   .6 ☐ 65 or older

8. Have you any additional comments about this book?

   _____ (51)
   _____ (53)

Thank you for completing and returning this questionnaire.

PRINTED IN U.S.A.

NAME _____

ADDRESS _____
(Please Print)

CITY _____

ZIP CODE _____

BUSINESS REPLY MAIL

FIRST CLASS   **PERMIT NO. 717**   **BUFFALO, NY**

POSTAGE WILL BE PAID BY ADDRESSEE

NATIONAL READER SURVEYS

901 Fuhrmann Blvd.
P.O. Box 1395
Buffalo, N.Y. 14240-9961

cult to hold in the mind's eye as the whiff of an elusive but haunting perfume.

As he'd told Michaels, there wasn't a male employee in the Bureau who hadn't at one time or another, secretly or otherwise, imagined himself in love with her. She'd gently ignored them all, until Thad Moses.

And Titan, the big man himself, Jade thought now in self-derision. How had he felt? Insulated by his layers of anonymity, had he really imagined himself to be immune? Ha! If he'd been so unsusceptible, why had he sometimes felt the need just to be near her, even if he could never let her see him, talk to him face-to-face...touch him? That time in Vienna, for instance, and others he hadn't told her about yet.

The trouble was, he knew better. He'd seen her in action. He knew where her talents lay. She could turn emotions, facsimiles of emotions, on and off like a faucet. They were the tools of her profession. And for years he'd thought her incapable of the real thing.

Then had come the Beirut assignment, and Thad Moses.

Jade's mind tacked sharply away from that shoal.

Then, two years later, he'd been given the chance to finally meet her. It would have made a tempting proposition under any circumstances. The chance to do it as a different person, with a fresh, clean slate, had been irresistible.

But he hadn't looked beyond that first move, a fatal and unforgivable error for a gamesman. He hadn't foreseen the possible consequences of that face-to-face meeting. He hadn't expected the chemistry to be so strong; he hadn't expected it to be mutual. He hadn't thought about what he would do if he fell in love....

"Your skin," he said abruptly, not surprised to find that his voice was hoarse. "It looks like it's going to burn."

"Yes, I've never been much for lying in the sun, getting a tan." Her head was bowed, muffling her voice. He could see the fine, velvety hairs on the back of her neck. The desire to touch them with his mouth was so strong, and his self-control so strained, it made his jaws ache. It was just as well, he supposed, that his hands were such a mess. It made it easier to remember not to touch her. And he knew he couldn't touch her. He couldn't account for himself and his actions when he touched her. And even with her head lowered and her back to him, he could feel her tremble with fear of his touch.

"Come, love," he said gently. "There's shade over there at the base of those rocks."

It wasn't hard, through the bright, warm afternoon, to maintain the distance that had come between them and which, for her sake, Jade knew he had to preserve. Conversational forays had become brief and sporadic, confined to the concerns of their immediate situation. After a while it seemed to Jade to be easier just to pretend to be asleep.

He lay on his back in a shady patch of sand at the base of a pile of rocks, his head pillowed on the wet suits, his arm across his eyes. He probably should have slept. His whole body felt like an open wound. His head ached; his muscles hurt; his hands and feet burned like fire. His hands were the worst. Not only did they hurt like hell, but he hadn't realized how important they were to him in the area of communication. It was odd. Without the ability to touch, he felt as if all that was gentle and vulnerable and tender in him had been trapped deep inside him.

Without touching, he had no way to let those feelings out.

So instead of sleeping he watched Rose from time to time, when he could do it without her knowing. Once she felt free of his conscious presence she got over her own self-consciousness. He found pleasure in watching her become comfortable with her near-nakedness, until she was again moving with that natural grace that always stirred him so.

He watched her spread her sweater and his shirt across the rocks to dry, fussing over them with little house-wifely tugs and pats that had a peculiar poignancy because they were so far from what he would have expected of her.

He watched her wade into the clear, quiet pool between the sandbar and the island, then duck her head under the water and scrub at her scalp with her fingers, combing through the fine hair that fanned around her like a dark, spreading stain.

He watched her rise from the water, arching backward so that her hair fell away from her in a sleek, weighted curtain. Her body was as taut and vibrant as a bow, the muscles in her torso clearly defined, buttocks firm and tight, small round breasts pointing to the sky.

The memory of the way she had felt in his arms became a tangible thing. By the time she waded out of the water and came toward him across the sand, squeezing moisture from her hair, it had become prudent for him to turn over onto his stomach.

The moving sun found him again and soothed his aches with its own particular kind of anesthesia. And after a while, because he was truly exhausted, he really did sleep.

He woke, chilled, to the sound of sea lions barking in the distance. He rolled over and sat up, started to rub his face, winced, and glanced briefly at his hand, then laid his forearm carefully across his drawn-up knee.

Rose was sitting a few feet away, hugging her knees, watching him with those unreadable dark eyes of hers. She'd put on her sweater. His shirt lay beside her on the sand.

"Sorry, love," he said hoarsely, and cleared his throat. "Didn't mean to leave you like that. How long have I been asleep?"

"All afternoon. The fog is coming back in, so it must be getting late. It's all right. You needed it."

"Hmm. What've you been doing?"

"Nothing much. Just exploring a little. Watching for boats. There weren't any."

"I told you we're pretty much off the beaten track here. Unless someone saw or heard that explosion, no one's likely to be by. Find anything interesting?"

She shrugged. "Lots of birds and seals and rocks. I think we're pretty much stuck here on this sandbar. You can't climb the cliff with those hands."

"No."

"Jade…" Her face was somber. "How long will it be, do you think, before anyone finds us? How long can we make that water last? How long can we last without water?"

As he gave her a reassuring smile something grew hard and strong inside his chest. "Don't worry, love. There's always a chance someone did notice the explosion and reported it. Someone may even get tired of diving off Anacapa and try a change of scenery. We'll survive, no matter how long it takes. We're survivors, you and I."

Her face suddenly lit with a grin that almost stopped his heart. "Yes," she breathed. "We are, aren't we?"

"You bet. Hey, if you survived that damned orphanage..."

"Oh, it wasn't so bad, you know," she said, tilting her head as if the thought had only just come to her. "The people were kind. And I'd decided early on that I wasn't ever going to be adopted, and that was a kind of security, you know? I didn't suffer the awful uncertainty and longing and disappointment. Will they like me? Will they want me? Why didn't they choose me? I never allowed myself to dream of parents, a home. The orphanage was my home, and it was good enough for me."

"What did you dream about, Rose?" The question surprised him. As Titan, he'd never allowed himself to probe her depths, probably because he wanted too badly to know, and because as Titan he would never have gotten past her sarcasm and hostility.

Her response surprised him even more. Another smile lit her face, this one a soft glow that stayed mostly in her eyes. "You asked me that once, remember?"

He nodded, though he hadn't remembered until that moment. That strange moment of discovery in his office seemed like something that had happened to two different people. "And you told me that dreams were for children."

"Oh, they are. I dreamed... silly romantic stuff, princes and princesses and happy-ever-after. And I dreamed of going away to far off, exotic places, wonderful places." The smile faded; her eyes slid sideways to the fog-draped horizon. "I think that's partly why I joined the Bureau. The only thing was, in my dreams there was always sunshine. I guess I didn't realize that in real life it's

almost always night. Once I figured that out, I stopped
dreaming.''

Her voice faded, leaving him with an aching sadness
and a need to comfort her that was worse than a tooth-
ache. As he sat there feeling desolate and helpless, she
surprised him again.

In a tight, hurried voice that didn't really sound like
her, she said, ''Speaking of night, it seems to be coming
awfully fast and I'm freezing to death. How do you suggest we keep warm?''

He stared at her for a time, not quite able to believe she
was asking what she seemed to be asking. Her body language was all walls and defenses; she looked to be closed
tightly against him. Over the protective barricades of her
drawn-up knees her eyes stared at him like gun barrels.
But at the same time, on another level entirely, he could
feel her vulnerability and her silent plea.

At last, when the silence seemed about to crack with
the burden of its own weight, he said, ''Rose.'' His voice
was hoarse. He persisted and managed to say, ''Come
over here, love.''

She unwrapped herself stiffly and, with elaborate un-
concern, picked up his shirt and stood up, then crossed
the few yards of sand that separated them and dropped
to her knees beside him. Her natural grace had deserted
her; her movements were coltish, touchingly clumsy.

''Here,'' she said with a bluntness that bordered on
belligerence. ''Put this on. You'll get cold. I'll help you.''
She held the shirt while he struggled to get his arms into
the sleeves. He felt her hands tremble.

That trembling, that tension...he'd thought they were
from fear of him, even revulsion. But now he looked into
her eyes, those lovely dark eyes he'd always considered so
unfathomable, and suddenly he saw the little girl she had

been. She was so vulnerable, so full of longing, so full of bravado. A little girl who'd always guarded herself so fiercely against the possibility of rejection that she'd never allowed herself to love. Understanding burst inside him like a warm, spring rain, the kind that nourishes the soil and makes things grow.

Without a word he leaned back against the rocks and held out his arms. After a moment's hesitation she moved into them and fitted herself gingerly against his side.

"Are you sure you're comfortable like this?" Her voice still had the uneven edge of belligerence.

"Perfectly." The rock was stabbing him in the back, but he wouldn't have told her that even if it had been slowly killing him. "You?"

"Umm..."

"Warmer?"

"Yes."

"Then relax. You're shaking."

"Oh." She snuggled against him like a kitten. He felt her hand curl on his chest, then flatten. She gave a sigh.

He felt handicapped—literally. With his hands he knew he could have had her purring in no time, but without them he could only hold her and touch his lips to her hair and murmur wordless reassuring sounds, and hope she wouldn't misunderstand the vibrating tensions in *his* body.

Her hand began to move back and forth across his chest, slowly and tentatively at first, and then as if searching for something.

"Jade." Her voice was soft on his collarbone.

"Yes?"

"It meant a lot to you, didn't it? It was more than just a thing to wear around your neck."

"Yes." He didn't pretend not to understand. "It had been with me a long time."

"I'm sorry it's gone."

He was quiet for a while, looking inward. What he saw there, and what he felt, surprised him. He chuckled softly. "That's funny. I'm not."

Her head bumped up under his chin; he nudged it back down and touched his lips briefly to her hair. "I feel... lighter, somehow. It's hard to explain. I don't know where I got the damn thing—maybe I stole it, for all I know. But it was all I had in the world. The only thing I brought with me from a life I can't even remember. I had no family, no name, no memories, but I had that bloody piece of stone. And it became all those things for me. Do you know what I mean?"

He felt her head move in the hollow of his shoulder, but she didn't speak. After a while he sorted out more of his thoughts and went on.

"I don't remember it bothering me particularly, the fact that I had no name, no... history."

"Roots," Rose supplied suddenly, as if she knew exactly what he meant. And he realized that she did. Of course she knew.

"Yes. Roots. But I guess maybe I felt kind of... fraudulent. The name I'd given myself had validity only because of that pendant, not because it stood for me. And even after I acquired that chemical company and changed its name to Castle Industries, I still felt that the name stood for the rock, not me. Because you see, inside I still felt nameless. And having a code name for so many years probably confused the issue a little. I had two names, and neither one of them belonged to me." He laughed painfully. The hand on his chest moved, curling suddenly into a fist, almost as if in response to his pain.

"And now the pendant is gone. And I still have my name."

"Jade..." It was a whisper, followed by a muted sniff.

"Yeah, Jade Castle. Of all things. But it's my name. Not a bad name, either. Beats the hell out of Homer."

"Or Eggbert," Rose said, sniffing again.

"Hmm. Or Bartholomew. I suppose I could have come up with something better, more dashing. What do you think about Lance?"

"Blaze!" Rose cried, getting into the spirit of the thing. "Rock! Steel! Sand!"

"Sand Castle?" Jade mused. "I think I like that one."

"Personally," Rose said, settling down as her giggles subsided, "I prefer Jade."

"Good," he said dryly. "It's on all my credit cards and important papers."

They sat in silence for a few minutes, and then Rose stirred restlessly against him.

"Jade?"

"Hmm?"

"I don't understand . . . something."

"What, love?"

"I'm sorry. I just don't understand how you got from *there* to *here*. You've come an awful long way from Singapore."

Jade's short bark of laughter rocked her head, and she tilted it to look up at him. He laid his own head back against the rock and stared up into the foggy darkness. "Oh yeah." He laughed again, softly, and shook his head. "Don't ask me to tell you everything that's brought me to this particular point, because you don't really want to know. Believe me. But basically, I inherited a great deal of money."

"From the smugglers?"

"Yeah. People in that line of work live on luck, and theirs ran out rather suddenly. Mine didn't, so I wasn't with them when their plane went down in the Cambodian jungles. But I knew where everything was, you see—everything they'd left behind. I took it all and went to Australia. It was enough to buy me a new life. A new beginning."

"I see. But . . ." She took a deep breath and let it out in a frustrated sigh.

"But what, love?"

"Jade, can I ask you just one question?"

She sounded so perplexed that he had to smile. "One," he said solemnly.

"Where did you . . . who taught you to *love*?"

He hadn't expected that. It caught him by surprise, and he had to think a minute to realize that, since she didn't really have any evidence that he *could* love, what she really meant was, who had taught him to *make* love? After a minute, when he hadn't answered, she went on to explain.

"You grew up...without gentleness, and yet you know how to be gentle. Your environment must have been almost totally masculine, even brutal. And yet you know . . . you can make . . ." She stumbled to an embarrassed halt, and he felt her throat move. Warmth stirred in his belly, like a sleeping cat stretching. His laughter was low and intimate.

"Totally masculine? Not by a long shot. Listen, those guys that found me thought a lot of me, but there was no way in the world they could have raised a six-year-old kid, and they knew it. No, they were pretty good at being uncles and big brothers, but they figured I needed a mother. So they took me to the closest thing they had." He was still for a while, remembering the first soft arms

that had ever held him, the first perfume he'd ever
smelled.

"Her name was Fanny. She ran an…establishment in
Hong Kong." He smiled, and let the smile into his voice.
"In fact, I imagine she was probably a pretty close
counterpart of a certain Mama Califa, who lives, I believe you said, in Cairo."

"Oh, God." Rose's hand moved from his chest to
cover her eyes. "Don't remind me of that, please. That
was such a dumb thing to say."

"Not at all. Michaels got a big kick out of it. He thinks
you can probably turn water into wine, by the way."

"I like him, too," Rose murmured darkly. "So Fanny
raised you? A *madam*?"

"She was a woman. And quite a lady. She taught me
to read and like it. She taught me arithmetic. And man-
ners. She taught me to appreciate music and art. She
taught me to play chess. She taught me to respect women,
and to appreciate them as people. She taught me to be
gentle, and when I got out of line, she beat the tar out of
me!"

Rose joined in his laughter, and when it had subsided,
murmured, "So…" Her fingers were open again,
stroking the flat, hair-roughened plane of his chest.

"So…" He tucked in his chin and looked down at the
top of her head. The sleeping cat inside him yawned and
stretched. "No, she didn't teach me loving—not that
kind. She was the only mother I'd ever known. She
just…prepared the ground, and then made sure the right
person planted the first seeds."

"Oh," she said. "I see." To Jade's relief, she fell silent.

It wasn't that he would have minded telling her; it
wasn't something he was ashamed of. It was just that that

particular topic of conversation, coupled with her nearness, was having a predictable effect on him. It was beginning to look like a very long night.

A shiver suddenly coursed through her body, and his arms tightened around her, an automatic reflex. But he couldn't seem to release her once the shudder had passed. And as his embrace hardened, her hand slipped downward to the bulge of his pectoral muscle and began to knead it with open palm.

"Rose," he said hoarsely, "are you doing that on purpose, or just fidgeting?"

"Why?" Her voice seemed as unreliable as his. "Do you want me to stop?"

"Only if you're fidgeting. If you're doing it on purpose, I wish you'd tell me so I can join the party."

"Feel free," she said, and lifted her face into the hollow of his neck.

He felt her mouth, hot and open against his skin, and a gentle, drawing pressure. He groaned softly. "Rose, do you know what you're doing?"

She said, "Yeah, using the oldest cliché in the book, the old 'I'm so cold, will you keep me warm?' gambit. Still works, though, doesn't it?"

"Works great. Why in the world do you need a gambit? You know I—"

"Because," she said fiercely, raising herself to look at him, "it's too damned hard having to eat my words!"

He stared at her, listening to the tension in her, feeling her need and measuring his own. And then he said gently, "I know, love. Come on, I'll make it easier for you."

With the firm pressure of his arm across her back he urged her into his embrace. But now, with the strange perversity that makes a person deny the thing she wants most, having irreversibly declared herself, she fought him. But Jade understood that the rigidity in her body, and even her shivering, were no more than measures of the depth of her need.

And that was something he knew how to deal with.

Chapter 14

Jade pulled her down into the cradle of his body, supporting her with his arms and murmuring soothing phrases, caressing her with words since he could not with his hands.

His mouth found her throat; her skin was so soft, and it tasted of salt. He wanted to keep the pressure gentle—soft nibbles and warm tongue strokes—because he knew his face was rough with stubble; but she sighed and caught his head between her hands, arching her throat against his face, seeming to revel in the rasp of his beard on her skin.

His own need blossomed like a match flame put to dry tinder. He sought her mouth and for a time tried to lose himself there, as an antidote for the fires consuming him. He worried that he was hurting her, going too fast, overpowering her. But her mouth opened under his, and she lifted herself into his kiss, matching his urgency, welcoming his power, feeding his passion. The firestorm had taken her, too, and it wasn't gentleness she wanted now.

The kiss became too much to deal with. Jade tore his mouth from hers and returned to her throat instead. He held them both still, pressing his lips to her racing pulse and listening to his own heart batter itself against his ribs. He began to move his open mouth back and forth across her chest, warming her with his breath, tasting her skin with his tongue. When he encountered the edge of her sweater he stopped, frustrated.

Without hesitation Rose jerked the offending garment over her head and dropped it onto the sand. She disposed of her bra as swiftly and deftly, then pulled his head hard against her. He turned his face to her, drawing his chin across the soft swell of her breast. She gave a sharp gasp and arched upward, offering him her body without reservations or restraints.

If he'd had the use of his hands he would have used them to soothe and gentle her, to calm them both into a sensuous languor. But he had only his mouth, the rough caress of his jaws and chin, the pressure of his lips, and the warm, gentle laving of his tongue. When he abraded a tender, sensitized nipple and then surged over it with his open mouth, soothing it with deep, drawing pressure and rhythmic, moist stroking, passion exploded in her. Her skin blazed; her chest rose and fell as if it took desperate effort just to breathe. When he touched the muscles of her belly with his lips she tensed and tightened, and a shudder rolled over her in hot, rippling waves. She cried out his name, "Jade!"

Her fingers raked through his hair, kneading his scalp, the muscles of his neck and shoulders.

"Yes, Rose...sweet Rose. Touch me, too, love...."

Her head fell back, her hair tumbling over his arm like a cooling rain. Her open palms followed the curves of his shoulders, sliding under his shirt to press hard against his back. And beneath the tight-stretched skin of her belly a muscle fluttered against his lips. He followed that tiny movement and encountered the edge of her panties. In sheer frustration he caught the elastic in his teeth.

Without hesitation her hands went to her hips and slipped inside the thin fabric. He lifted her with his arm so she could slide that last barrier down and away.

Her hands and his mouth... It was all he had, and her body was so tight, so tense! He laid his cheek against her leg and felt it tremble. He touched his mouth to the tight curls between her thighs and found her hot and moist and throbbing. He stroked her, then entered her gently with his tongue. When he did, he heard her sob his name.

He heard the panic in her cry and knew that her need had a sharp and terrible edge; to release her that way would bring her more pain than pleasure. Instead he pressed his lips to her in a gentling kiss and, raising his head, whispered hoarsely, "Love, come to me."

He had only to guide her a bit; she moved into his arms and astride his lap as if she'd read his mind. He buried his face in her hair and chuckled softly. "Rose, sweet love, I need your hands again."

She muttered a funny little breathy *"Oh,"* and released him at last from the confines of his bathing suit.

Then she moved over him again, but slowly now, holding his head between her hands and flattening her breasts against his chest, sliding her belly sinuously against his, fitting herself to his body like a fine, soft glove.

With his arms he held her firm, bracing her to meet his thrusts, and entered her swiftly, surely, completely. She gasped once, sharply. Her head fell back; he felt her hair like healing balm on his hands. His mouth found the curve of her throat; his tongue touched the pulsing hollow. He felt a turbulence inside himself that he was only just beginning to recognize, a great thundering stampede of emotions he wasn't ready yet to put a name to. So he just said hers, "Rose."

"Yes," she sighed. And as she had once before, she whispered, "Love me, Jade."

He tried to be careful at first, knowing the penetration was deep...very deep. But he might as well have tried to control a hurricane. In the end all either of them could do was ride with the storm and go where it took them. And when the storm had hurled them ashore, exhausted and spent, they clung to each other, stunned but jubilant, like the survivors they were.

Rose's body was shaking with sobs; she couldn't help it. They were joyful sobs, but Jade couldn't know that. Or could he? He was holding her tightly, with his face buried in her hair, and his words stroked and soothed her.

"Yes, Rose, I know. I know, love. Hush now."

Presently, without leaving her body, he lay back on the sand and drew her down with him. When she would have pulled herself from him, his arms tightened around her, and he whispered, "Let me stay a while, love. If I can..."

So she sighed and adjusted her body to his, sliding her legs along the outsides of his until they lay comfortably relaxed and beautifully entwined.

She thought she knew what had just happened, where that passion-storm had blown from. In the midst of catastrophy and tragedy there is a natural instinct to affirm life; in the midst of destruction, a passion to create. That she and Jade should have made love under these circumstances to satisfy their mutual need was understandable. It would be a mistake to read too much into it.

Just as it would be a mistake to read anything at all into the habit he had of calling her "love." It was an Australian colloquialism. He and Tessa called each other that; Tessa called *everyone* that. It would be foolish of Rose to imagine subtle differences in the way he said it, at certain special times, to *her*. As if he meant it . . .

Damp, chilly fog touched her where he couldn't, and she stirred, seeking more of his body heat.

"Cold, love?" His voice was sleepy.

She murmured an affirmative. He groped with his hand for the shirt he'd abandoned in the storm and draped it over her. His hands seemed stiff, his movements awkward. He rolled her sideways and half under him, and in that warm, protective embrace she slept.

She awoke alone, stiff and plagued with a variety of discomforts. She was cold, of course. She seemed to have no other options on this godforsaken spit of sand than to be either too hot or too cold.

And she was thirsty. The yellow plastic canteen lay in the sand at the base of the rocks. She picked it up and shook it, listening to the sloshing sound it made. After a moment's hesitation she unscrewed the cap, took a careful swig, rolled it luxuriously around her mouth and swallowed it. The water level in the canteen didn't seem to have gone down at all since yesterday. Rose wondered whether Jade had had any at all. She wondered if he was saving it . . . for her.

She slapped the cap back on the bottle and stood up, pulling Jade's shirt over her arms and hugging it across her body. Then she saw Jade. He was standing hip-deep in the shallow pool, head back, eyes closed, soaking his hands in the seawater.

The morning fog was already beginning to burn away; the sun had lit it to a lovely golden haze. The world had become a tiny island of sand, some craggy whitewashed rocks, a quiet pool. The dark cliffs streaked with white and the endless turquoise ocean surrounded them, isolating and protecting them. The world was lovely, and it was theirs.

Jade opened his eyes, and saw her standing there and called, "Good morning."

"Good morning," Rose called back, cherishing strange shivers of joy. "Doesn't that sting?"

He lifted his hands from the water, shook them and put them back in again. "Like hell. But salt heals. How are you, love?"

"Fine," she said huskily. "Except I have sand in places you wouldn't believe!"

He grinned at her. "Come join me. I'll help you rinse."

For a moment Rose stood very still in the center of that quiet, golden world. And then, with a strange sense of being newly born, she slowly opened the shirt and dropped it onto the sand.

Jade's eyes caressed her body while his smile warmed her soul. He lifted his hand, held it out to her and said simply, "Come, love...."

She walked across the sand and stepped into the water, then waded toward him until she reached his outstretched hand. Taking it carefully in both of hers, she laid it against her cheek.

"Your poor hands," she murmured. "How are they?"

"Better. Stiffer, but not as sore." His smile grew tender. "They'll be fine."

"Oh good." Her voice had a funny catch in it. "I love your hands."

For a time they just gazed at each other, memorizing each other's faces as if they expected to go blind any minute.

Jade broke the spell at last. "Rose," he sighed, and, hooking his arm around her neck, he pulled her into his embrace.

She went with a feeling of homecoming, like a boat going into its own slip. The shape of his body in her arms, his scent, the texture of his chest hair against her cheek, all felt familiar and right. She felt warm, secure, happy...loved.

Home. In all her childhood dreams she'd never allowed herself to dream of home. She knew now that, if she had, it would have felt like this.

Jade's cheek moved on her hair. His chin nudged her forehead. She tilted her head back, lifting her face to look at him, then laughed and kissed the heavy growth of stubble on the underside of his chin.

"Like me beard, do ye, me pretty?" he growled villainously.

"Never saw anyone grow one faster. What's it been, three days?"

"Or four. I can't remember. Time flies—"

"When you're having fun!" Rose joined in, laughing. It felt so good to laugh. So good to hold him, and be held by him, as if neither of them wanted to do anything else ever again.

But... *three days*? Had it been such a short time ago, the first time they'd made love? Incredible. They'd been such strangers then. The man who had made love to her body that night wasn't the same man who held her now. That man had been only a part of this one. The man in her arms was whole.

A thought struck her, something that, with all that had happened since, she'd forgotten. "Jade..."

"Yes?"

"That offer you made, is it still open?"

"What offer is that?"

"You asked me...to stay with you. Live with you. Is that—"

"No." He shook his head. "Sorry. That offer's been withdrawn."

"Oh. I'm sorry, I—"

"I've got a better one. I think."

"A better one?"

"Yes. Marry me, Rose."

She pulled away, staring at him, then abruptly turned her back to him so he couldn't see the shock, the hope and the despair that were fighting for control of her face. She felt cold and suffocated, as if the water that lapped around her hips had suddenly surged over her head.

"Rose, what's the trouble, love?" She felt him move close to her, felt him touch her hair, then take his hand away. "If you don't want to marry me..."

"Oh, Jade." Her voice broke, filling her throat with aching sadness. "People like us don't *marry*!"

"People like us?" He'd gone very still, very cautious. "What do you mean?"

She made a quick, angry gesture with her hand. "We've lived all our lives in the shadows, Jade. We're night people, you and I. We've dealt with intrigue and danger and deception for so long we don't know how to live like normal people! Love, marriage, kids—those are daylight things. Jade, we wouldn't even know how to live in the sunshine!"

"Rose." Forgetting his injuries, he put his hands on her shoulders and turned her to face him. She didn't want

to see his face, but he took her head between his hands
and tilted it, compelling her to look at him. His was
strained and grave. "Rose," he said again. And then,
"Do you love me?"

Her mouth opened, then closed. She was only a little
bemused to discover that she had no pride at all where he
was concerned. With stark simplicity she said, "Yes."

His face seemed to blur; its rough places grew fuzzy, its
sharp edges soft. His image shimmered; for an instant she
saw him through rainbows, and then the tears slipped
from her eyes and ran down her cheeks.

Jade touched them away with his thumbs and murmured, "You do?"

She nodded. "Yes."

"That's funny. I love you, too."

"You do?"

"Yes."

She gazed at him, entranced. She noticed that even
though the tear-glaze wasn't in the way anymore, the lines
of his face had stayed soft.

"Rose, if love is a sunshine thing, and we've managed
it, why not the rest? Marriage, kids, all of it."

"That's what I love about you. You have such a logical mind!" Laughing tearfully, she lifted a hand to her
face. "But, Jade, neither of us had a family. We wouldn't
know how to be parents!"

Jade frowned thoughtfully. "I suppose we wouldn't
have to be parents."

"But I'd want to be! It's just..."

"Then we'll learn," Jade said fiercely, turning her and
pulling her hard against him, his arms crisscrossing her
breasts. He lowered his head, laying his face against her
ear. "We'll learn. And we have one advantage over most

people: we sure as hell know what we missed! We'd never take parenting for granted.''

"Or children, either. Jade, I just realized something. Not only did we never have parents, we were never children! How can we know anything about children when we never got a chance to be children ourselves?''

He was silent, holding her close and thinking. "Hmm," he murmured after a while. "That's an interesting thought. I guess we'll have to learn that, too."

"Learn to be children?"

"Umm-hmm." His lips found her ear and delicately nibbled its edges.

"Jade, I'm thirty years old!"

"And I'm forty. So what?" His breath was making tiny explosions in her ear. She suddenly became aware of the slippery coolness of his body against her buttocks.

"How...does one learn...to be a child?" she whispered, lifting a hand to touch his hair.

"I don't know. We'll work on it. Right now I don't feel very childish."

Rose tilted her head, listening to responses somewhere inside her body. "Me, either," she decided, feeling groggy. Jade's tongue was exploring the convolutions of her ear. She closed her eyes and melted against him. Her hand slipped to the back of his neck; it was sun-baked and vibrant with strength and virility. Love and wanting came together inside her, bursting through her in a wonderful kaleidoscope of sunlight and colors.

"So how about it? Will you marry me?" His tongue was doing magical things to her neck. One hair-roughened arm chafed her nipples, while the other hand slipped slowly down over her rib cage to splay wide over her belly.

"I ... don't know," she murmured, and gasped when his finger found the dimple of her navel.

"What's wrong now?"

"If I say 'yes,' are you going to stop trying to persuade me?"

"Say yes and I'll spend the rest of my life persuading you it wasn't a mistake."

"Yes...."

With a swift, fierce movement of his head Jade swept her hair aside and captured her nape with his mouth. Desire exploded inside her. As her head fell forward the hand on her abdomen dipped below the surface of the water to cup her between her thighs and pull her hard against him.

"My goodness," Rose gasped, her voice weak with wonder, "how did you do that?" She moved sinuously, sliding her bottom against him.

"I didn't do it; you did." Jade's husky growl broke into laughter. He released her and spun her into an embrace that was equal parts passion and exuberance, lifting her high with his arms tight around her waist. She hung on to his neck, laughing and breathless, until he eased her, with exquisite, excruciating slowness, down his body.

Her breasts felt swollen; her nipples burned where they dragged against his chest. A shivering emptiness opened up inside her. Suddenly hungry for him, she tangled her hands in his hair and brought her mouth to his. With a low murmur of pleased surprise he opened his mouth for her. Made brave by his approval, she ran her tongue along the insides of his lips, teasing. His tongue touched, then stroked hers, inviting her in. Her tongue sank into his mouth; she clung to him, famished.

It seemed a natural thing to wrap her legs around him. He cradled her bottom in his arms and pressed her, soft and open, against his slippery, water-cooled skin.

And then they were moving through the water, and yet no longer in the water. The earth tilted and rose up against her back.

"Rose, open your eyes. Look at me." Jade's voice carried an odd urgency.

She lifted lids that seemed weighted and tried to focus on his face. "Jade?" He looked tense, and strained. She lifted her hand to touch his lips and smiled. "Jade, I love you."

His smile was sunshine. He touched her smile with his and brought their bodies together with one sure thrust . . . and the sunshine flooded her inside.

Making love in the sun made them thirsty.

Rose took the cap from the canteen and held it out to Jade. Her silent gaze was unwavering, so he took it and drank sparingly. When he gave it back to her, she shook her head and said, "I'm not thirsty."

Jade said softly, "You never could lie to me, Rose."

She drank, still holding him with her eyes, and then put the cap back on the bottle and gave it a shake.

"One more swallow apiece," Jade said cheerfully. "We'll save it to toast our rescue, when it comes."

Rose's empty stomach complained painfully. To soothe it, she pulled her knees up and hugged them tightly to her chest. "Jade," she said, staring at the empty horizon, "what about Tessa? What's going to happen to her?" When he didn't answer immediately she went on intensely, "She's as much a victim as we are—maybe more so. It's so cruel, what they did to her. They *used* her,

Jade. They used her hopes and fantasies, her dreams that her mother—''

''I know,'' Jade said softly. His mouth was grim. ''And if I have anything to say about it—''

''Will you have anything to say about it?''

He chuckled. ''Well, now that my name has been cleared, I should think so. After all, it would be up to the Bureau to bring charges, and I was director of the Bureau for over ten years. That and the facts Michaels and I have uncovered, with your help, should carry some weight, don't you think?'' He stood up suddenly and held out his hand. ''Come on, love—let's do something to take our minds off our empty stomachs.''

They bathed away the sand in the shallow pool, then dried each other with Jade's shirt. They sat in the shade with their arms around each other and talked, and watched the horizon for boats. One went by now and then, but much too far off to be worth hailing.

When the evening fog came again Jade opened the canteen and held it up like a crystal wineglass.

''Here's to us, love, a couple of survivors.''

''To us,'' Rose echoed. Her smile was radiant.

They both drank, draining the last drops from the canteen; then Rose ran her tongue across her lips, glazing them with precious moisture. Moisture glistened, too, in her eyes.

''Jade, I love you. Whatever happens, I'm glad—''

''Hush!'' He stopped her with his kiss, then drew back to look into her eyes. ''We're going to make it, Rose. We're going to have our time in the sun. Believe it.''

''I do,'' she whispered.

They slept with their arms around each other.

In the morning they were awakened by the throbbing of powerful diesel engines and the wail of a foghorn. As they stood hugging each other an amplified voice blared, echoing off the fog-shrouded cliffs: "Ahoy the island. This is the United States Coast Guard...."

She had the pride of Nantucket in her spirit and the passion for one man in her blood.

Until I Return
Laura Simon

Author Laura Simon weaves an emotional love story into the drama of life during the great whaling era of the 1800s. Danger, adventure, defeat and triumph—UNTIL I RETURN has it all!

Available at your favorite retail outlet in OCTOBER, or reserve your copy for September shipping by sending your name, address, zip or postal code along with a check or money order for $7.70 (includes 75¢ for postage and handling) payable to Worldwide Library to:

In the U.S.	In Canada
Worldwide Library	Worldwide Library
901 Fuhrmann Blvd.	Box 2800, 5170 Yonge St.
Box 1325	Postal Station A
Buffalo, NY	Willowdale, Ontario
14269-1325	M2N 6J3

Please specify book title with your order.